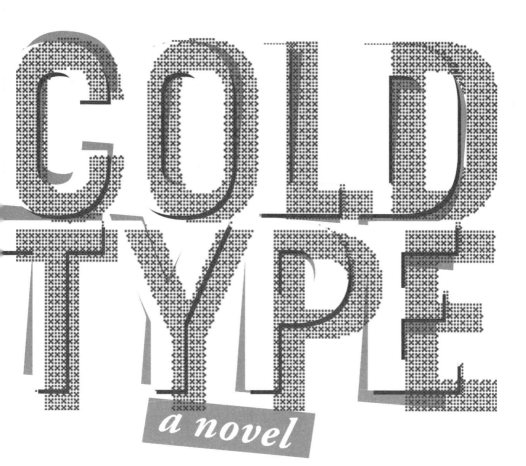

COLD TYPE

a novel

COLD TYPE

a novel

HARVEY ARATON

Cinco Puntos Press
EL PASO, TEXAS

FIRST EDITION
10 9 8 7 6 5 4 3 2 1

Library of Congress Cataloging-in-Publication Data

Araton, Harvey.
  Cold type / Harvey Araton.
     pages cm
ISBN 978-1-935955-88-7 (cloth); ISBN 978-1-935955-71-9 (pbk.);
ISBN 978-1-935955-72-6 (e-book).
  1. Fathers and sons—Fiction. 2. Journalists—Fiction. 3. Journalism—Politital aspects—Fiction. I. Title.

  PS3601.R356C65 2014
  813'.6--dc23

2013040574

Cover and book design by Anne M. Giangiulio
Proud mother of Little Lulu and John Jacob Jingleheimer Schmidt.
Dah dah dah dah dah dah dah!

To my friend Paul Needell,
who crossed with me, in and back out.

Day One: Monday, November 7, 1994

CHAPTER ONE

The clock in the middle of the newsroom reported five past midnight. Jamie's Sunday—his planned day off—had ended with a frantic deadline rush.

It had begun so serenely over a three-egg omelet at his favorite café, with newspapers scattered on his table by the window overlooking the neighborhood's busiest commercial street. He'd had an overcast, unseasonably warm morning to himself and was looking forward to seeing his nearly two-year-old son later in the day. But, no question, he'd made the classic reporter's miscalculation—going home after his meal and answering the telephone without letting the machine pick up.

Cal Willis barked at him, "I want to run your piece tomorrow, Kramer. You said it was ready, didn't you?"

Jamie hesitated, unsure about arguing with his boss' inventive memory.

"Well," he said. "I guess…"

"Good," Willis said. "Get the piece in as soon as you can."

Jamie hung up the phone and swore under his breath. The truth was that he hadn't yet organized the scribble that was scattered in three different notepads. On the other hand, he knew he had enough material to squeeze out nine hundred words on the squalid conditions and care in a Brooklyn nursing home.

The tip had come from a friend who'd found his Alzheimer-stricken grandfather in urine-soaked pants. Jamie followed up with a surreptitious inspection of the facility, interviews with two other concerned families in the parking lot and with an official from an advocacy group for the elderly. The story was no prize winner. It probably wouldn't even rate a front-page tease. But it had been weeks since he had generated anything remotely enterprising, a point he had been reminded of earlier that week—though not by Willis.

"Got anything good?" Steven Kramer had asked when they'd stepped out for lunch.

It was just like Steven—his older cousin by six months and the Kramer whose face *Trib* readers were well-acquainted with from his twice-weekly column—to make Jamie feel defensive about his output. It was also a subtle reminder that he owed his very existence in the newspaper business to family connections. Steven, conversely, had a degree from the Columbia School of Journalism.

Jamie wanted his story published but wished he'd had the courage to tell Willis he needed another day. After he hung up, he called his ex-wife to tell her that he had no choice—he had to work and would not be coming up to deliver his son's birthday gifts. His excuse was airtight, entirely legitimate. He *still* was upset but not so much at Willis as he was with himself—and Karyn.

"Why can't I just bring Aaron's presents to his party?" he asked her.

She sighed.

"It would, you know, just be uncomfortable for me and by extension for Aaron," she said.

He returned fire with a sigh of his own.

"You can see him on *your* birthday next month," she said.

"I'll be 32, a little old for a party," he said. Sarcasm got him nowhere.

"Let me know when you want to bring the gifts—*before* Friday," she said.

He hung up, collected the notepads from his desk, stuffed them into his shoulder bag and left for the office.

Four cups of coffee, two apple cinnamon granola bars and a small container of lo mein later, he made the 11 o'clock first-edition deadline, with about forty-five minutes to spare. He helped himself to a call on the *Trib's* dime to a high school friend who had migrated to the California Bay Area. He flipped through sections of the voluminous Sunday *Times*, waiting for the fresh stack of Monday's first edition *Tribs* to be dropped on a nearby desk.

Jamie made a beeline for a copy, glancing at the front page headline (**DOOM FOR DEMS?**) that hopefully raised the possibility of a mid-term rebuke of the Clinton White House agenda in the election that was two days away. He folded the tabloid and stuffed the lower half into the back pocket of his jeans. He scraped away a few stray noodles on his desk and rolled the greasy refuse into one disposable mass. He treaded carefully by Willis, who didn't look up.

"Not bad. Need the copy earlier, as usual," Willis said. He always needed copy earlier no matter what time it was submitted.

Willis' dark, bald dome glistened under yellow-tinted fluorescent light. A platoon of cigarette butts overflowed an ashtray on the left side of his desk.

"And we had to trim," he said.

"How much?"

"Fourteen lines."

Willis, as usual, disclosed the damage with no apparent remorse.

Damn, Jamie thought. *I spent so much time making the transitions work. Now it'll read like shit.*

Other reporters—Steven certainly—would have complained. Why shouldn't he? *Say something,* Jamie thought. He didn't. He reasoned that he owed Willis every line he'd published, not to mention the paycheck that supported him, his son and his ex-wife. Besides, his copy *was* late.

"See you tomorrow," he said. Willis grunted a response that didn't much sound like goodnight.

The decrepit elevator leading to the rear of the old waterfront building reeked of antiquity and groaned all the way down before shuddering to a halt. Jamie pulled the paper from his back pocket, opened it to his story at the top of page five and held it up to his face to read. He lowered his left shoulder into the metal door.

He'd been unwilling to walk the five blocks to the subway when he knew he'd be working late. That meant surrendering a cherished Brooklyn Heights parking spot to make the short drive over the bridge and lock up under the highway across the street. There he could count on the security of the post-midnight bustle, the fraternal, profane chatter of the drivers at the end of the production line as they waited to leave on their runs.

But something was different outside the building, unfamiliarity permeating the cold night air. There were unmistakable sounds of anger, the scent of disorder. One of the deaf guys who worked the presses was sitting in a chair in the dimly lit lobby, reading the paper.

"Something going on out there?" Jamie said, hoping the guy could read his lips. He just shrugged.

Jamie leaned a shoulder into the door. One step onto the sidewalk was not enough time for him to prepare for the force of nature hurtling toward him, about to tear through his flimsy newspaper shield.

In that immeasurable blink of time between detection and reaction, impact and consequence, Jamie could only create a vague mental recording of the brawny forearms that snapped the glasses off his face, knocked him to the ground—and out cold.

CHAPTER TWO

"There's some blood," Carla Delgado said. She cradled Jamie's head on her thigh. Someone from the small circle of onlookers produced an ice pack.

When Carla applied the compress, the cold jolted Jamie back to consciousness.

"Small cut," she said, pulling back to inspect the damage. "Just a little blood."

Eyes still closed, Jamie recognized the husky, accented mix of San Juan and New York. It was the sultry yet robust voice of the *Trib's* office manager.

"He got lucky," Carla said. "Looks like when he fell, his head landed on his bag and not the sidewalk. I don't think it's going to need stitches, just some ice and a Band-Aid. But the eye, it's starting to swell up a bit."

Caressing his cheek, she shouted: "Jamie, can you hear me?"

He opened his eyes. He wasn't quite sure where he was but he liked the feeling of her hand on his face, the light but scratchy touch of her long fingernails. What felt even better was his head resting on the stocking covering her thigh. Her breath smelled of spearmint gum.

"One of the drivers ran you over."

"I got hit by a car?"

"No," Carla said, shaking her head, giggling a bit. She couldn't help but be amused by his incoherence.

"Not by a car. One of the drivers, our truck drivers, happened to be running by just as you walked outside and knocked you over. This guy here saw what happened."

The haze lifting, Jamie was able to place himself outside the building. He remembered more now—the forearms extended, the clenched fists, even the breathy aroma of potato chips.

"This guy…came at me…don't know why…"

He lifted his head off her thigh. Carla continued to apply the ice pack and pushed him back down.

"It was an accident, he didn't mean to take you out," said a man in a navy blue hooded sweatshirt and a Mets cap pulled so low that his eyes were hidden.

"Jamie, listen," Carla said. "The drivers just walked off the job a little while ago. Management is trying to move the trucks with scab drivers they must have had hidden nearby. All hell just broke loose. Someone was running by here just as you stepped outside. You understand?"

In the distance, there was more obscene shouting. When Jamie turned to look into the street, blurry as his naked night vision was, he could make out a *Trib* delivery truck, immobilized in the intersection. Its windshield was smashed. The dumped contents were burning, dozens of bundles of Monday editions—hundreds of copies of Jamie's story suffering the worst of all possible trims.

Carla and the handful of bystanders anxiously watched a cavalry of ranting *Trib* drivers moving in the direction of the trucks that were lined up behind the one that was attacked. A phalanx of city cops was trying to push them out of the street. Police cars were haphazardly parked with their driver-side doors flung open.

"I must have just followed you down in the elevator," Carla said. "When I opened the door, you were laying here."

"For how long?" he asked.

Men rushed past them, wielding baseball bats. One yelled, "Scab bastards."

"Jamie, are you listening to me? Should I send someone up to get your father?"

The acrid air from the drifting smoke seemed to act as a stimulant—unless it was Carla's request to call his old man.

"Why would you do that?"

"So he can drive you home," she said. "You don't look so good."

He sat up and took the ice pack from Carla.

"I'm fine," he said. "I can drive."

He noticed his broken glasses on the ground next to him. He unzipped his shoulder bag to find the extra pair of tortoise shell glasses he always carried there. Back on his feet, his head throbbed, as if someone had cranked up the bass too high.

He straightened up, replacing the bag on his shoulder.

"Take the ice pack with you," Carla said.

"What exactly did you say is going on?" Jamie said.

Her first-aid mission complete, Carla was already moving off in the direction of the mob.

"Go home," she called back, glancing sympathetically over her shoulder, pressing a palm to her eye. "Keep using that ice."

Jamie decided to take her advice. He'd had enough excitement for one night—and enough damage done. His jeans were torn at the left knee and his right ankle felt like he'd twisted it during his fall. It took him several seconds to remember where his Corolla was parked. He walked away with a slight limp and made the short drive over the bridge into downtown Brooklyn for what he hoped would be a decent night's sleep.

With any luck, the drivers would be delivering newspapers again by the time he woke up—not burning them.

CHAPTER THREE

Jamie squinted to meet the sun streaming through the half-drawn blinds. It wasn't the most prudent idea—the swelling beneath his left eye made any optic movement a chore.

He picked up a ringing telephone from the night table next to his bed.

"What's up?" he said, closing his eyes and letting out a noisy yawn.

"Are you?"

"Yeah, sort of."

"Heard you took one for the team last night," Steven Kramer said.

"Some team," Jamie said, his head back on the pillow. "An asshole walks off his job and thinks I'm a human turnstile."

"Unless that asshole gets back to work today, my guess is that we're going to be out with him. That's what I'm calling about, actually. The Alliance is meeting this afternoon at headquarters. Big vote. You should come."

Jamie closed his eyes and frowned.

"You there?" Steven said.

"Still here."

"It's at twelve-thirty."

"I'll try," Jamie said.

"Don't try, be there. We're in this."

"In what?"

Too late, Steven was gone. He was questioning a dial tone.

It was a few minutes after ten. As usual, Jamie hadn't been able to relax and fall into a deep sleep. He had battled insomnia since preadolescence. He typically slept well in the morning but invariably woke up feeling he needed more. Today was no different.

He inspected the discoloration on his face in a wall mirror beside his bed. There was a spot of dried blood that could be washed off but it didn't look as bad as it felt. Sunglasses would hide the worst of it.

He brewed coffee, waited in the cramped kitchen, feet bare on the linoleum floor. He returned to the edge of his bed, clicked on the television to catch a report about what had happened at the *Trib*.

Drops of coffee, tasteless as tofu, slid off his lips, down his chin and onto his bare chest.

"Trucks attempting to leave the plant were halted by *Trib* employees, who smashed windows, hurled rocks and set bundles of papers on fire," the anchorwoman said. "Three of the non-union drivers attempting to man the trucks were injured. Police estimate about two dozen arrests. By one a.m., *Trib* executives were admitting that the paper would not be on today's newsstands. For more, we go to Deborah Givens, who is with the drivers' union president, Gerard Colangelo, outside the *Trib* plant in downtown Manhattan."

Jamie had run copy at the *Trib* with Debbie Givens, a diminutive blonde with a pristine complexion and immovable shoulder-length hair. She was from a small town in Iowa. She also had a master's degree in broadcasting from the University of Missouri—enough to land her a general assignment reporter's gig at the city's cable news station.

When Jamie was still married and living out of the city in a suburb that some wintry nights seemed north of Yonkers and south of Maine, they had gone out for a drink, commiserating the meaninglessness of their work and pondering the prospects of elevation, or escape. For Jamie there weren't many.

Gerard Colangelo was almost a foot taller than Givens. His combed-back black hair left a three-inch scar uncovered high on his forehead—a remnant of his days as a boxer who cut too easily. With his lined, angular face, Colangelo bore a fair resemblance to Pat Riley. But he was not exactly giving the kind of corporate motivational primer for which the famous Knicks coach demanded a working man's annual haul.

"We tried…we begged the *Trib* to negotiate with us like human beings," Colangelo said. His scratchy voice suffered the effects of a long, argumentative night. "Lee Brady doesn't want to work with the unions. He doesn't want contracts. He doesn't seem to believe in them. And our workers, all the unions, have taken enough from this bully who thinks he can come to New York and do what he did to the unions in Dublin and London. New York is not Dublin or London. Now we show this guy what New York is all about."

There were cheers and a mix of obscenities from the mob of drivers behind them.

"Mr. Colangelo, we have reports of injuries to the non-union drivers…"

"You mean *fuckin'* scabs," a voice from the rear yelled out.

Givens winced. An irritated Colangelo turned and lifted a resolute index finger to his lips.

"What happened last night, those were isolated incidents," he said. "We can't control every man. But you've got to remember that these union brothers have kids to feed, mortgages to pay. We opened our arms to this billionaire when he sailed into our city on his fancy boat to buy our newspaper. We've already sacrificed jobs and made other concessions to make it easier for him. He seems to have already forgotten that."

Givens began to pull away, phrase another question. Colangelo leaned forward, almost making contact with the crown of the mike.

"He wants our jobs, our homes, so now we do what we have to do," he shouted. "Now…now we close Lee Brady down."

The pause for dramatic effect set off the drivers behind Colangelo. It was the perfect segue for Givens to throw it back to the studio. Jamie pointed the remote at the screen and clicked it off. He tossed it over his shoulder onto the bed.

"I need this right now like a damn root canal," he mumbled.

He sat for a spell, sipping more coffee, feeling slightly flush from the effects of the sun-drenched room.

He headed for the shower and let the warming water drench his hair and soak the unblemished side of his face. He wished he could wash away the echoes of Colangelo's voice.

Now we close Lee Brady down.

As if Colangelo's face were etched into the shower tile, Jamie said aloud, conviction enhanced by the bass echo chamber: "You think you're the only one who has a mortgage to pay? Child support? A kid to feed?"

He thought about the stack of bills sitting on his desk—the cable and electric bills, the credit card on which he would have to make the minimum payment. Again.

And, he thought, *Lord knows what Karyn will call and ask for.*

He closed his eyes, took a deep breath and let his forehead rest against the tile.

CHAPTER FOUR

Jamie checked his watch and quickened his pace through the newspaper-strewn and otherwise filthy outskirts of Chinatown. It was warm for early November, the sky a cloud-pocked blue. He wore his checkered-colored flannel shirt tied around the waist of his jeans. A light corduroy jacket was draped across his right shoulder. His tangle of nappy brown hair was still wet.

On frigid days, his habit of procrastinating at home and rushing from the shower to make an appointment would create frozen clumps he feared would snap like small pieces of gnarled, uncooked pasta.

On the train, Jamie stretched his neck—a chiropractic tic he resorted to when it was sore or he was stressed.

The musty union hall was already jammed by the time he arrived and hurried through the long narrow corridor. Rows of folding chairs were filled, with standing room scarce along the cracked and vomit green walls. Jamie stationed himself near the entrance for what he hoped would be a convenient exit. At the same time, he scanned the crowd for his cousin so he could make eye contact and his presence might duly be noted.

He nodded to a sports guy who occasionally dropped by Jamie's desk to talk NBA hoops—the only sport he seriously followed. One of the police reporters casually scanned the *Sun's* front page. Dotty, the nice lady in charge of the morgue, flipped open a mirror to check her makeup.

Jamie suddenly smelled the odor of nicotine breath in his ear, felt a hand on his back.

"Strike three, yer out."

Without turning, he knew it was Patrick Blaine, the *Trib's* senior columnist.

"You see my cousin?" Jamie said.

Blaine winced at the discoloration around Jamie's eye that was visible through his glass frame. Jamie cursed himself for forgetting his shades.

"You piss someone off at the bar?" he said. "As for John L. Lewis, he's in the back—with the big boys."

Jamie smirked, as if he knew who this Lewis was.

"What're you hearing?" Jamie asked.

"Matter of fact, I talked to Robbins earlier this morning. He told me what happened last night."

An unlit cigarette dangled from Blaine's mouth. He lit it.

"Fuck the fire codes," he said. Jamie found himself in the familiar position of admiring the old man's disdain for rules and political correctness, in no particular order.

"Robbins is back in the conference room, probably on the phone to Colangelo and the other union guys. They'll come out soon to talk it over with the membership but—forget it—this union will be out on strike in less than an hour with all the others."

The way Blaine said it—matter-of-factly, like they were all on the way to some Disney theme park—was unnerving.

"And I'll have to head back to the office and cross a picket line for the first time in my life," he said.

Jamie looked up, just in time to inhale a cloud of smoke.

"I'm not one of you anymore," Blaine said. "I'm under contract. Signed a three-year deal a couple of months before the old broad sold the place to that cocksucker Brady. He owns me now."

Blaine took another languorous drag, his eyes narrowing as he sucked the smoke into his lungs.

"Why'd you do that?" Jamie said.

Blaine rubbed the thumb of his left hand against his index and middle fingers.

"Did the column twenty-three years and maybe twice I got something more than the union-scale raise. I think, in the end, Maxine felt bad about that. She knew I wasn't going anywhere, not at my age. Any kid she hired—like your brilliant cousin, for example—she had to pay market value. So she calls me into her office one night as I'm finishing up a piece. She's sitting behind her desk, stocking feet propped up, reeking of Dewar's. She pushes a piece of paper at me and says, 'Sign this.'

"I say, 'What is it?'

"She says, 'Just sign or you're off the goddamned column!' I sign. She pulls it away and puts it in her drawer."

In his next check, Blaine explained, he discovered an extra two-fifty and no standard union dues deduction.

"So what if you don't go in?" Jamie said.

"Contract's null and I'm void."

"You sure we're going out?"

"No choice," Blaine said.

He scratched a wide landing strip of a nose containing more colored lines than the city transit map.

"You know what happened last night, how it started?" Blaine said.

Jamie nodded, in the way he would when bluffing his way through an interview. He understood that Blaine was going to give it to him "Blaine and simple," as the columnist was fond of describing his writing style. The young *Trib* reporters considered it corny as Barney and Blaine generally as outdated as the dinosaur. But if anyone had the right to tell them to go fuck themselves with their RAMs and ROMs it was Blaine.

He was a throwback and damn proud of it. Out of spite, it seemed, he was still tapping out columns on a typewriter and handing the copy to a clerk—Jamie, in fact, not all that long ago—to load into the system.

Blaine was the kind of shoe leather reporter who seldom emerged from the city's blue-collar taverns as tipsy as the civil servants he had fleeced of secrets. He still wore a tie every day to the office and an impeccable starched blue shirt with an off-white collar, even as he reeked of tobacco, needed a shave and more than a few nose hairs clipped.

"The drivers were baited but they fucked up by walking out last night," Blaine said. His voice was raspy from decades of smoking. The cigarette dangled between his right index and middle fingers.

Blaine explained that the drivers had played right into Brady's hands by hitting the street. The drivers walked out, everyone would follow and Brady would proceed to produce the paper with management personnel, wire services and assorted flunkies. He would get what he wanted—the unions in the street and the paper on the stands.

"It'll be ugly for a few days but he's banking on what happened with the unions in Ireland and England, especially on Fleet Street with him and Murdoch," Blaine said. "Even without a contract, Brady couldn't start changing work rules because he couldn't know how the feds at the National Labor Relations Board would react. So he kept baiting the drivers, hoping they'd lose their heads."

"Which they apparently did," Jamie said, patting the discoloration around his eye.

Blaine ignored him and kept talking. "That guy they fired last night? Young polish guy, long name I can't even pronounce. He's been working half shifts for two years since he hit a pole with his truck in a snowstorm in the suburbs. The kid's in a coma for almost a week, then he wakes up and he's not all there. Not incapacitated, still able to work, just not quite the same. So they let him stay on half a day, drive a short route. Then suddenly

Brady's guy is telling him he's got to drive a full shift. He freaks out, says he can't because of his condition. They give him a full truck anyway. He refuses to get in, they fire the poor fuck, escort him out of the plant. A dozen guys follow to see what's going on. That's it—they've left their posts without authorization. They're fired too. All hell breaks loose. The drivers are out in the street, carrying on. Here come the scabs, on cue. The whole thing was organized by the strike-busting lawyer from out of town that Brady has had negotiating for him. The Mayor went along with the police protection because Brady helped put a Republican in a Democrat's town in office. And now you're all here, taking a strike vote."

"Yeah," Jamie said, "but you know a lot of city room guys don't see this as their fight. They know there are no jobs out there. Papers are cutting back—if not closing. I'm not so sure we vote to go out in sympathy."

Blaine laughed—too derisively, Jamie thought.

"Listen, kiddo, sympathy has nothing to do with this—and neither does right and wrong. It's only about power and leverage, about which jobs are more essential in putting out the damn paper. That's the drivers, not us. They got wire copy to replace us with—or I should say *you*. There are guys working in subway booths who think they can do what we do—tell a story and put their name on top of it. So the drivers are steering this ship. And when I say strike vote, I don't mean like this is some fucking democracy. This union isn't run by everyone in here. It's run by *them*."

He jerked a thumb in the direction of the union chiefs, making their way to the front. They were led by Sandy Robbins, president of the Alliance—the union representing the *Trib's* editorial and advertising employees. Right with them was Jamie's cousin, beaming as if he were standing in front of the Pulitzer committee.

"If they want the Alliance out with the other unions, then the Alliance is going out," Blaine said.

"So what are you doing here?"

Blaine pulled a notepad from his back pocket and held it up like a school-bus pass.

"I'm the local guy, remember?" he said. "I don't do Hillary health care, unless she's got some sick aunt holed up in White Plains. I don't do Contracts with America, unless it's a mob hit ordered by one of the New York families."

For once, Blaine looked and sounded more sad than cynical.

"Whatever happens here, it's a story," he said. "And I'll probably be the only one with a staff byline in tomorrow's paper."

He laughed. Mainly, it seemed, at himself.

"So be thankful that you're on the side going out," he said.

CHAPTER FIVE

Sandy Robbins was a roundish, smallish incongruity, unimposing except for a commanding baritone voice. Gray wisps above his ears and a few loose strands spared him total baldness. His oval-shaped face was embellished by a bushy mustache. His stubby arms and barrel chest made him look like the image of a small prehistoric creature in a children's book.

The more benevolent likeness was Danny DeVito.

His tough talk never seemed to find its way into any new contract. The annual 1.5 percent raises he negotiated for the *Trib's* editorial union—officially known as the Alliance of Editorial and Advertising Workers—drew collective sighs. He'd been called a weasel by disgruntled rank-and-filers for so many years that even he had to grudgingly answer to the handle Wheezy. Robbins maintained it dated to his days on the *Trib's* advertising team when allergies could set him off on an extended sneezing seizure.

The truth was that most Alliance members understood the newspaper business was not thriving. Robbins would defend his work with heartfelt speeches at union meetings. "You have to understand that the most profitable papers are in cities that are only able to sustain one," he had said when Jamie attended a recent meeting—for the first and only time. "This is the country's most competitive market. The *Trib* is struggling. It was losing money for years with Maxine."

Maxine Hancock was the matriarchal owner who had generally played by contract rules, even as she pinched pennies to keep her losses from getting out of hand. But this was the first contract showdown with Brady, whose anti-labor reputation preceded him. Every *Trib* union had been on edge.

"Sandy, explain one thing," a voice called out from the back of the room. It was Paul Shapiro, the *Trib's* Albany bureau chief. Shapiro lived in the woods between Saratoga and the state capital and looked the part. His dark wavy hair was worn shaggily long. His Smith Brothers beard needed serious grooming. An avid hunter and outdoorsman, Shapiro liked to chide his downstate colleagues as liberal gun control wimps and brag to them that he had the paper's best assignment. When Jamie's copy boy and clerk duties included answering phones, Shapiro would call in and ask, "How's life in the cesspool?"

"The drivers walk out after everyone agrees that's the last thing we should do because the climate isn't very good for a strike and no one wants to be out with the holidays coming up," Shapiro said. "What I want to know is, are we talking about going out because they went out, or because we've reached an impasse in our own negotiations and think Brady won't negotiate a fair contract with us?"

Robbins legitimized the question by nodding vigorously.

"Paulie, I know what you're getting at, but let me say this. We have been without a contract now for six months and have had talks with Brady's lawyer for nine. We've gotten nowhere on any of the pertinent issues. They did make one offer, as you know. It was so regressive on job security and guaranteed work hours that the negotiating committee was compelled to unanimously reject it.

"Now it's true that we said we would stay on the job for as long as it took to get a deal done. But we learn what's in store for us by the negotiations that take place before us. And we learn by the provocation that management is engaged in now that unless we show them it doesn't work, that's what we'll be facing down the road. We don't see the drivers as having gone out. We see them as locked out. Gerry Colangelo told me this morning that the first thing he did when he got to the plant last night was to propose that the matter of the driver who works the half day go to arbitration. Management said no. Then he proposed that the men who left their post be allowed back in. Management said no. That's a dozen men fired for no other reason than being worried about a colleague."

"Yeah, but that's them, not us," a guy Jamie recognized from Sunday Arts yelled from a seat in the middle of the room. He was a short, slender man in a tweed sports jacket, with thinning dark hair and plastic white frames that were too large for his narrow face.

"They're the ones who Brady says are getting paid for shifts they don't even work, and you know that's true. They're the ones Brady's after, and they're also the ones who run into the street as soon as something doesn't go their way. They don't represent our values as journalists. They're a closed union shop, almost all white. Why do we even want to risk everything for those assholes?"

The room was stunned into momentary silence, followed by murmurs that quickly increased in quantity and volume into a collective expression of anti-driver sentiment. Someone yelled, "If we walk out, we're committing professional suicide." Another voice from somewhere on the side wall near Jamie groused, "This is all a goddamn setup."

Jamie could feel a surge of passion from those who wanted no part of this. He, too, wanted to shed his veneer of neutrality, leap on top of this surge of politically incorrect passion, ride it right out the door and back to work. But he kept his opinion to himself.

From the row right in front of the original voice of dissent rose a shrill, "What the...?"

Carla Delgado wheeled in her seat, turning to stare down Sunday Arts.

"Let me tell you something, those *assholes* saved your pitiful ass four years ago. They supported you and everyone else in here when Maxine wanted to make all of us pay through the nose for our health insurance. Am I right?"

Sunday Arts frowned but obediently shook his head.

Carla, fueled by her access to expense accounts, wasn't about to let the ingrate off the hook.

"And who the hell are you, Henry, to accuse people of stealing? I see the crap you run by every goddamned week. When was the last time you paid for dinner? How'd you like me to run back to the office right now and bring over a copy of that crap you turned in last year, a week in Bermuda doing some bullshit—what was it?—weekend getaways to fuck your bitch from the art museum?"

"Art museum?" someone along the wall snorted. "She looks like she's from The Museum of Natural History."

Carla sat back down, crossed her legs, pulled her black skirt closer to her knees and crossed her arms. The room grew quiet. The protest seemed successfully squelched by the office manager and Jamie's emergency nurse.

Jamie thought, *Damn, she is some piece of work. A good thing I kept my mouth shut.*

Up in the front, he noticed Steven edging his way forward, placing something in Robbins' hand while whispering in his ear. Robbins delightedly held up a security pass that buzzed employees into the *Trib* building during nighttime hours when there was no one manning the front desk in the lobby.

"Carla, I can tell you that you couldn't just run back to the office," Robbins said. He was grinning like the gap-toothed Letterman after another bland monologue joke.

"We had someone over at the building a couple of hours ago. These cards don't work anymore. They've already installed a new security system. In effect, they've locked you out too. Since the *Trib* has taken a position of not wanting to negotiate a new contract with our union, I move that we officially are on strike, as of this morning."

Jamie couldn't believe it or didn't want to believe it.

Half the people in here are reporters—and no one is going to at least ask who the source of this information is? This is such bullshit!

"Let's show this bastard who we are," Robbins yelled. He shook his fist and punched the air.

That was the last thing Jamie heard before he was caught in a tide of humanity pressing through the corridor, surging toward the street.

On the way through, to Jamie's left, he spotted Blaine, pinned against the wall, the proverbial fly. In the midst of another long drag, holding the cigarette high to avoid setting fire to someone's hair, he caught Jamie's eye.

Blaine smiled, wickedly. He mouthed the words, "What did I tell you?"

Jamie didn't respond. He only lamented that Blaine had been right—*damn straight this is no fucking democracy. We didn't even get a show of hands.*

Needing no effort to move forward, Jamie felt as if he were floating on a raft, about to go over the falls. He was pushed along until he was out the front door, into the street, meeting the flash of cameras and the glare of television lights.

He recognized some reporters from other media outlets. One spotted him and called out his name. Too late, he was shepherded past and handed a cardboard picket sign by an Alliance member who had clearly been positioned before the meeting was over.

Jamie had a flashback to an awful night when a boy from down the street slept over and his striking father and uncle paraded around the apartment wearing picket signs on their heads with their pants down around their knees.

At least they had an excuse—they were drunk.

Feeling stiff, almost programmed, certainly silly, Jamie slipped the picket sign over his head without looking what was printed on the front. It might have said, "Kick me, I'm Unemployed," but all he knew was what he felt: *This string feels like a damn noose digging into my neck.*

His tic got worse. If only he could spin his neck 180 degrees and exorcise himself from this fast-developing nightmare.

CHAPTER SIX

"Molly, has Louie called yet?"

Morris waited ten seconds for an answer that didn't come. That could only mean his wife was in the back bedroom, on the phone again with their daughter. Their marathon conversations exasperated Morris because Becky lived in the downstairs apartment of their two-family home.

"What's the big deal?" Molly would say. "If someone calls, it'll beep and I'll get off."

It had been weeks since Becky's last failed attempt at getting pregnant. That meant another mourning period could commence at any moment, leaving Becky in bed, depressed and refusing to report to her teaching job. Molly's maternal mission was to talk her back on her feet.

Next to Jamie's divorce and his living more than an hour from his ex-wife and son, Becky's unrelenting infertility was the family's worst source of tension. The most benign baby chatter risked sending her on a tearful trail to a bedroom with her husband Mickey in immediate and reluctant pursuit.

Molly's prescription for her first-born child seemed to be inexhaustible patience. "Next time," she would say. "You'll see."

Morris sat on the living room sofa, facing the old console he stubbornly refused to part with. The color on its television faded in and out like out-of-town AM radio. The stereo had not been touched since the kids flap-jacked those revolting Rolling Stones albums on it.

The radio was on, set to the all-news station. Morris was dressed in his standard home uniform—boxer shorts and a sleeveless T-shirt covering but in no way hiding his pot belly. He needed a shave and a comb for his thinning gray hair. His calloused bare toes were perched on the wood trim of the glass coffee table.

He had already heard several updates on the *Trib* story, one every twenty-two minutes, hoping for a new nugget of news.

Next to him on the couch was the *New York Sun*. Its front page, ignoring the mid-term election, screamed in red banner delight—"CLOSED!!"—of its rival's sudden shutdown.

Morris only bought the *Sun* because the other option in town, the *Times*, was out of the question. He couldn't handle the microscopic print and the constipated writing. So he indulged the *Trib's* tabloid competition, read it for its excellent coverage of baseball, the only sport he followed.

Even now, confronted with his own work stoppage, he was fuming over the baseball strike that had forced the cancellation of the World Series—and just when it looked as if his beloved Yankees were making a run. Morris' head told him the players were spoiled and overpaid. His union heart could not root for an owner.

Molly called out to him from the bedroom to pick up the telephone in the kitchen.

"It's your brother," she said.

Morris rushed to the phone. "Louie, where are you?" he said.

"Kelly's," Lou said.

"What's going on down there?"

"Cops are everywhere. There's barricades and broken glass from the trucks all over the street in front of the docks. I haven't heard from Stevie yet but someone said that the Alliance and some of the other unions were meeting today to decide what to do."

Louie was breathing hard, talking a mile a minute. When Louis Kramer was troubled, independent thoughts crashed into each other like bumper cars. It was that way since they were kids, two grades apart, walking home from school in East New York.

Lou was the talkative one, forever pestering his older brother with questions that followed no narrative pattern. *Do you think I could take that kid who cursed me out in gym? Why do you like the Yankees and not the Dodgers when we live in Brooklyn? What should I tell mom about that D, the one I got in History?*

Morris would listen until he'd had enough. Then he would hold up one hand like a stop sign. "Don't worry about it, Louie, OK?"

Lou hated to admit it, but as long as Morris was around, he felt calmer, safer, better.

"Mo, listen, I'm a little concerned here," he said. His hushed voice meant he was using the pay phone near the bathrooms at Kelly's Pub, a few feet from the back room table that for years had been unofficially reserved for *Trib* printers.

Morris didn't respond. Lou kept talking.

"Some of the guys are here. Red, Tommy Isola, couple of others. The word going around is that Brady's a maniac, swearing up and down that he's not going to let the unions shut the paper. Tommy's heard that they've got a shitload of scabs to drive the trucks, even more after what happened last night."

"Lou, just because he says he wants to put out the paper doesn't mean he puts it out," Morris said. "He didn't put it out last night, did he?"

"Yeah, but they're saying the cops are going to make sure the trucks get out tonight, that the Mayor won't let them turn the other cheek and let the drivers do—well, you know, what they do. As long as Brady keeps the paper open, whether it gets out or not, we're in a bind, with the lifetime job guarantee thing."

"So…"

"So a couple guys are saying that we might have to…"

"Who said that?"

"Naw, forget who. It's just…"

"No way."

"Yeah, but…"

"You hear me, Lou? No *friggin* way do we cross anybody's picket line!"

Lou took a deep breath. "Mo, I'm not telling you that I think we should cross."

"Good, Louie, because you know me well enough to know I'm not going to do that."

"I know, Mo. I know. But I'm just telling you that these guys are wondering what'll happen with our deal if we don't. Some of the guys want to meet this afternoon. You should get down here, soon as you can because they're pushing me for answers and I keep telling them, 'Talk to Mo.' They're not going to listen to what I say like they do with you, you know what I'm saying?"

"I do, Louie."

Lou waited for his brother to offer something more. Uncomfortable moments passed.

"Louie, don't worry," Morris said.

"OK, Mo," Lou said. "But please come, OK?"

Morris hung up the phone and returned to his seat on the couch. He picked up the *Sun* again but his mind wandered far from the sports page. He would never admit this to his brother, but *this time* Morris Kramer was worried.

CHAPTER SEVEN

Morris was dozing when Molly returned from sitting with Becky. His snoring served as a soundtrack to the radio news anchor. Part of the newspaper lay precariously on his lap. The other part had slipped onto the worn lime carpet.

She knew better than to rouse him. If Morris was lights-out before noon, he must have been exhausted from sheer tension. Long ago she had come to realize this was how her husband believed he could not only contain his emotions but also defeat them.

Morris' mother had taught her to let him be when he was stressed out. The day before they were married, more than forty years now, Morris told his mother he needed a nap at ten in the morning. He didn't wake up until the morning of the wedding. Molly called a half-dozen times before taking the bus over to the Kramers' apartment in East Flatbush. She was suddenly panicked at the thought of Morris fleeing Brooklyn to become—she didn't know—a stowaway on a slow boat to Jerusalem.

"What should I do, Mrs. Kramer?" Molly said.

His Russian immigrant mother, so tiny that her apron sagged well below her knees, smiled and told her that Morris had been sleeping away stress since he was a small child.

"You don't have to do anything," Morris' mother said. "He'll wake up, God willing, and be happy to marry you."

As far as Molly was concerned, Morris was still content, if not blissful. In relaxed moments he could admit to her that their marriage could have turned out much, much worse. She took it as his best compliment.

Molly decided to let Morris sleep another few minutes. She dialed Jamie's apartment. The answering machine picked up after four rings. She hung up without leaving a message.

"Who're you calling?" Morris asked from the sofa, roused by the dialing.

"Jamie—he's not home."

She heard him mumbling.

"You want me to call back and leave a message?" she said, stepping into the living room. Molly was small in height and body type, standing maybe an inch and a half over five feet. If she weighed more than a hundred pounds, that was after her biggest meal. She wore her straight graying hair in a bun. Often she looked like she was smiling because she was squinting—never comfortable wearing the glasses that dangled from her neck on a chain.

"You would think he would call on his own," Morris said. "You would think he would know what's at stake here."

"Why do you think he wouldn't?"

"Who knows with him?"

Molly shook her head and left the room.

She confided in Becky that she had all but given up on Morris ever forging a closer relationship with Jamie. "I wish I could do something," she'd say. "But it's gone on for so long—since Jamie was a boy—and all I ask is that they don't fight in front of me."

When Jamie lived at home, Morris' long work hours and union responsibilities had helped in that respect. But weekends became especially difficult during Jamie's teenage years. Avoiding one another was next to impossible in a five-room apartment on the second floor of their two-family home—no matter how hard they tried.

Jamie could lock himself in his room for hours, watching basketball games on the black-and-white portable television and reading comic books starring *The Amazing Spiderman* and other Marvel superheroes. Morris would retreat to the bathroom and sit on the toilet for the better part of an afternoon with his newspapers. Confrontation was still inevitable.

"Dad, I have to go," Jamie would yell from the hall.

"Damn it, just wait a while, it won't kill you."

Jamie would sink to the floor, falling against the wall, rapping his knuckles on the door after every passing minute until Morris emerged, red-faced and mumbling *son of a bitch*.

Who knows with him? There were times when Morris felt as if he'd been asking that question from the days he schlepped his frail and allergy-afflicted son from one doctor to another.

Jamie never cried, as best Morris could recall, even as other kids wailed all around him. He had narrow brown eyes that at first glance almost looked Asian. The pediatrician called them *sleepy* but Morris worried because that's how his son acted most of the time.

When Morris scored seats ten or twelve rows behind home plate at Yankee Stadium, Jamie munched on a hot dog during the first inning and fell asleep in the second. Granted, he was only eight, it was 1970 and the Yankees were lousy. But it was his first ballgame and when they got home, all he could say was, "Baseball stinks. Nothing happens."

"You think so?" Morris said. "What game do you like?"

"Basketball," Jamie said. "They jump really high. Walt Frazier is so cool."

At work that night, Morris recounted the unhappy experience to his brother.

"Can you believe it, Louie?" he said. "I take him to see his first baseball game—*Yankee freaking Stadium*—and he tells me how he'd rather watch a bunch of *schvartzers* run around in their underwear."

"Yeah, Mo, I know," Lou said. "But Stevie doesn't like any sports."

"What are you comparing?" Morris said. "Stevie's a little genius—his teachers have been telling you that since kindergarten. What the hell does he need to worry about sports for?"

"Yeah, I know, Mo," Lou said. "Just don't be too hard…"

"Ah, forget it," Morris said, waving him off.

Morris and Jamie didn't bond any better when young Jamie made the occasional excursion with his father to the *Trib* on a day off, usually when Morris had quick union business. His chest swelled the first time he led the boy by the hand into the cacophony of the old composing room, pulling him through the labyrinth of clattering linotype machines.

"What do you think, Jamie—pretty cool?" Morris said.

Jamie frowned.

Morris had imagined explaining to his son that reporters and editors may have been the glamorous heroes of Hollywood's version of the newspaper game, the men about town and taverns. But not until these printers clocked in, brown bags dangling at their side, could there be a tangible production, a creation. If Jamie had ever asked what this awesome collection of sights and sound amounted to, Morris would have told him, "This is where we make the paper, son. They don't make it without us."

Jamie never seemed to get close enough to the men in the hats made of carefully folded newspaper to hear them say, "So this is little Mo?" The rhythmic clacking of the type set on forty-pound blocks and the shouts of "Watch yer back" by thick-armed men rolling the finished pages on the metal carts made Jamie recoil. He would cup his hands over his ears and crouch against the wall.

"He's so timid," Morris complained to Molly. "He has no—you know—*oomph*."

"He's just a little boy, what do you want from him?" she said. "The machines scare him. Let him be."

Morris eventually gave up trying to connect. He had more urgent matters on his mind those days—the increasingly clear fate of the printers.

It would be years before Jamie stepped into the *Trib* composing room again. By then, all that had been so intimidating was gone. The energy. The power. The heat. The remains of his father's once-dominant trade had vanished like some ancient civilization. The need for the human eye and touch to distinguish typeface and size had been replaced by clusters of computers in specialized work areas rendered numbingly docile by the vague hum of climate control.

For the printers, automation was a man-made earthquake. It condemned them to a long, cancerous decline, sustained by the guarantee of lifetime employment negotiated by their union leader, Jackie Ryan, at the dawn of the 70s. The formerly omnipotent Local 11 of the Typographical Union of America—the Ones, as it was known in New York trade circles—could not stand in the way of the technological parade. Ryan knew it. He signed away the craft and they all set out together on the road to virtual irrelevance.

The printers were soon pasting up strips of computer-manufactured copy onto grids they called slicks. Morris dismissed the work as child's play. "Like the Colorforms we bought for the kids," he told Lou. "It's embarrassing."

"I know, Mo," Lou said. "But some of the guys like the quiet. And let's face it, it's safer."

"So was the composing room if you knew what the hell you were doing," Morris grumped.

Eventually, all page-makeup could be done by editors at their terminals. By the 90s, printers were left with nothing to print. They identified and directed pages for editions like transit cops waving traffic through busy intersections.

At the *Trib*, Morris Kramer remained shop steward and night foreman, but he was no longer concerned with job description—only with the preservation of employment for the men who had earned that much. He'd fought hard for the privilege from the beginning. Having scoffed at his father's bluster that the *goyim* who ran the union would always take an Irishman or Italian over a Jew, he feared the old man was right when he tried to break in as a sub and was ignored by the supervisor for nights on end.

He'd report with the other subs and resented being left standing there, reminded of the hapless dockworkers in his favorite movie, *On the Waterfront.* He dreaded the subway ride home to the third-floor walkup in the Brownsville section of Brooklyn. He hated pushing open the door to the first sighting of Molly's sympathetic face.

"You hungry?" she'd ask.

"Just tired," he'd say.

Just the same, she would fix him a sandwich or heat up some macaroni and cheese, embellished with a touch of tuna—the way he liked it.

"It'll work out," she would say, with the brand of optimism she would later use on her infertile daughter.

The foreman eventually learned Morris' name, a grimly pronounced "*Kram-uh.*" He went on to a long proud career, mastering all the main operational facets of the newspaper print shop—linotype operator, proofreader and handman. He attended every union meeting he could, volunteering at headquarters and eventually networking his way onto Jackie Ryan's slate of trustees.

"My lawyer," Ryan called him. Morris took it more as praise than an anti-Semitic slur. Morris had, in fact, been in the room two decades earlier—though it seemed like two lifetimes ago—when the automation agreement was reached.

Ryan promised Morris that not one of the printers would lose his job before they were ready to retire. "You're owed that much if you've risked losing a finger or a foot working one of those damned machines," he said.

Now these were Morris' men. They needed him to make sure that

Leland Brady—an outsider with no understanding or sentiment of the sacrifices they'd made—honored Ryan's pledge.

"I'm taking a shower and then I'm going down to see the guys," Morris told Molly.

"You want me to give Jamie a message when he calls?"

"If he calls."

"Morris, you know I don't like to hear that," she said.

Ninety minutes later, Morris climbed the steps from the subway onto Fulton Street. He headed through the mid-afternoon crowd, down toward the maze of city housing projects that stood like eight-story sentinels guarding the undeveloped waterfront. He couldn't remember seeing a bigger law enforcement presence at a strike scene. Police cars were everywhere.

He hurried around to the back of the building and crossed the street into a bar, nodding to the owner Kelly Murphy. He went directly to the back, caught his brother's eye and settled into the open seat that Tommy Isola pulled away from the table for him.

"Guys," Morris said.

"Mo, this just came for you," Louie said.

Lou pushed a white envelope across the table.

"Brady's son brought it down and left it with Kelly about an hour ago," Louie said. "She told him we were back here, but the prick just told her to give it to us."

"You kidding?" Red Duggan said. "There's no way that jerk-off dares come back here."

The back room of Kelly's was the printers' lair. As a makeshift union hall, it had its charms and benefits. Free rent and an occasional burger were among them. Kelly Murphy, daughter of a one-time *Trib* printer, made her real money off the buffalo-chicken-wing-eating editorial and advertising staff which stayed in front. She'd decorated that area in the popular sports bar motif. A new TV satellite dish beamed sports games from all over the country. But the back end she left alone, a jumble of bare walls and splintered wood tables with no coverings. *Trib* printers had the back of the bar to themselves, clubhouse of the lost boys.

Morris tore open the envelope and pulled out a letter on *Trib* stationary, addressed to him. He read loud enough for everyone—including Kelly twenty feet away at the bar—to hear.

Dear Mr. Kramer:

As you are well aware, the *Trib* is currently experiencing an unfortunate stoppage by its unionized workforce. As you also know, the strike was precipitated by employees following routine disciplinary measures taken by the *Trib* in response to work place intransigence, in accordance with specified conditions in past labor contracts.

Despite the strike, and whatever support the United Deliverers Association may draw in its conflict with the *Trib*, the newspaper's parent company, Atlantic News Corp., has determined that it will continue to publish, without delay, and therefore expects all management employees and those still under personal or organized labor contract to report for work. Failure to do so WITHIN A REASONABLE TIME FRAME will result in the termination of existing agreements and the possible dismissal of said employees.

Sincerely,

Leland F. Brady, Publisher

Morris jammed the letter back into the envelope, ripping it in the process. The others at the table, waiting for his response, said nothing. A cute freckled waitress brought a menu for Morris and asked if anyone needed a drink. Lou pushed his empty bottle toward the edge of the table.

"Another Bud, thanks," he said.

Lou avoided his brother's eyes and checked his watch. His foot tapped a steady beat against the floor.

"By the way, anyone heard from Sean Cox?" he said. "He left a message on my machine, said he was coming down. He needed to see us about something."

Nobody answered. They were anxiously waiting on Morris.

"Guys, I think this is just a formality," he said, lifting the envelope a couple of inches and setting it down. "They have to cover themselves legally. On the one hand, they say we should *report to work*. Then they say within a reasonable time frame—but what the hell does that mean? They know we're not going to cross a picket line. They're expecting this thing to be settled by the end of the week."

"Maybe we should have a lawyer look at it," Red said.

"Why do that?" Morris said, reaching for the menu. "It would be a waste of money we don't have. Brady's bluffing."

There was an uncomfortable silence before Lou said, "Mo's right. The scumbag is bluffing."

The others nodded and glanced nervously around the table. Not another word was spoken until the waitress returned with Lou's beer. She asked Morris what he'd like to order, but he didn't answer. He continued to stare at his menu which he was holding upside down.

CHAPTER EIGHT

Jamie actually swelled with rebellious pride as he chanted an improvised battle cry, "Don't buy the *Trib*." Any tabloid editor who submitted so unimaginative a headline for the first edition would have had it rewritten for the second. But Jamie's newly discovered ardor faded soon after a smiling brunette in an unbuttoned black coat, dark business suit and very high heels made brief eye contact and passed by.

The strikers cut a circuitous swath on the way back to the *Trib* building, picket signs swaying as they marched through the Fulton Street business area, past the fish market and along the East River. Some in the lunch crowd seemed amused. A few passers-by volunteered a thumbs-up. But Jamie recognized this common response he had seen while reporting at crime scenes and accidents, too many places where the curious couldn't help but gape at a spectacle while hurrying back to their comparatively sane lives.

In fact, Jamie considered himself an accredited representative of those who wanted to have a general idea of what was happening and not much more. He didn't fancy himself a journalistic insider as much as just someone who crossed into the disaster zone on an abbreviated fact-finding mission.

Truth be told, he was never very much at home around the sudden and occasionally shocking messes that commanded a few paragraphs in the next day's paper. *Get through it*, he would tell himself. Get what you need and get back to the solitude of your partitioned workspace, to the anesthetizing clatter of computer keys. There he could enjoy the challenge of organizing the chaos of the street, of life itself, into an orderly and publishable six hundred words.

By the time the Alliance contingent was within a few blocks of the *Trib* building, Jamie's throat was dry. He was chanted out, starved for lunch. His limp fist, when he bothered to raise it, would not have knocked out a horse fly. He only feigned a surge of energy when Steven, working his way back from the front of the pack, found him languishing in the middle.

"So, what do you think?" Steven said, walking alongside.

"I think we're on strike," Jamie said, impassively.

"It's going to be a fucking war, you know?"

"I guess."

"Listen, when we get to the building, we'll need to start organizing picket duty right away. And then set up a meeting to create a longer-term strategy because you know that moron Robbins hasn't thought of anything beyond getting us out of the building."

Jamie nodded obediently. He watched as Steven, his body typically caffeinated, rejoined the front of the pack. Steven had inherited his father's wiry frame—he was almost six feet tall, with dark brown eyes and a prominent nose that fit his angular face. His straight black hair, worn stylishly long, flapped in the breeze blowing off the river. Six months past his thirty-second birthday, Steven could still pass for a scruffy Columbia undergrad with jeans ripped at the knee and his hand on the tight ass of some poetry-reciting coed.

When they both were in college, Steven would occasionally invite Jamie to a party at his off-campus apartment on the Upper West Side with the promise of an introduction to a cute freshman he might get into bed with minimal effort and charm. But Jamie hated the inevitability of having to reveal himself as an interloper from Hunter College, a city commuter school. College life had been a mostly graceless, sexless tedium that concluded with him graduating after five years as a communications major. He minored in film studies, which more or less had credentialed him to consult the movie reviews before choosing which one to see.

Right out of school, he took a summer job teaching basketball three afternoons a week to semi-coordinated pre-adolescents at a Jewish Community Center day camp. In the fall, he was hired to work afternoons in the center's after-school programs. One afternoon it was cooking class— tapioca pudding and grilled cheese sandwiches left uneaten by the kids for Jamie to pick at and dispose of. Another afternoon it was dodgeball in the gym. Finally, he agreed to replace the Cub Scout den mother whose pregnancy required sudden bed rest.

Most of the letters Jamie sent out seeking full-time employment went unanswered. He found a full-time job selling shoes in a department store. He sold magazine subscriptions making cold calls. Two years after graduating from Hunter, he went home one day and, with all the rehearsed humility he could muster, asked his father to help him secure a job at the *Trib*.

Morris looked at Jamie as if he'd requested a ride on the space shuttle. Molly shot Morris a hard stare.

"Why couldn't you?" she said. "People do these things for their children. At least ask."

Jamie was hired within the month as a copy boy, with the promise of promotion to editorial clerk if he handled his initial chores well. Six months after Jamie pioneered a second generation of Kramers at the *Trib*, Steven graduated from the Columbia School of Journalism. He was snapped up right outside those august gates of academia as a general assignment reporter.

"Don't worry, I won't make you get coffee for me," Steven told him during a family dinner at a Chinese restaurant. Only Becky, with whom Jamie made eye contact, seemed to acknowledge what a shitty thing it was for Steven to say.

Jamie, as usual, hid his envy and did his best to tolerate Steven, who always looked like he was ready to make a smart-ass remark—and often was.

When they were boys, Jamie would complain to his mother that his cousin was a braggart and that he made Jamie feel like he was good at nothing. Molly would say, "He needs to make himself feel better because he hasn't had it so easy." Jamie could at least understand Steven in that context.

They were in grade school when Steven's mother, Aunt Marge, began substituting scotch for her husband's companionship while Lou worked night shifts in the composing room. By the time Lou caught on, she was deep into an alcohol-fueled affair with Freddie the mailman from down the block. They ran off when Steven, an only child, was in sixth grade. Uncle Lou raised him alone. Steven spent many a night doing his homework on the floor in Jamie's room, sleeping on a cot a couple of feet from Jamie's bed.

"My mother's a drunk," he said one night with the lights out. "I'm glad she's gone."

Jamie didn't answer. He liked Aunt Marge for how she playfully teased his father for "only smiling on the day he gets a tax refund from the government."

On nights before non-school days, Uncle Lou would take Steven to the office, where he would sneak away from the composing room to spy on editors and reporters hunched over keyboards—index fingers pecking away, covering for other fingers untrained. Steven was drawn to that life early on.

"He wants to be one of the big shots," Lou would say, affectionately grabbing his teenage son around the neck. He said this once in the company of Morris and Jamie. Jamie wished his father had a comeback regarding Jamie's future plans. But Morris had not a clue what Jamie was contemplating and neither for the most part did Jamie. They would stand by quietly, awkward and resentful.

When he was hired as a reporter, Steven scoured the streets for little people under siege by landlords, city agencies, anyone in power. His writing was filled with bold, effusive commentary—leaving Cal Willis rolling his eyes and a finger on the delete key.

Occasionally Willis even wondered about the veracity of Steven's quotes. They were so well-timed and pithy that any editor worth his salt and cynicism would question if they originated from the notes of a meticulous journalist or the imagination of a Hollywood screenwriter.

"You sure he said this?" Willis would say.

"Here, it's right in my notes," Steven would respond.

There was no arguing with the fact that his cousin produced front of the paper copy. Within three years, he was off the general assignment schedule and given the freedom of an enterprise reporter. The column came soon after, before Steven turned thirty. It was more specialized than Pat Blaine's—a demagogic, union-touting, Wall Street-bashing voice for the worker. Steven volunteered the title—"In Labor"—and even rendered a crude drawing of an old waterfront boss choosing his crew from a ragged crowd of workers. It became his logo.

The column was relished by the city's unions, admired by some editors uptown at the *Times*. One of them called Steven to say, "We might consider you after you've matured as a writer and toned it down."

He immediately went to Maxine Hancock and informed her of The Gray Lady's quote-unquote interest. She offered him a raise and a contract.

"How would it look if I signed a contract and quit the union?" he said. Of course he gratefully accepted the raise. Mission accomplished, salary upgraded, he ridiculed the notion of going to the *Times* and writing stories he compared in style to text book math.

He proclaimed the *Trib* "my paper" and its readers "my people."

But Steven's column seemed to become an endangered species in the early reign of Leland Brady. He was too much the bleeding-heart to suit a publisher who had made his fortune in his native Dublin and later London and the Canadian provinces by generating readership less with personal conviction than sheer ambition. While longtime Brady associates described him as an avowed conservative, the editorial position of his newspapers was typically opportunistic. In New York, where the *Times* spoke to the liberal majority, Brady's mission was to steer the *Trib* to the far right, to become so much the enemy of the *Times* and of Godless New York that even the Man Upstairs might sign on for home delivery.

Leland Francis Brady was well known in Ireland and the U.K. for his cozy relationships with the well-heeled and connected. Leveraged with a string of publishing houses, he rewarded his new friends with lucrative book deals. He fashioned himself as a more eccentric, flamboyant Murdoch and became known for his posh gatherings aboard luxury yachts. He reveled in being referred to by the broadsheets and trade magazines across the Atlantic as the hottest press lord. He conferred on himself the eminently bogus title of Lord Leland Brady—and ordered his companies worldwide to do the same.

He arrived triumphantly aboard the Vanessa Queen—named for his wife—in New York harbor to stuff enough cash into Maxine Hancock's account to allow her to live luxuriously for her remaining days. The newsroom mourned her departure and welcomed Brady with a front page that read: **LORD, HELP US.** The staff's true feelings were expressed in the late edition when the comma between **LORD** and **HELP** was mysteriously dropped.

Two days after the sale was complete, Brady rented the ballroom at the Waldorf and threw a bash for the city's power brokers. Mimicking his social rituals abroad, he began throwing the occasional and extravagantly catered Friday night dinner party aboard his yacht. He drew up the guest list on Monday mornings for the city room manager he inherited, Carla Delgado. Rare was the invitee who declined, who wanted to risk not being a friend of the man who had come to New York to expand his influence in the New World.

In the blink of an eye, the *Trib* went from Hancock's rugged and unaffiliated coverage of City Hall to unquestioning support of a conservative agenda. With an election coming up, Brady threw his editorial might behind Republican challenger Harold Zimmerman, summoning his city editor Willis into his office every day for a review of the next day's political news. Armed with a bright red marker, Brady would check off stories or draw a large X right through the ones he didn't approve of. The incumbent Democrat's coverage was cut in half. When Willis groused, Brady offered him early retirement, with four weeks' pay.

Willis was the first black city editor in the history of mainstream New York City journalism, still the highest-ranking African-American at any of the papers. He loved the *Trib*. He spent so much time in the newsroom—routinely working twelve-hour days—that reporters joked he had no apartment and slept on a Greenwich Village bar stool.

The upshot was that Willis was not about to surrender his job to Brady that easily.

Steven, conversely, was emboldened by the union protection he had for as long as the union could protect itself.

"Mr. Kramer, the champion of organized labor, if I am not mistaken," Brady said when he made his introductory newsroom rounds. He was a massive man, six-foot-four and more than three hundred pounds, with thick dark hair that belied his sixty-four years. He had a taste for exquisite silk scarves.

"I write about jobs for New Yorkers, Mr. Brady—the ones who are your readers," Steven responded.

"If our readers need a job, they may consult the want ads," Brady said.

"The ads we run are for minimum wage jobs," Steven said.

Brady laughed, much too smugly, in Jamie's opinion, who was standing nearby.

"Travel the world as I have, young man, and you may discover that most people live terrifically contented lives on no great abundance of money," Brady lectured. "What they most want is to have the faith that they can live and worship peacefully, without fear of being shot by a mugger or blown up by fanatics. Their newspaper has a moral obligation to help them with that, unless you believe—like many members of your Congress—that we ought to be in the business of guaranteeing them employment."

With the last word, Brady moved on. Steven turned to Jamie and half-joked, "I'll be pounding a beat by tomorrow." But the only newspaper passion of Brady's that outranked his ideology was his undying devotion to the bottom line. He set about operating the *Trib* on a shoestring, not even bothering to bring aboard financial or editorial people from his parent company. He merely installed his son Maxwell, bestowing on him the title of executive editor. Maxwell Brady took to proofreading the paper every night from the bar stool of the trendiest East Side haunts.

Lee Brady had apparently surmised that Steven's column had too much readership to kill outright. The column continued, though Brady and occasionally his son grew into the habit of spiking one for every three printed.

Weeks before the strike, Steven had managed to deliver one dear to Brady's own political sensibilities. He blistered the teachers union for threatening a job action if the city continued to explore its plan of reducing classroom crowding by operating a year-round school calendar.

Teachers want it both ways. They complain about overcrowded classrooms. Then they threaten to walk out when the Mayor sits down with the Chancellor and comes up with a viable working plan to ease classroom crowding by extending the school year. They say an extended summer vacation is essential to the well-being of students but it sounds like a self-righteous attempt to preserve the great American essay, "How I Spent My Summer Vacation."

The column got the wood—the front page. The next morning, Brady stepped out of his office with the paper rolled under his arm. The newsroom came to a standstill.

"Pardon, pardon. The work today of Mr. Kramer was the finest example of what we set out to do here and must not pass without an appropriate show of appreciation. I have therefore instructed our accounting department to award our esteemed columnist a $250 bonus for his extraordinary essay."

At which point, before the startled newsroom had fully ingested

Brady's spontaneous and uncharacteristic largess, Steven climbed right up on his desk and shouted, "Attention…attention, please."

Brady, walking back toward his office, turned around and did a double take.

"I would like to thank Mr. Brady for his generosity. But columnists do not accept cash awards for their convictions. We only wish for every opportunity to express them, without editorial interference."

Brady shook his head and walked away. Just as he stepped inside his office and closed the door, he unleashed a mighty, convulsive sneeze.

Steven bent his, slender frame into a perfect bow and bellowed, "Bless you, Lord."

The city room broke out in laughter. Steven's line was etched in *Trib* lore, contemptuous employees all over the building mouthing those words the moment Brady's back was turned.

Brady continued to have the last word. The same day Steven rejected his gesture, he returned to work on a Sunday column about former welfare mothers being harassed by city workers. It was a controversy bound to land in the lap of the new mayor, Zimmerman.

Willis gave him the thumbs-down sign when he trudged back from his daily showdown with the publisher.

"Didn't it occur to you that Brady might fire you on the spot for showing him up?" Jamie asked Steven the next morning.

He shrugged. "Fuck him. When the contracts run out and the shit hits the fan, this place will be a war zone—and then we'll see how tough Lord Brady is."

Jamie knew his cousin had been waiting for the strike, almost to the point of invitation. "The paper is already lost to this lunatic," he said at Kelly's one night, going over each slanted story, getting angrier by the beer.

"Steve, I don't think there are too many people who actually want to go out," Jamie said. "Things aren't good out there in this business or in the economy. And the holidays are coming."

Steven chugged more beer and kept talking.

"The only way we can get it back is to kick his ass in a fair labor fight," he said. "He won't keep it if he can't have it his way. He'll sell the damn place lock, stock and barrel twenty minutes after we shut him down. We'll get our paper back. I'll get my column back."

Jamie listened to his cousin rant. He wondered if only a drunken fool—or a well-paid columnist with no dependents—could be so anxious to walk out.

CHAPTER NINE

Jamie stepped away from the marching strikers as they neared the *Trib* building and the wooden blue barricades that were set up by police. Keeping his distance from the picket line, he hid across the street behind a parked van.

His cousin, along with Carla Delgado, had taken over organization of the line. Steven, he conceded, was a natural leader. He always had been. When they were kids, in school or at summer camp in the Catskills, there was even a modicum of status in it for Jamie when others discovered that Steven was his cousin.

While Steven hung a picket sign from a low branch of a small tree, Carla stepped into the street and yelled, "Listen up."

The assembled staff once again gave her its full attention.

"Unless you sign up at headquarters, you will not be eligible for union strike benefits. You can get a hundred bucks a week, two-hundred if you are the only working member of your family and have at least two kids."

His ex-wife would be thrilled with this jackpot news, Jamie thought. The notion of midnight patrol on the deserted waterfront already fatigued him. The afternoon sun had faded behind the clouds and taken with it the last vestige of autumnal comfort. Jamie almost started to walk toward the picket line but held back. Steven didn't seem to be looking for him. He had more than enough people to organize for the war that he insisted would bring Brady down.

Jamie decided to leave, shielding himself from view behind parked cars. He headed for the subway, thinking *Steven won't even notice I'm gone.* Just the same, the train back to Brooklyn Heights couldn't come fast enough.

With no destination in mind, he walked the narrow streets lined with handsome brownstones and brick-faced apartment buildings. He had fallen hard for them and the entire neighborhood from the night he nearly emptied his gas tank in search of a parking spot and was forty-five minutes late for his first date with Karyn.

They met in the spring of 1990 at a mixer for Hunter College graduates. Karyn failed to mention that she had transferred to Hunter from Princeton after two years. Having fared so poorly in the Columbia pickup scene, Jamie might have wished her well and gone on his way had she told him. Instead, he and Karyn topic-hopped from his business—newspapers—to hers—book publishing—until finding more mutual territory: a love of Jackson Browne, every Seinfeld episode from the show's inception in 1989 and the NBA playoffs.

Jamie was for Magic Johnson and the Lakers because they were, beyond *Showtime*, the essence of unselfish team play. She was for the Pistons and Isiah Thomas because he had "the cutest ass and an irresistible smile."

Given that standard, Jamie decided not to elaborate on how much of a basketball junkie he really was—and how much of his adolescence he had devoted to the game.

He looked more like a wrestler than a basketball player. A shade over 5' 8" without the verticality of his hair, Jamie was on the stocky side, a body replica of his father. The curvature of his back made his shoulders look stooped. Nor was he the most graceful or fluid of athletes. But he had spent hours as a kid launching weathered balls at backboards and rims in schoolyards and in cramped neighborhood backyards. From the time he played his first games of three-on-three, he loved basketball's freewheeling nature and simplicity, the ease with which it was organized, controlled, without parental supervision or intrusion.

By late middle school he was the proud owner of a magnetic dribble with a surprising quickness for the proverbial stout white boy. For Jamie, the beauty of playing his position, of being the point guard, was that he was in control of making things happen for others. The process of creating off the dribble and finding the open man was instinctive. You had to make an immediate decision and live with it. There was no time for second guessing—a Jamie specialty—because the next play was coming up fast.

He made his high school freshman team and became friends with several black kids who lived in the housing projects a few blocks away. In the 70s, Farragut Houses was no isolated fortress of poverty and despair like other developments around the city. Blacks and whites, European immigrants and those from the Caribbean co-existed. But there was never a proprietary question around the basketball courts that were smack dab in the middle of the cluster of buildings. The black kids reigned. And Jamie had an open invitation to get chosen in.

They called him J—so what if he bore no resemblance to the gravity defying Julius Erving, Dr. J? At least his curly hair, worn stylishly long, could from a distance pass for a reasonable imitation of Erving's trademark fro.

The courts were quiet on Sunday afternoons when Erving's Philadelphia 76ers played on national television. Jamie often watched from the crowded apartment of the boy he liked best. Ronald Allen was a gangly six feet tall—gap-toothed and so skinny that the other boys called him Bones. His favorite Knick was Earl Monroe, though his attempts to mimic Monroe's classic spin moves were comical. His bank shot, however, was money.

"Man, we should go to your house and watch the game," he said to Jamie one Sunday when Dr. J and the 76ers were playing the Knicks—his favorite team but only a shell of the early 70s championship teams. "Bet your family's got a nice color TV, better than this old piece of shit."

That was true, but Jamie made up an excuse that his family was having relatives over. For one thing, he was suspicious of how welcoming his father would be. He hated it when Morris and Uncle Lou used that word—*schwartzer*. Their attitudes convinced Jamie to make sure that what happened in the projects stayed in the projects.

Beyond basketball, there were other adolescent adventures going on there. He smoked his first joint in a chilly, dark stairwell. He copped his first feel.

Sarah Tompkins' breasts were fleshy and Milky Way brown. In the half-dozen times they slipped away from the crowd, she confidently guided him under her sweater, never bothering to complicate matters with a bra.

Morris had no clue that his son's incursions into the projects were producing such interracial indulgences. He still hated that Jamie spent time in a place that his generation believed symbolized failure. They had worked so hard to escape from it.

"I just go there to play ball," Jamie told him. But Morris learned otherwise one hazy summer afternoon between Jamie's freshman and sophomore years. Jamie's team had lost a game and stepped off the court for the boys who called *next*. Jamie wandered outside the fence where the girls watched and flirted. Sarah Tompkins and a friend were among them.

The friend sidled up to Jamie and said, "You're not bad for a white boy." Sarah promptly elbowed her aside.

"Don't be getting ideas," she said. "Jamie and I got a little thing going. We have our secret meeting place."

Jamie blushed, uncomfortable with the public display. Just the same he was aroused by Sarah's seductive playfulness. She was wearing a spaghetti-strap top with tight shorts that highlighted the tautness of her thighs.

She winked at Jamie and said, "Maybe we'll meet up soon if you promise to take me on a date."

"Like where?" Jamie said.

"You know, like a movie."

The thought of being with Sarah outside the projects terrified Jamie. He played along though, asking her what she wanted to see.

"Something sexy," she said, rubbing a shoulder against his. This led to a game of pretend fighting and a round of kissy face. Jamie was feeling his fifteen-year-old oats until he felt a hard tap on the shoulder.

He turned to face his father.

"What are you doing here?" he stammered.

"I need you to come home now," Morris said, red-faced and in no mood to argue.

"Why?" Jamie said. He sensed the others were watching.

"Because your grandmother had a heart attack and is in critical condition. We're all going to the hospital."

Morris turned and walked off. Jamie looked at Sarah, who had overheard them. She shrugged her shoulders. Jamie left without saying a word. One of the mouthier boys yelled out, "Don't worry, Big Daddy. J's cool. We weren't taking his money—only his motherfucking Cons."

It was a reference Morris wouldn't get—Jamie had bought a new pair of black Converse sneakers that were the envy of the playground.

He got why his father had to come looking for him and why he had to follow him home, lame as it looked to the others. But only the gravity of his mother's health had eclipsed the shock of what Morris had stumbled upon—his son in the arms of a black girl. He didn't say a word about it to Jamie, but Jamie read the disapproval in his eyes.

Jamie told his mother, "Every time I pick up my basketball and walk toward the door, he looks at me like I'm going out to join the NAACP."

"Talk to him about it," Molly said.

"Yeah, *right*," Jamie said.

He knew it was pointless to explain—and why the hell should he? Morris would never understand what his social acceptance in those outdoor courts meant. Even Jamie was incapable of fully getting it until years later when he explained it to his brother-in-law Mickey, who liked basketball. "Going into the projects helped me play all four years in high school. I sat the bench on varsity as a senior because I didn't have the speed the other kids did. That didn't matter. I was on the team. I was accepted as a *player.* Not that it mattered to anyone at home."

"Your dad didn't go the games?" Mickey asked.

"Not one."

"Why not?"

"They were played weekdays, late in the afternoon," Jamie said. "He'd already left for work. But he had some days off. He just didn't like, you know, the element. His greatest fear was that I was going to date black girls."

Jamie, in fact, could still picture the relief on Morris' face when, years later, he brought Karyn home to meet his parents—the first time he'd brought *any* woman home. A few bites into dinner, he announced they had decided to get married. Molly cried. Morris hugged Karyn tight. She had him at the mention of her last name—Kleinman.

Jamie had called her a few days after they met. He took her on a dinner date in Brooklyn Heights.

"I thought you would be here at 7, 7:15," she said when she answered the door. Her one-bedroom, second-floor apartment was in a corner building two blocks from the famous Brooklyn Heights Promenade.

"Your neighborhood has lots of personality but no parking," he said.

Her building was run down, its hallways musty and dark. But Karyn's apartment was well-furnished and spotless, painted in light, cheerful colors. Framed posters decorated the walls. The pillows on the couch were set perfectly in the corners. Magazines were carefully laid out on the coffee table as if it were a dentist's office.

Karyn wore a short black skirt, turtleneck sweater and earrings that fell even with her neck-length light brown hair. She appeared taller than five-foot-four, thanks to a slender frame and the heels on her black Frye boots. She wore granny glasses that slid down her nose just enough to cover a slight bump. On both wrists were bangle bracelets, different colors all—her trademark wardrobe accoutrements. She had on a lemon-scented perfume that Jamie found too pungent but would never have the audacity to complain about.

They ate sushi, which he labored to feign a taste for, on Montague Street. They bought ice cream cones at a Baskin-Robbins next door to the newsstand. Eight months later they were married in the neighborhood in a brownstone synagogue and celebrated modestly with a small delegation of family and friends in a private room at Junior's restaurant on Flatbush. Jamie moved into her one-bedroom apartment. He quickly grew to love the irregularly shaped neighborhood on the promontory of Long Island—about eight blocks wide and fourteen long at its principal range—that took form as New York's so-called first suburb after the establishment of a steam ferry between Manhattan and Brooklyn in 1814.

It all seemed so long ago now. So much had since gone wrong. So much had changed. Baskin-Robbins had turned into a florist. Jamie and Karyn had left what had been *her* neighborhood together and Jamie had come back to it, alone.

He walked along Montague, picked up a *Times* from the newsstand and settled in at a Greek restaurant where they had occasionally eaten. Jamie set the paper on the table and scanned the front page. The lead story on the mid-term elections headlined: **CLINTON STRATEGISTS SEE GLOOM FOR NEXT TWO YEARS.** The middle of the page featured an investigative look into security advancements that had apparently been proposed at the World Trade Center following the car bombing of an underground garage in February 1993.

Jamie had played a small role in the *Trib's* reporting of that story, manning the phones and recording information from reporters in the field. He was grateful for the mention he received in the box identifying the many who had contributed to the coverage.

Below the fold, near the page index, was a small headline over a single tease paragraph: **SHUTDOWN AT** *Trib*, **METRO, PAGE 3.** He pulled the Metro section from inside, folded over the front. He found himself staring at a familiar sight—burning stacks of *Tribs* alongside the hobbled delivery truck.

The strike news seemed dated because, after all, this was a story he was living. By the time Jamie's dinner of lamb and potatoes arrived, he had downed his Coke and wasn't much hungry. He picked at the meat and called for the check. He resumed his wandering of the streets and strolled onto the Promenade. There he could stare at the twilight majesty of downtown Manhattan. He could watch the boats drift by, framed against the backdrop of office buildings, dwarfed by the Twin Towers of the World Trade Center.

Jamie loved the view though he always seemed to be admiring it in passing or when jogging or braving the potholes on the Brooklyn-Queens Expressway.

Darkness came. The bulb on a nearby lamppost flickered. A tugboat foghorn bellowed, momentarily drowning out the rumbling of the highway traffic below. Jamie felt no urgency to go home. He was content to stretch out his legs and to dwell on his predicament without having to do anything about it. An hour passed, then another. He closed his eyes, napped intermittently until distracted by high school boys in droopy sweats woofing on each other, bouncing basketballs that echoed in the evening chill.

Jamie glanced at his watch: ten after eight.

He trudged wearily up the exit ramp, past a young couple embracing against the fence of the toddler playground. Jamie swung around to Hicks Street, where he had taken refuge after his divorce from Karyn in a red brick, four-story building. All he could afford was a three-hundred-fifty square-foot studio, sublet to him by an unemployed attorney relocated to Philadelphia to live with a girlfriend. The rent was marked up from a subsidized $199 a month to $300, still a bargain and less than the cost per night at most Manhattan hotels unfrequented by cockroaches and crack heads.

Jamie posed as the attorney's cousin and endured the three-floor walkup and occasional act of sabotage on the part of the Israeli landlord. Once a month on cold winter nights, the jerk would sneak into the basement and cut the heat in an attempt to chase out the tenants. Then he could renovate the apartments and sell them as marked-up co-ops. Considering the portion of his earnings that were owed to his ex-wife and son in Westchester, Jamie invested in a space heater.

He bounded up the stairs, two at a time, pushed his way into the cramped room and saw that there were two messages on his answering machine.

Molly: "We're having dinner tomorrow night. Your father wants you to come."

Sure he does. Jamie fast-forwarded to the next call.

Karyn: "Call me," she said. "Want to know what's going on."

He dialed Karyn.

"It's me," he said when she picked up.

"Well," she said, "what's the latest?"

"What do you mean?"

"I mean, how long before this strike is over?"

"It just started."

"Do you at least have a choice of whether you work?"

"I don't know," he said. "Not with anyone's blessing in the union—and definitely not my father's."

"I heard on the news they're saying they'll start replacing anyone who doesn't report to work."

"That's what they're saying."

"What if they do?"

"I don't know, I really can't say."

"Well, I actually have something to say…"

"OK…"

"I've been meaning to talk to you about this," Karyn said. "And now with this strike, I may as well let you know I have a job offer."

"Great, congratulations," Jamie said. He thought, *Well, at least that's good news.*

"It's in publishing. Well, not exactly publishing. You remember the guy I knew from my two years at Princeton? Jeffrey? We ran into him one night in the city, coming out of the movie theater on Twenty-Third Street?"

"The guy who dated your roommate, but you thought might have been more interested in you?"

"Not the point," Karyn said. "He's got this business idea, and he remembered from our conversation that night that I was working with Harper. He called there looking for me, and they gave him my number up here. He's got an idea for a startup company, selling books."

"Wasn't he a Wall Street guy?" Jamie said.

"Wall Street guys make money and invest it in other things," Karyn said. "He's apparently done pretty well and wants to go into the book-selling business, except he wants to sell them electronically."

"How do you do that?"

"On this internet thing everyone in the business world is so excited about. They're saying that a huge segment of goods and services are going to become available through the computer."

Jamie stifled a chuckle and rolled his eyes, but decided if he knew what was good for him he had better be positive.

"So, that's good," he said. "Will it pay more than the real bookstore in Chappaqua?"

"Yes, it will. Plus benefits. Plus…moving costs."

"Moving? To where?"

"Seattle."

"You're kidding,"

"No, actually I'm not."

"Yes you are."

Silence convinced Jamie she wasn't.

"Wait a minute," he said. "Just wait. Are you saying that you're going to pick up Aaron and move him all the way across the country without talking to me about it?"

"I am talking to you about it."

"Yes, I hear. I'm on strike from my job for one day and already you're telling me you're moving three thousand miles. And if this—pardon me—bookstore is supposed to be in a computer, why would you have to move to Seattle to work for it?"

"Look, I told you. This guy…Jeffrey…we had lunch and he said he is launching the company out there and that there would be a good position for me if I was willing to make the move, take a chance. He called the next day and offered me the job. I told him I needed some time to think about it, given the circumstances."

"I don't get it," Jamie said. "Why would you even do the interview?"

"Excuse me, aren't you the critic who's always complaining about how little I make? You're the one who was so pissed when I quit Harper to have Aaron to begin with. Remember? How many times have you accused me of making fourteen cents an hour?"

"I didn't suggest you could make more money in fucking Seattle."

"Jamie, for one thing, *fucking* Seattle is a lot closer to Los Angeles, where my father lives, than New York. Aaron and I see him—what—once a year? And when I heard about the strike at the *Trib* this morning, it got me to thinking that you were right about how I can't put off my career forever. I owe that to Aaron. I've been home all day with him pretty much for two years, working nights just to get out of the house and make a few bucks. What I make basically pays for sitters while I'm working. It was a long shot that I would move when I did the interview, but when I heard today you were on strike, it made me think, what if something really goes wrong with your job? Then what would I do? How would I pay for this house? His clothes? His future?"

"Karyn, I'm on strike one day. That doesn't mean I'm unemployed."

"Jamie, the real issue here is *me*, not you. You have nothing to do with this…"

"Aaron is also my son, no?"

"That's not what I mean. I've got to resume my own career. And if that means I have to move, then I'll have to move, and we'll have to deal with it."

"You mean I'll have to deal with it."

"I never said I didn't want Aaron to have his father…*you*…in his life. But what about his future? What about college? It's not like either of us is ever going to inherit any real money. You pay the mortgage, the bills, but you don't have a cent in the bank, and neither do I."

"Karyn, I don't know what's going to happen, but the last time we went out it was over in a couple of days. Most of these things don't last. Don't take this job because of the strike."

"I told you, this is about me. I need to give Jeffrey an answer by the end of the week."

Jamie paused, working hard to hold back his agitation. "Give it a few days, we'll see what happens," he said. "Maybe you could look for a job in New York."

"I've been looking for six months."

Jamie had no response for that. The inevitable suspicion of whether Karyn had developed a romantic interest in her old college friend—and vice versa—crossed his mind. He knew better than to broach that subject or she'd hang up on him and somehow manage to not be home for his next visit—her standard tactic when her custodial mood turned sour.

"Just don't do anything for a day or two," he pleaded. "Seattle—how in the world would I ever see…?"

"The other line's beeping," she said. "I've got to go."

Jamie hung up, pulled the receiver up again and froze in mid-slam.

He walked over to the bed, sat down and looked up at the inoperative ceiling fan. He realized that in the shock and confusion of Karyn's thunderbolt, he hadn't asked to speak with Aaron. He thought about calling back. But his mood, not exactly sunny to begin with, was as gray as the sky over Seattle—or so he had heard.

Day Two: Tuesday, November 8, 1994

CHAPTER TEN

Not this one again. Oh, please, no, the voice providing the narrative to Jamie's morning dream was pleading.

Deadline was approaching. The phone on the night table kept ringing. Jamie knew it was a source with information he needed for a story. But when he reached out to answer, the cord was severed from the receiver. He tried frantically to reattach it, but Karyn materialized, brandishing a shopping list for Aaron's birthday party. She chastised Jamie for forgetting plastic spoons.

The exception being that Jamie's subconscious had given her a makeover. She had Debbie Givens' blonde hair and was demanding an apology with a microphone aimed at his chin.

The ring came again—twice, a third time. Jamie's recorded voice intervened and delivered a shot of psychological caffeine that awakened him to the cognitive realization that he was better off asleep.

For the second morning in a row, it was Steven rousing him from the deep morning slumber that is so precious to an insomniac.

"So where the hell did you disappear to yesterday?" he bristled.

"What time is it?"

"Eight-fifteen."

"What's your problem?"

"Better question," Steven said. "Are you out with the rest of us?"

"What do you mean?"

"I mean," Steven said in his most provident tone, "you made yourself scarce after the meeting yesterday, and we need everybody we can get on the line today because they got the damned paper out..."

Which Jamie received as promising news...

"...and we're hearing that the sportswriters may be ready to cross and maybe the photographers and..."

This is really getting good, Jamie thought. He would soon have ample ammunition in a campaign to convince Karyn to cease and desist on her relocation strategy.

He propped himself up on his right elbow, the phone now wedged between ear and neck.

"...once that happens, the Alliance is finished, Brady can isolate the other unions as blue-collar thugs and there's a good chance the asshole wins..."

"Why are the sportswriters crossing?" Jamie asked casually.

"Couple of guys at Jersey papers supposedly got calls, offered jobs," Steven said. "I don't know who in his right mind would leave a job, even at a smaller paper, to come to one on strike. But our guys panicked and went back in. Got to get back to ripping the baseball owners for forcing the players out and killing the World Series."

Steven left Jamie a window of silence to acknowledge his sports association and, better yet, his wit. Jamie respectfully declined. For the most part, Steven didn't much know a foul ball from a football. He had managed, however, to sneak one summer column past Brady that condemned the owners for their attack on organized labor after the Fall Classic was taken off life support and interred in disgrace.

"We've got calls out for everyone to show up early this afternoon for a rally with a few speakers," Steven said. "A couple of guys from the national office—Robbins said they're trying to get Mario Cuomo—if they can guarantee some television coverage."

"I'll be there, I guess, if that's what you woke me up for," Jamie said, feeling blindly for the television remote in the tangle of blanket and sheet.

"It's at noon," Steven said. "I'll be speaking too."

"Hey, nice," Jamie said coolly.

"Not to change the subject," Steven said, "but didn't you once go out with Deb Givens?"

"Deb? How informal we've gotten."

"OK, excuse me, Deborah."

"I wouldn't call it going out," Jamie said. "We had drinks after work a couple of times. Why?"

"She's doing a studio thing on the strike over at the station," Steven said. "The producer called. I'm going on tonight."

"Nice person, a bit hyper, talking to the world while she's talking to you, like everyone else on TV."

"You sleep with her?"

"We had drinks, I said. I was married at the time, remember?"

"Remember who you're talking to."

"I'll tell you what, if she starts asking tough questions, why don't you change the subject and ask her if she'll sleep with you? It'll be better television than discussing that fat fuck, Brady."

On the screen of Jamie's set, speaking of the Lord, Brady's massive frame swallowed up the pretty morning anchor, making the NY1 set look out of balance, like a seesaw. Brady was smiling and holding up a copy of the morning's *Trib*, its front-page welcoming itself back into circulation. The banner headline read, **AS WE WERE SAYING**, as if clearing its throat. There was a large color photo below of a scab *Trib* driver with a sheepish smile, unloading bundles of papers in front of a newsstand.

Jamie could make out the actual lead to the story in the sub-head.

Driver Beaten in Late-Night Attack.

He turned up the sound just in time to hear Brady congratulate the city on the return of its God-fearing daily.

"…assure our readers that there will under no circumstances be further interruptions of production or delivery of their favorite morning paper. Today's edition is on the stands, with all the hard-hitting, insightful analysis that *Trib* readers have long been accustomed to and…"

Jamie had a vision of Pat Blaine propped up on a midtown bar stool, hoping the strike would be finished by the time he sobered up and remembered his contract. *Poor Pat*, he thought.

"Mr. Brady," the anchor interrupted before Brady could continue. Her voice was calm yet challenging, her demeanor pleasant but firm. Her brown hair was clipped just below her ears, her makeup inconspicuous, as if done in defiance of the more flamboyant network brand.

"Before we go live to Deborah Givens at the *Trib's* downtown Manhattan plant, could you explain how the newspaper was able to publish this morning without its union work force?"

"As you know, the untimely work stoppage by the drivers and the other unions has compelled us to employ a new staff of deliverers, as well as replacements to man the presses and numerous other positions. Some of these workers have come from our sister papers in Canada and others are new *Trib* employees. And I must compliment all of these men who have embraced a most difficult situation, in many cases leaving their homes and families, risking danger. But they recognize that the threat of violence is not enough to turn church-going men away from the opportunity to support their families.

"Our new employees are determined to help us build a prosperous future for the *Trib*, as opposed to continuing along the disastrous road the unions have been forcing one of our city's great institutions to travel with their intractable and militant negotiating practices. I want to personally thank and commend these men and promise them all good jobs, good benefits. God bless."

"Are you willing to negotiate?" the anchor asked. "And if not, aren't you engaging in union-busting tactics?"

"Our employees have voluntarily vacated their positions and at this time we cannot make the presumption that they plan to return," Brady said. "In the vernacular of the industry, the people we have hired are called permanent replacement workers. And permanent means permanent."

Jamie swallowed hard, then rested back on the pillow and pulled the blanket up to his chin as Deborah Givens appeared.

"It was a long, demoralizing and ultimately violent night for the striking workers here at the *New York Trib*. Inside the plant behind me, the presses rolled shortly after midnight, manned by replacements. The bundles of papers were then loaded onto trucks, and with the escort of a *Trib* security force and a massive police contingent ordered to the scene by the Mayor, they moved past the strikers, who screamed obscenities at the replacement drivers. Otherwise, the strikers were kept peacefully behind barricades, unlike the first night, when the trucks were obstructed from leaving the plant.

"Once the drivers were out onto the streets, it was another story. Roving bands of strikers tracked down trucks in various neighborhoods in the early morning hours, halted them in the middle of the street and pulled drivers out from behind the wheel. There were reported beatings, including one replacement driver who was hospitalized after being attacked in the Greenpoint section of Brooklyn..."

The shadowy video was rolling now. Across the night shadows on Jamie's screen, a small gang in hooded sweatshirts was pummeling two men who were on the ground, screaming for mercy.

"Fucking nigger scab!" one of the attackers yelled, with only the expletive deleted. More shouting ensued, followed by the sound of breaking glass.

"...A NY1 crew followed this *Trib* truck to an ugly scene in St. Albans, Queens until the strikers turned on our camera crew..."

The camera, still recording, was on the scattered bundles of papers in the street, before careening wildly as the crewman pulled back inside the car, speeding off with his coveted tape.

"Police this morning reported several arrests. But as *Trib* Publisher Leland Brady just announced, live in our studio, most deliveries of the paper were completed to outlets around the city and suburbs. We go now to City Hall for a live statement from Mayor Zimmerman…"

The Mayor was a fitness fanatic who jogged to work every morning rush hour. He waved to commuters, occasionally slowed to press some flesh with a startled construction worker or stockbroker. His first press conference of the day often found him still in his running suit, tufts of thinning hair resembling an untended garden.

Zimmerman announced that the city, while taking no sides in the dispute, was obligated to protect the replacement workers now producing and delivering the *Trib*. When a reporter asked if the rank-and-file police force was unhappy having to assist non-union workers, the Mayor stretched as tall as his five feet, five inches would allow. His chest seemed to swell with indignation.

"They have their jobs to do, like it or not," he said. "This is about fundamental protection under the law."

Jamie clicked off the set, closed his eyes and tried to unscramble the events of the previous nights. *Brady's an inveterate gasbag, a bully and a union-buster too. I can see that.*

But Jamie could also see the other side, enough to carry on an imaginary one-way conversation with Steven.

How can you be on the side of such a segregated union? Men who can summon enough rage to kick a guy as he lies helpless, who can shout, "Motherfucking nigger scab!" as easily as they could recite the Pledge of Allegiance?

To whom did Jamie owe his allegiance?

Didn't he at least have the right to ask?

He was always amazed by how the city's tabloid legends—the Hamills,

Breslins and Blaines—could furnish an instant take on the issue of the day. How they could summon moral outrage, seemingly without considering the other side of the story, much less contemplate the possibility they were wrong. It was as if someone out of the blue had walked up, put a hammer in their hand, pointed to a nail and said, "Right here." His cousin was like that. Jamie, conversely, could dwell for hours on an issue and end up more confused than when he began.

"Life is more complicated than you make it out to be sometimes," Jamie had told Steven once.

"Only if you make it that way," Steven said, as if nuance was an affliction. "You're just too concerned about how people are going to react."

Jamie couldn't deny that. His mother always told him he worried too much, and that was why he had so much trouble falling asleep.

His insomnia began in earnest when Jamie reached adolescence. He would lie awake for hours, changing positions, until he couldn't stand to stay in bed anymore. He would prowl the apartment into the wee morning hours. Molly would tell him, "Look at your father, he carries around everyone's problems, and he sleeps like a baby. Just don't think."

"How do you not think when you're still awake?" Jamie said.

"Then think good thoughts."

He would read—comic books, newspapers, even a school assignment that was particularly dull and might put him out. He would wrap himself in a blanket on the floor and watch television with the sound turned down to a whisper. Eventually he would fall asleep—he always did. But it was only for three or four hours in the early morning. At least Molly let him sleep until the last possible minute on school days, knowing he needed every minute he could get.

As he lay in bed, contemplating the rally, the picket line and another day on strike, weariness set in. Jamie had gotten maybe four good hours sleep. He napped for another ninety minutes. He got out of bed and trudged into the shower. He ate a bowl of cereal and downed a glass of orange juice. It was time to go to the rally—or not.

He went out to his car and pulled two shopping bags from the trunk. He walked to the subway and took it to Grand Central. He bought a roundtrip ticket to Pleasantville. He went to a phone bank and dialed Karyn's number. She answered on the fourth ring.

"I'm bringing Aaron's gifts up today," he said. "If you want to plan something during lunch hour, I can sit for him. If not, I'll drop them off and come right home."

He hung up without waiting for her to respond. He dragged the shopping bags to the platform and boarded the train. Steven would have to address the union masses without him, Mario notwithstanding, while Jamie attended to business much more personal.

CHAPTER ELEVEN

Pressed for an explanation of why he'd agreed to move to the suburbs, Jamie might have blamed it on a childhood passion. He loved trains and had since riding the New York subway with Molly and Morris as a small boy.

In theory, commuting by rail to the city was appealing, a chance for Jamie to get in touch with his inner quaint. But he immediately wished they had never left Brooklyn. The streets in Pleasantville were so empty and quiet. He missed walking out his door and seeing people. He preferred continuous white noise to silence interrupted by a car motoring past his house.

"These crickets are insane," he told Karyn on their second night in the house. "I can't sleep."

"You couldn't sleep in Brooklyn either," she said.

"It's worse out here," he said.

Who knows? Maybe I would have gotten used to it, he thought as the train left Grand Central. Jamie sat by a window, his bags of birthday gifts propped next to him. There were two other passengers—an elderly dark-skinned man wearing a turban and a long blue coat and a tall young woman with turquoise streaked hair, partially braided, in a clingy knee-length red skirt.

His neck was still tight so Jamie continued to rotate it gently, trying to crack it loose. He made sure to wear sunglasses to hide the damage from Aaron as best he could. When he arrived at the house, Karyn told him he could have Aaron for a couple of hours.

"I'm going to run to the gym and then I have a few errands to do," she said.

He resisted asking if any were related to moving to Seattle. He didn't want to risk another geography discussion that might dampen, or derail, his visit. Jamie only wanted to give Aaron his gifts before the Friday party brought a deluge of toys from friends. Most would be played with once or twice and finally heaped onto the mound of plastic rising in the corner bedroom with sloping ceilings.

Jamie had admittedly overdone the shopping. He had driven the previous Saturday to the big toy store off the Belt Parkway and wandered the aisles like a tourist. He filled his cart with a Lego assortment, Candy Land, (the only board game he recalled playing with either of his parents), a plastic ball and bat, a miniature set of cars with accompanying garage and a five-pack of Sesame Street books. These were all in addition to the starter tricycle Karyn had purchased and agreed to share as the gift from the two of them.

"Don't go crazy—he has enough junk," she'd said, prematurely consigning Jamie's generosity to the pile of excess. More than anything, she hated messiness, anything left out of place. Jamie's habits made her cranky.

"You leave shoes by the front door, clothes on the floor by the bed—why do I have to pick up after you like I would for a child?" she would say. "It's not my job."

"You're right, it's not," he'd say. "So don't."

To keep the peace, he did make more of an effort. But she went too far when he would carry cookies or a bowl of rice into the living room and onto the couch. No sooner had he gotten up, Karyn would unleash a dust buster on his loose crumbs.

"I had roaches in the city," she said.

"What are you worried about in the suburbs—a bear breaking in?" he said.

When it came to buying gifts for Aaron, Jamie dismissed her aversion to clutter on the grounds that he, the father in absentia, had to at least distinguish himself from Pleasantville's general friend populace.

The mere consideration of himself as Dad was still something of an out-of-body experience for Jamie. But he relished the time spent with his son, preplanned as it was. He thought Aaron was as beautiful a little boy as he'd ever seen. He had Karyn's rich lips, sparkling green eyes and even a small birthmark, as she did, below the right side of his mouth.

Aaron looked more like Karyn and, given the living circumstances, she made Jamie feel as if Aaron belonged solely to her as well. Early on, she tried to schedule Jamie's visits around Aaron's nap times. When that failed, she felt the need to supervise a routine diaper change, as well as a feeding and burping.

"You're hitting him too hard," she'd say. "You'll hurt him."

"I'm barely touching him," Jamie would say. "At this rate, it'll take a week."

Several times he had come close to telling her to *knock it off* but he realized she had the final say on when he could come. When she left, he would rebelliously lift Aaron out of the crib, gently deposit him on the blue bed quilt in Karyn's room—his too, once upon a time—and lie alongside him. He would nuzzle the baby's warm reddened cheeks, carefully stroking his hair.

Occasionally he would tear up and whisper, "I'm so sorry."

Aaron could not grant him clemency for his role in this nuclear calamity. But as he grew into a toddler, his eyes brightened at the sight of Jamie—or *dah-dee*.

Three weeks before Jamie's gift-bearing visit, Aaron had clomped over, carrying a mini-basketball and wanting to be hoisted up to a plastic rim for a dunk shot. A basketball connection! Jamie was a mess of conflicting emotions, joy mixed with melancholy. The truth was that it felt damn good to feel something, *anything*, since the chain of life-altering events that followed their move to the suburbs.

It was late winter, 1991, when he and Karyn bought the charming colonial with the glass-enclosed porch from the elegantly dressed blonde real estate broker with the model's legs and the William Buckley syntax. She insisted they could afford the monthly payments without mentioning that they *both* would have to continue working—along with everything in the 85-year-old relic for which they would owe almost a quarter of a million dollars.

"Lovely starter, walk to the train," Buckley had said with her lips barely moving. They had a deal by the following morning.

Hours after the movers hauled their stuff from Brooklyn, Karyn welcomed him to his new country palace with breaking news: the hot water heater had burst, flooding the finished basement and ruining the carpet.

The carpet was no big deal, she said. It could wait to be replaced, but not for too long because the real bulletin, the lead that she had calculatingly buried, was that within roughly nine months a little rug rat was coming.

One year earlier, Karyn's almond-shaped eyes had glistened with unbridled sincerity as she promised to not even think of starting a family until Jamie was doing better in the take-home department. Now she would be requiring a shopping spree to accommodate a waistline soon to undergo biological alteration.

"Can you believe it?" she said, shaking her fists and nodding vigorously. "You're going to be a father."

A father.

A father?

Shit, Jamie thought. *How can I be a father when I haven't cracked the code yet of being a son?*

"The one night we didn't use the diaphragm, remember?"

"You said it wasn't that time of the month."

"I guess I just miscounted."

"Jesus…"

"You're not happy about this, about having a child, even if we didn't plan it?"

As he stood on the threshold of the quarter-million starter—his feet suddenly feeling as if they were tacked to the welcome mat the sellers had graciously left them—did it really have to be a choice between delight and devastation? Jamie would soon enough embrace the notion of impending parenthood. It was the marriage he didn't quite know how to nurture.

He realized he had gone along with the move to the suburbs because he had somehow convinced himself it was consistent with a new pattern of accepting change in his life. But the thought of leaving Brooklyn had never occurred to him—and not to Karyn as far as he knew—before she came home from work one evening, furious and near tears.

She had spent forty-five minutes trapped in a stifling, packed elevator that delivered commuters from the Clark Street subway platform to the street-level station lobby. The city was beating her down, she said. She needed to breathe. She wanted a yard, a porch, her own retreat from the daily publishing grind.

"I'm willing to commute," she said. "The train is therapeutic."

But she gave notice at work six weeks after the move because the electrical field along the rail tracks couldn't possibly be healthy for the baby—nor could stressful work for forty-five hours a week. Her aunt, who lived a mile up the Saw Mill River Parkway, happened to know someone who knew someone who could land her part-time work at a small bookstore in nearby Chappaqua Village.

"How can we afford this?" Jamie asked.

"You want the baby to be brought up with neither parent around?" Karyn said.

Implicit in this last loaded question was the weight of her being pregnant and not having her mother—lost to breast cancer during Karyn's sophomore year at Princeton—live long enough to see it. Her father, since remarried, had relocated to Los Angeles.

"My aunt is like a mother to me," Karyn said. "Who else am I going to lean on?"

As the pregnancy progressed, even Jamie's clumsy attempts to pursue meaningful communication in the bedroom were rebuffed. In the beginning, Karyn was tired, nauseous, immersed only in the climax of a good novel. By the second month, she was downright dismissive. In one tearful tirade that Jamie could only pray was hormonal, she accused him of plotting to use his penis like a sword to abort an unwanted child.

Out of sheer financial panic, and, yes, as an excuse to escape mounting tensions, Jamie lobbied Cal Willis for extended night hours. He began staying in the city, alibiing that he didn't want to risk navigating the darkened parkway for fear of falling asleep at the wheel. It was easier and less stressful to stretch out on the bed in his old room at his parents' place.

Then came a night when Jamie went with the flow of late-afternoon office banter and career commiseration. He landed in a taxi with Debbie Givens after drinks at Kelly's, her hand massaging his crotch, her tongue locked in his. Jamie thought better of it by the time they reached her place in the Village. "I'm married and my wife is pregnant," he said in excusing himself. Left unsaid was that he had no interest in awakening next to a body—tight as it was—and having to participate in another round of career-advancing chatter without the alcoholic inducement.

Stepping out of the cab, Debbie announced herself impressed with Jamie's conscientious rejection. She kissed him on the cheek and sent him back to the office and on to his parents' apartment. Jamie went home early the next evening after work, determined to make a sincere plea that he and Karyn figure out some way back onto the same existential track.

She wasn't home. Her note on the kitchen table said she was out shopping for baby furniture with her aunt. They would have a late dinner too. He shouldn't wait up.

What Jamie read was an unambiguous directive: keep your damn sword in its sheath.

CHAPTER TWELVE

Downtown Pleasantville looked as if architectural planners had established one side of Bedford Road as Then, the other as Now. The diner on the west side of the street was an old boxcar configuration wedged between the hardware store and the local pizza joint. Directly across were the headquarters of three real estate brokers and an upscale supermarket. Its entrance was obscured by three men and one woman carrying picket signs denouncing the company for anti-union practices.

Jamie glanced uncertainly at the picketers, wondering for a moment if they had been strategically placed there by Steven. He laughed off his paranoia and let Aaron lead him by the hand, up the two steps to the glass door of the diner.

"Go *he-uh, dah-dee.* Go *he-uh.*"

Stepping inside, Aaron crouched to brush permanent scruff marks off the little Nikes Karyn's aunt had bought for him. He rose nonchalantly, took Jamie's hand and led him to one of the window booths. Each one contained an old-fashioned wall-mounted jukebox. Jamie slid in alongside Aaron and reached across to inspect the selections. At the top of the first page, he flipped to an oldie he remembered from his sister's collection of ancient 45s. The Righteous Brothers: "You've Lost That Loving Feeling."

The waitress was notably short, with fleshy arms and hair dyed orange, cut a few inches below her ears. She enthusiastically greeted Aaron while sizing up Jamie with a peripheral but poorly concealed gaze. Jamie turned to face her, lest she get an angled view behind his sunglasses of the swelling under the shades.

"How's it going, little buddy?" she asked Aaron. "You want the usual?"

Jamie, unable to share in this insider information, turned to Aaron, hoping he would place his order on cue.

"Cute boy," the waitress said. "Love those pudgy cheeks and the way you cut his hair short in the front so you can see those big green eyes. He'll be a ladies man for sure some day. Are you Dad?"

"*Gill-tee, dah-dee,*" Aaron said, pulling on Jamie's left pinky.

"I am," Jamie said.

"He comes in with his mom a lot," she said. "I don't think I've seen you around. Playing hooky from the office?"

Jamie shrugged. "I guess you could say that."

He looked past her to the clock on the wall behind the counter. It was ten past noon, the rally presumably underway downtown. Jamie imagined Steven at the microphone on a small stage in front of the *Trib*, strumming chords on a guitar and expressing his labor outrage in verse. Jamie took some comfort from recalling how Steven, who had fancied himself a folk singer in high school, could barely carry a tune.

"*Gill-tee, dah-dee. Gill-tee.*"

"Well, my ex, he used to commute to the city, but that was back in the 60s and 70s, before the money poured into town and you could actually afford to live here without being a banker or doctor," the waitress said. "We had a nice little place over on Beaver Creek Road, behind the high school. He worked in this print shop, all the way downtown, by Wall Street. It took him a couple of hours, one-way sometimes, because the train was so slow. Winters, *forget* it."

Trying to avoid the subject of Aaron's usual order, Jamie said, "So, your husband, he still commutes?"

She coughed up a loud, derisive *heh*. "Oh, he stopped a long time ago, and that's a story right there too. Started with him calling a lot and saying the train was late, or he was delayed with some order the boss had thrown at him, last minute. Then he started not coming home for two or three days, said the commute was killing him and we should even think about moving to—I don't know—maybe the Bronx. And then he called one night to say he had met someone, it just happened, he's real, real sorry but he'd be coming home by the end of the week to pick up his things."

"I'm sorry," Jamie said, consciously shielding the vacant ring finger on his left hand.

"*Gill-tee, dah-dee*," Aaron said, turning over the peppershaker. "*Gill-tee*."

"Never even saw him again, not once. The whole divorce thing was done by mail. I got remarried to a nice fellow who made a living running a landscaping business out of Katonah. We moved all the way up to Putnam County when we found out that the taxes there are, like, half. Two years ago, actually almost three, he passed away. Skin cancer. Melanoma. All those years, outdoors in the sun, he never put on a spot of sunscreen. Stubborn fool. But what are you going to do? You got to make a living, right? Got to put food on the table. We didn't have kids, mind you, but I had a lot come through this place that I got to know pretty well. Just like this little guy."

She reached a hand across Jamie's face to tousle Aaron's hair.

"My little buddy."

"*Gill-tee, dah-dee. Gill-tee*," Aaron said, stuck on his mantra.

Jamie ordered himself a well-done burger and a Sprite. By the time the waitress had turned to Aaron to say, "And that'll be a grilled cheese sandwich with the crust cut off for you, sweetie," Jamie was lost in thought, back in time more than two years, to when the bills piled up for him and Karyn at their idyllic suburban retreat. And he, like the waitress' philandering husband, found reasons to not come home.

CHAPTER THIRTEEN

"We need to think about upgrading this kitchen," Karyn told Jamie two minutes after he walked in the door from work one night. She was four months pregnant and showing. He was getting lighter in the wallet with each passing week.

"What's wrong with it?" Jamie said.

"The counters and cabinets are ancient," she said. "The wallpaper looks like my grandmother's. The linoleum is gross and warped. When the baby comes, people are going to visit—don't you think it'll be a little embarrassing?"

"I'd be more embarrassed to not be able to feed them because I spent thousands of dollars updating a kitchen that is working just fine," Jamie said.

Karyn rolled her eyes, shuffled into the living room, turned on the television and ignored him the rest of the night.

The old kitchen stayed—a rare victory for Jamie. But while the pregnancy advanced, Karyn made liberal use of their credit cards in preparation for the baby. Jamie compensated by working every extra hour he could squeeze out of the *Trib*. Lucky for him the city never slept or stopped making news and the night desk was understaffed.

As he worked later and later, the less appealing the drive north became and the more frequent Jamie's commutes to his parents' place in Brooklyn became. The drive took about half an hour and was a study in the borough's diversity—from the affluence of Brooklyn Heights to the Orthodox Jewish neighborhoods along Ocean Avenue to Caribbean Hispanic to African-American on the way to the outer sanctuaries of middle-class whites.

Jamie would turn left off Ocean onto Foster Avenue, take it all the way past the Flatbush Junction and Brooklyn College. Soon he would come upon the neighborhood of neat, identical two-family homes where he was born and lived until he was sixteen. Now it was one more area abandoned by whites, who after the exodus would invariably refer to it as *bad over there.*

How many times had Jamie heard that thinly veiled commentary from his father or Uncle Lou? *Everybody's gone, all schwartzers now.* At various times during the second half of the twentieth century, few once homogeneous Brooklyn strongholds could withstand the tide of demographic change. The minority encroachment continued and there went the neighborhood— house by house, block by block.

Jamie never understood why his parents had to leave Fifty-Eighth Street in the first place. He loved living dribbling distance from the courts inside the projects—now it would take him twice the time to walk over. Weeks before the move, he befriended a couple of black kids who had just moved onto the block; he took them into the courts and introduced them around. He was embarrassed to say his family was moving. He couldn't tell them it was for the same reason as everyone else. They would know anyway, he figured.

He wondered what it must have been like for their families to be welcomed with the news that nobody who was white wanted to remain on the street, much less next door.

But Morris and Molly fled with everyone else. They bought a newer two-family brick home on Ninety-Fifth Street, between Avenues L and M, where they much later would grant the ground-floor space to Becky and Mickey, rent-free, as a wedding gift. By the early autumn of 1992, when

Jamie called one evening to say he'd be working late and sleeping over again, he got Becky instead of his mother. Jamie could hear Morris and Molly arguing nearby. He could see them in his mind at the kitchen table—Morris in his coffee-splotched V-neck T-shirt and Molly in a housedress with an apron around her waist.

"What are they carrying on about?" Jamie asked.

"Oh, just about what's happening down the street, with the Kravitz house," Becky said.

"What'd they do," Jamie snorted. "Sell to blacks?"

"How did you know?"

"I didn't," Jamie said, thinking at first that Becky was teasing.

"Well, that's it, give yourself a prize," she said. "Everyone on the block has already heard and they're up in arms. You'd think Al Sharpton is coming."

"To them, every black may as well be Sharpton," Jamie said. "Including you know who."

"Oh, cut Dad a break," Becky said. "He doesn't mean the things he says. It's just what he heard growing up. He's actually one of the few who doesn't really care. To him, anyone but drug dealers and newspaper publishers would be an improvement over the Kravitzes. He doesn't want to move."

"Did anyone force him the last time?"

"Don't start," Becky said, "or you'll start sounding like your holier-than-thou but full-of-shit cousin. You know it's about the real-estate value."

It occurred to Jamie that if his parents were going to sell, Becky would have to relocate too. No doubt she was in a foul mood herself, though it seldom took much for her to disparage Steven, whom she had branded an "instigating brat out of hell" when they were all in their teens.

Nonetheless, since Steven was the journalist of note in the family, Jamie dropped by his desk later that week and mentioned what was happening on Ninety-Fifth Street. He and Uncle Lou lived two blocks away but as renters in a smaller apartment. Jamie could tell right away that Steven's interest was piqued.

"Could be a piece about what it's like being the first black family on an all-white block," he said.

"That's what I was thinking," Jamie said.

"Not a column but it might be something I could do for a Sunday read," Steven said.

"I was actually thinking about pitching it myself," Jamie said.

"What do you mean—you're a clerk?"

Jamie's face reddened. "Clerks have gotten bylines. They get promoted."

"Do you know how much time a story like that would take? You'd have to set up camp on the block and Karyn is due in—what—a few weeks?"

"Two months," Jamie said. "She's also made it clear she's not going back to work full-time and I've got to figure out a way to make more money. The only way I can think of is to get promoted to reporter."

"Who told you to buy a house in Amityville?" Steven said.

"Pleasantville—and, believe me, I am going fucking crazy there," Jamie admitted. "There's plenty of space, trees, yards, just no people on actual sidewalks. They just wave as they go by in the car. I'm waving to people I never say a word to and pushing the damned lawn mower into a tree."

Steven shook his head in a pitying way. He had never professed great love for Karyn in the first place. He'd become especially antagonistic after the move, correctly predicting that Jamie would be miserable. He took to sarcastically referring to her as "Karen with a y," and later shortened that to "K with a Y."

"Want me to talk to Willis for you?" Steven said.

Jamie considered the offer. Allowing Steven to run interference was tempting. Cal Willis wasn't big on features, especially long ones that required a jump from one page to another. He claimed *Trib* readers on page sixteen were pathologically incapable of remembering what they'd read on page four. But it also occurred to Jamie that if Steven went to bat for him, Willis might just like the story and tell Steven to do it. Jamie thanked his cousin for offering, but said he would do it himself.

For a while, he was content to relish his plan for professional advancement. But he took Steven's advice and practically moved in with his parents after a few weeks. He stayed in his old room, where nothing much had changed, including the Magic Johnson posters.

Morris mumbled under his breath about him leaving Karyn pregnant and alone. In her quiet, unthreatening way, Molly asked Jamie about that too. "I need the overtime for when the baby comes," he said. "We need to fix up the house."

"The kitchen could use it," said Molly, who had visited once. Jamie glared at her suspiciously, wondering if she could possibly be in cahoots with Karyn.

He watched closely for activity around the Kravitz house. One morning, he peeked out from behind the living room blinds and spotted a red moving van, boxes stacked nearby. Jamie casually wandered across the street and introduced himself. Thad Greene was beginning residency in the maternity ward at a nearby hospital. His wife Brenda had a new job there too, as a nurse. They had one child, a five-year-old girl.

No one else on the block was quite as welcoming. Two *For Sale* signs appeared on the street a few days after the Greenes moved in. Both signs belonged to the broker, Brookwell Associates. One was on the small patch of lawn of Molly and Morris' neighbor, Sam Grabstein.

Sam and his wife owned several storefronts in the neighborhood. He had lived every day of his seventy-two years in Brooklyn, always wearing the Dodgers cap his father had tossed in the trash the day his beloved Bums quit Brooklyn for Los Angeles. Jamie liked Sam, who was gregarious and loud. Like Mickey, he liked to tease Morris for being too serious. He called him a stick in the mud.

On the day that Sam's house went on the market, Jamie returned from buying a newspaper and spotted him at the corner, walking one of those yappy terriers that practically induce self-strangulation while leaping at every pedestrian within ten feet.

"I'm a little concerned about my parents, this housing thing," Jamie said.

Sam nodded. He cupped his hand around the left side of his mouth, as if they were about to speak confidentially—or conspiratorially.

"To tell you the truth, we'd been thinking of going in about two or three years, but decided it's time now after the Kravitz house sold. People here begged them not to do this, but the old man couldn't take the cold anymore, said he wanted to be in Florida by this winter. Said his mortgage was paid off and a few dollars here or there didn't matter to him. Said the family answered the ad in the paper, nice people, and he didn't give a shit what anyone else thought. Said there's a housing recession going on, you take what you can get. If you ask me, the guy's always been a stubborn SOB. Remember when his kid was living at home years ago? They'd go away in the winter for a couple of weeks, and there'd be parties until three, four in the morning. Loud music, kids getting drunk, pissing in the street—you name it."

Jamie didn't recall that or his parents ever complaining. He nodded to keep the conversation going.

"Then the old man would come home and blame everybody else for calling the cops. 'What's the big deal? They're kids, having some fun!' What the hell did he care? He was sound asleep in St. Petersburg. Anyway, once the word got out they sold to a black family, we start getting calls from the broker. See, it's just business. They call up and say they have a lot of nice families who want to buy now. The longer you wait, the less you're going to get because the neighborhood is changing. But with so much housing stock, the prices are bound to go down. They sell a bunch anyway and make a killing on broker fees. We get our money and get out. And *they* get the block."

The Greenes, he meant, and the unnamed black families to follow. It didn't take long for Jamie to realize the time had come to pitch his idea to Willis—now or never. At work that night, he followed Willis into the bathroom. Standing side-by-side at the row of urinals, he took a deep breath and let it spill out—the Kravitzes, the Greenes, the Grabsteins, the calls to the neighbors from Brookwell Associates.

"That's your story," Willis said.

"What is?"

"The broker is panicking whites into selling, probably only showing the houses to blacks. Racial steering, it's called. It violates some civil rights legislation. It was a big deal about twenty years ago. Look it up. Get back to me."

Willis shook loose the last drops and zippered up. Jamie had no chance to discuss his empathy for the Greenes, the courage they had to have to be the first blacks on the block. How that would make for a poignant read. Willis' suggestion wasn't quite what he'd bargained for, but now he had gotten his attention. He had to follow up.

Fortunately, Jamie had become something of a wizard with microfilm and clips. It took him thirty minutes to discover that the Civil Rights Act of 1968 had outlawed any form of racial discrimination in housing, including the steering of races into a particular area. A 1976 *New York Times* article on a landmark racial steering lawsuit brought against real estate brokers in Bergen County, New Jersey was especially helpful. A group of open-housing advocates had caught the brokers in the act by sending out black and white couples, who had been steered to different towns. He was startled to learn that one of the young lawyers involved in the lawsuits against the brokers was David Stern, who eventually became the NBA commissioner.

Jamie suggested to Willis that the *Trib* send out its own people to set a trap for the broker. If the advocates could use that strategy, why couldn't a reporter? Willis liked the idea. Within days he had helped Jamie recruit four fake couples from the newsroom. Two were black. Two were white. The following week—Jamie would never forget the date, Wednesday, November 11th—the couples were dispatched to inquire about the houses for sale on Ninety-Fifth Street.

Jamie stationed himself in a booth at a neighborhood diner. He nervously read the paper. He ordered a burger. He drank refills of Coke. He thought about checking in with Karyn at home, but he didn't have change for the pay phone in the diner's vestibule and was soon distracted by one of the couples rushing in to find him with good news.

The Brookwell broker had taken the bait. The minority couples were shown the houses in a neighborhood that was in transition. The white couples were encouraged to look on all-white blocks a few miles away.

Jamie took copious notes when the couples reported in. He called Willis that night.

"Go with it," Willis said. "Make sure you get reactions from the broker, a fair housing attorney and the Brooklyn DA."

The headline on the front page of the Sunday *Trib*, with an "Exclusive" red banner, read: **BROKERING THE RACES**. Jamie's nuanced lead about the uproar created by one black family's purchase of a home on an all-white Brooklyn block was rewritten to brag of an exclusive *Trib* investigation that had exposed the illegal practice of racial steering by one of the largest real estate firms in Brooklyn.

The Greenes were only mentioned as the lone black family to have recently purchased a home on Ninety-Fifth Street. Below the story a sidebar with Jamie's tagline offered reaction from city officials, who vowed to investigate. The real estate company's records were subpoenaed. Housing activity on the block ground to a halt. The *Times* interviewed the Greenes for a story in its Metro section that read more like the one Jamie had originally intended. But Jamie had the scoop. It was a coup for any *Trib* reporter to force the *Times* to follow up.

Back at the office, Jamie was drinking coffee in what passed as the

Trib's cafeteria—vending machines that carried sandwiches, drinks, candy and coffee. Willis came up from behind.

"Do you realize you look like crap?" he said. "And that's something coming from me."

The truth was that Willis looked remarkably good for a man his age. He had the most unlined skin Jamie had ever seen for a man over sixty. His waistline had made only minor concessions. His chest and shoulders looked like the football player he had been at the historically black Howard University.

"If I do, I actually feel worse," Jamie said.

"You sick?"

"Yeah, to my stomach."

"Then you probably shouldn't be drinking the swill they sell in that effin machine," he said.

Willis turned away to cough up phlegm in the way people who smoke too much do.

"It's about the story, right?" he asked.

Jamie hesitated, not wanting to whine to Willis of all people. But he needed to tell someone.

"It's just that it wasn't what I set out to do. I wanted to write about what it was like for that family to move onto that block. Something, you know, in depth."

"In depth? That's for *New York effin Magazine*," Willis grumbled. He shook his head. "People there are giving you grief?"

"They're all pissed off. Everyone," Jamie said.

"That's right, you pissed people off. And as a black man, I'll tell who that story *really* pissed off. Me! That's what good journalism does."

Jamie was unsure of what to say. He hadn't had even a decent night's sleep in days. The bags under his eyes felt like they were filled with sand and were sagging down toward his cheeks.

"Listen, you had a plan, Jamie. But the plan isn't the story. It's only what gets you off your ass so you can go find it."

Jamie couldn't remember the last time Willis had addressed him by his first name, if ever. And he had to admit: he liked it because being called Kramer had always been an unwelcome reminder of how and why he'd been hired, as the product of patronage.

"But look where it got me," Jamie said. "My parents are hated on their own street. My father wants to kill me if this guy Grabstein, who can't sell his house and has already bought a condo in Sarasota, doesn't do it first."

Willis shook his head. "You got a story, that's what reporters do. And you want to be a reporter, don't you?"

"I guess," Jamie said.

"Don't guess. Say you do and I'll give you the chance. Six-month tryout, soon as we can replace you on the clerk schedule."

He stood up, patted Jamie's shoulder.

"Good job," Willis said.

Jamie stared at coffee stains at the bottom of his Styrofoam cup and forced a smile.

"Oh, and congratulations on the other thing—the baby," Willis said.

The other thing was a competing newsbreak on the day Jamie had flawlessly executed Operation Brookwell—a plan he had been so obsessed with that he never did check in at home with Karyn. Her urgent call to the office had gone unreturned.

He blew a story which couldn't be rewritten. His son was born three weeks premature, almost strangling himself on a tangled umbilical cord, initially kept alive by a respirator. All this occurred in the sole, tearful company of the baby's mother and her aunt.

CHAPTER FOURTEEN

Jamie returned with Aaron from lunch to find the house empty. Karyn was still out making her rounds, tightening her abs. Aaron toddled into the living room and made a beeline for the television set.

"*Sez-me, dah-dee,*" Aaron said.

"Ok, buddy," Jamie said. "Let's see if Sesame Street is on."

He picked Aaron up from behind by the armpits and told him to press the red button. Jamie clicked on the PBS station with the remote. Aaron climbed onto the wicker couch with the off-white cushions—a wedding gift from Morris and Molly. Sesame Street was not on, but Aaron happily settled in to watch another program featuring a very tall man posing as a tree whose branches were being decorated by children with red and yellow streamers.

Jamie bent over to kiss his son's cheek. He tasted bread granules from the *gill-tee* sandwich. He reached for the *Times* on the edge of the coffee table, knocking it to the floor, along with a thin paperback that was sitting underneath it. It was a travel guide for the American Northwest. The bookmark opened to a section on Seattle, wedged between the introduction and a color photo of the city's famous space needle.

Shit, she's really serious about this. Overnight Jamie had almost convinced himself that Karyn had merely been angling for leverage in what she imagined might become a financial crunch. She couldn't really be thinking about picking up a two-year-old and moving across the country without knowing a soul in the new city?

Jamie stared at Aaron. His stomach began to knot. The telephone rang and provided a welcome distraction. But Molly's voice surprised him, as much as his disoriented her.

"I was just calling, you know, to ask what the baby needs for his birthday," she said.

Molly always referred to Aaron as *the baby*, as if she wasn't allowed too personal a relationship in a family torn asunder. But Jamie had to grudgingly admit that Karyn did make an effort to include his parents, out of respect, he guessed, for Molly.

Several times, when visiting one of her friends in Brooklyn Heights, Karyn had driven out of her way to drop in on her former in-laws. Molly, so appreciative that Karyn would make the effort, would extol her generosity to Jamie. He recognized this as a wistful if hopeless appeal for reconciliation.

"I'm here with Aaron until Karyn gets back," Jamie told Molly. He turned away from the couch and whispered. "I came to bring him his birthday gifts, but he's not going to open them until Friday, when he has his party. Karyn wants him to get them all on one day."

"Mine will be late then—unless I send it overnight mail," Molly said.

"It's alright, Mom," he said. "Whenever it gets here—and whatever it is will be fine. Don't get carried away."

"I'll call her later," Molly said.

"Great," Jamie said.

"So…you'll be here later?"

"For what?"

"Dinner. Everyone's coming. We talked about it. I thought you said you were coming."

"Actually, we didn't talk about it," Jamie said. "You told me about it on the answering machine. But let me think for a minute." What he meant was,

"Let me think of an excuse," but he couldn't produce one fast enough.

"I guess I can make it," he said.

"Good," Molly said. Jamie noticed Aaron's eyes were closing. "I'll tell your father."

"OK, fine," Jamie said.

He hung up. Aaron was asleep, head drooping onto his shoulder. Jamie lifted him from the couch and carried him into Karyn's room and laid him on the blue quilt. He climbed in alongside him and kissed his cheek. He checked his watch—it was just about time for Karyn to return.

Please, just another half-hour—this is so peaceful.

Jamie closed his eyes. Two minutes later he was sound asleep.

CHAPTER FIFTEEN

Molly pulled back the front door of the upstairs apartment. Jamie stepped inside and kissed his mother's cheek. He was famished for a good meal but wary of what he would have to endure to enjoy it.

Thanksgiving was still two weeks away, but Molly figured that the striking Kramer men were in more immediate need. She blew her weekly food budget for a roast, some lamb and broiled chicken that was just tasteful enough but didn't cause four-alarm blazes in Morris' tender stomach.

"You hungry?" she said, pulling Jamie by the elbow into the cramped kitchen. "Come. Sit. Eat."

And then, from his father, in so many stares, if not actual words: *Leave*.

As always, the number of dishes overwhelmed the table and there was no place setting for Molly. She usually prepared a plate for herself on the counter and picked at it between chores.

"Don't worry about me," she would say, though they had all given up years ago trying to get her to stop fussing and sit down. She never seemed to stop moving from one chore to another. If someone picked up a plate from the table to bring to the sink, Molly would appear suddenly to whisk it away to its destination as if she were running the final leg of a relay race. Morris would observe her from his seat, forever amused by and accepting of his wife's determination to do everything.

Molly cooked as if she had been tipped off of a coming potato famine, with five variations available: roasted, mashed, boiled, sweet and the obligatory container of potato salad.

"Where're the fries?" Becky asked, making eye contact with Jamie, her longtime partner in spoofing the family's culinary habits.

Her frosted dyed hair was tied back with a red ribbon that matched the color of her sweater, accessorized by her trademark Star of David. The Kramers were far from religious though Jamie had had a bar mitzvah mainly to make his grandparents happy. Becky, who was three years older, got off easier. The old folks believed the religious passage into manhood was, well, for males. Becky liked to say she was devoutly Jewish, culturally speaking.

She was small, like Molly, but more full-bodied, like Morris and Jamie. But she and Molly were as simpatico as a mother and daughter living in virtually the same house needed to be to survive. They were not aggressive, demanding women. But somehow their husbands had an intuitive understanding that they were not to be trifled with.

"Ma, did you make the vegetables?" Becky said.

"Oh, good lord, I forgot to put the broccoli up," Molly said, making a move away from the table. "Mickey, I'm so sorry. It'll take me a minute…"

"No, Ma, it's OK," said Mickey, the vegetarian oddball in a family of dedicated carnivores. "I'm fine. There's plenty."

Jamie cut a piece of lamb onto his fork. Morris carved up the chicken without comment. The bathroom door opened in the hall. Uncle Lou whistled his way back to the table.

"Jamie," Lou said, drying his hands on his gray slacks. "Good to see you. Were you at the rally today?"

Jamie considered lying but figured Molly, who knew better, might give him away. "Couldn't make it," he said. "I had to go see Aaron today. His birthday's coming up."

Jamie could see a smile form at the corner of his mother's mouth.

Approval, Jamie thought, *what a wonderful concept.* Molly was too damn easy when the matter was related to her only grandchild.

"So," Jamie said. "How did Steven's big speech go?"

"Where is Steven?" Molly interrupted. "I thought he was coming too."

"No, he had plans, something to do with the union," Lou said.

"He's doing a television interview, I thought," Jamie said.

"Television, that's right, he mentioned that," Lou said. "I don't know where that kid gets it to speak in front of all those people. Not from me."

"What'd he say?" Mickey asked.

"Hell of a speech," Morris said, without looking up.

"Word came down that Brady has started hiring new reporters," Lou said, looking at Mickey.

"Scabs, you mean," Morris said.

"Soon as they heard that, most of the sportswriters went right in," Lou said. "And I guess some of the other reporters were getting nervous, like they'll actually keep these losers on after we settle," Lou said. "So Steven gets up with this *schvartzer*, Carmen…"

"If you mean Carla, she's actually Puerto Rican, not black or whatever you feel you have to call her," Jamie said.

"It's just an expression. Doesn't mean anything."

"Never mind," Jamie said.

"Yeah, Carla something…?"

"Delgado," Jamie said, sighing. "She's the office manager."

"Mario Cuomo was supposed to be there, but he didn't show," Lou said. "So a bunch of the union guys talked, the drivers' guy, Colangelo, and then Stevie gets up. He's wearing a suit—didn't even know he had one. He's looking like some executive hotshot and he says, 'I just want to say something to my fellow journalists—the real journalists—not the cowards who run back because Brady puts a little pressure on them.' So he starts going on about how the reporters are the conscience of the newspaper, the shapers of—what'd he call it, Mo? Moral something…?"

"Moral responsibility," Morris said.

"Yeah, he starts telling stories of how workers get treated when there's no union. 'Forget raises. If they say the economy is bad, you get a pay *cut*! You get your health benefits slashed, and that's if you don't get laid off. If you don't believe that we have an obligation to be out here fighting a monster like Brady, well, you shouldn't even be in the newspaper business.' Then he shakes his fist and starts yelling, 'We are the journalists. *We are the journalists!*'"

Lou, his voice deep with mock authority, pounded a fist on the table and then cracked up.

"The next thing you know, they're all cheering, 'Brady sucks! Brady sucks!'"

"So all the reporters stayed out?" Mickey said.

Lou turned back to Jamie.

"You know of anyone going in?"

Jamie shook his head. "Other than the sports guys—I mean, no, I don't. Not today at least."

"You mean some still might cross?" Mickey said.

Jamie could sense them waiting for him to let something slip.

"I don't know, Mick," he said, turning away from his father and uncle.

Like Morris and Lou, Mickey was a staunch union man. Or at least one in the making when Ronald Reagan fired him and most of the air traffic controllers at Kennedy Airport in 1981. He was twenty-five and, fortunately, young and resourceful enough to change career course by enrolling in a Brooklyn College early education graduate program. He met Becky, a third-grade teacher in a public school where Mickey had landed as a kindergarten teacher.

Five years older than Becky, born in 1953, Mickey had grown up with Vietnam and Watergate. He was suspicious of what he called "the crooked corporate establishment" and, in retrospect, relieved that Reagan had forced him to pursue more fulfilling work.

"Ronald Reagan, my hero," he would say, sarcastically.

Mickey's most endearing quality, as far as Jamie could tell, was being blessed with the ability to evaluate whatever misfortune had befallen him as a prank engineered by some higher authority. The medical indignities of his and Becky's ongoing infertility were the perfect example.

"We go to the clinic for an insemination on a Sunday morning because that's the targeted day," he confided to Jamie while he was working the Brookwell story and they had stepped out one night for a run to a Chinese restaurant.

"There's like six other couples in the office, waiting for the nurse. She comes out and assigns all the husbands to a different numbered room, where there's a little plastic cup waiting and a stack of pornography that could service an entire high school football team. She tells us, 'After you finish, just put the lid on your specimen and bring it out here to the desk.' The wives are left looking at each other, probably trying to be the first one not to break down and cry. But then you're sitting there, behind the locked door, the magazine in your lap, your dick in your hand and you're thinking, 'Do I want to be the first one back or should I be last?'"

He asked the question so casually that Jamie failed for a few seconds to process the hilarity of the predicament.

That was pure Mickey, and that was also the moment when Jamie realized how much he had wanted Becky to be pregnant too, especially after Aaron was born. More than two years later, he was still rooting, though the subject was now entirely too stressful for even Mickey to make light of.

He was forty, Becky thirty-five. Time was no longer their ally.

"What I'm sensing and hearing is that there's some anger with some reporters about the way this all went down," Jamie said.

"How do you mean?" Mickey said.

"People feel like we were forced out, like the unions don't realize how hard it's going to be to win. They're worried, and I'll tell you something— they should be because they could lose their jobs. All this talk about Mario Cuomo, as if he or anyone else gives a crap about what happens to us. And for most of us, it's not as simple to just be out in the street."

He paused a few seconds.

"I mean, it's not as easy as it is for Steven."

"What's that supposed to mean?" Lou said.

Jamie turned back to his uncle. He could feel his father's eyes on him.

"Some people have real financial issues here, Uncle Lou. Steve's a single guy—no kids, makes a lot of money, at least for what we do. You've got family people out on the street who can't afford to go a month without a paycheck, much less put their jobs on the line."

"Jamie, you don't think we know that?" Lou said. "Do you know how many times we've been through this?" He glanced sideways at Morris. "Maybe you don't remember when you were a kid that we had families who lost their apartments and houses when we struck for months, and had to stay with us, sleep on the couch, on the floor…"

"I remember, but that was a different time. How many papers were there, how many jobs? I was talking to Pat Blaine the other day. He said Brady's been setting this all up, baiting us, just like he did at his other papers."

"What other papers?"

"Dublin…London."

"What does London have to do with us?" Lou said.

Lou's interests in labor were strictly related to his own local. He had a lifelong habit of relying on Morris to tell him what he needed to know.

"It involved the printers, mainly," Morris said. "Murdoch started it when he bought the biggest paper there, and he wanted to take back the power the unions always had. He and Brady got the government to pass laws that made it almost impossible to halt the printing and distribution of the papers during a strike. Then he built new plants that were like armed camps."

He looked straight at Jamie for the first time.

"But that's not happening here, no matter what one of your friends is telling you."

"Look," Jamie said. "All I'm saying is that we're all putting our jobs at risk knowing if we lose them we may not be able to find another one."

Lou looked at Morris for help. Morris looked like he'd already had enough of the discussion.

"Jamie, you want to talk about risk?" Lou said. "What about our union? We've got lifetime job guarantees that we all fought like dogs for when they automated the paper, when you were kids. How many times we were told to get out into the street if we want to save a job that's worth having—you don't think we were scared?"

"You know, Uncle Lou, maybe being scared or tough doesn't have anything to do with it," Jamie said. "Maybe it's about loyalty to your own members first. I mean, these drivers, they go around beating the crap out of people—poor guys just trying to make a buck…"

"Poor guys?" Lou said. "They're scabs—just goddamn scabs."

"Oh yeah? Then what's all the *nigger* shit about on the television?"

Lou again looked over at Morris, who started to say something but settled for waving a hand in the direction of Jamie.

"Louie please, you're not getting anywhere with him," Morris said. "How's he going to have any loyalty to his union when he doesn't even care about his own flesh and blood."

"Morris, don't start with that…" Molly said.

"What I cared about was the truth, and that's what my story was about," Jamie said.

Morris put down his knife and fork and spit a piece of chicken off his lips.

"No, I'll tell you what the truth is." He pointed a finger across the table. "The truth is that you cared more about that story than your own son and the woman who gave birth to him. You'd still rather be in the projects, playing ball and fucking around with colored girls."

"Morris, please…" Molly said.

Becky stiffened. Mickey rolled his eyes.

"*Colored* girls?" Jamie said. "How 1950s of you. Why don't you just get it over with and use the N word too?"

"Morris, you're getting everyone upset. You'll get Becky…"

"It's all right, Ma," Becky said. She leaned a shoulder into Mickey.

"No, Ma," Jamie said. "He wants to still bring up that I missed Aaron being born—fine, I did. I'm not proud of that. But maybe I was only doing what he taught me. Business first. Isn't that right, Dad? Union this, union that. The almighty Jackie Ryan called, it didn't matter what else was going on. What did you ever come to? One basketball game I ever played in, one school function? I guess it was nice of you to at least make an appearance at the bar mitzvah. You got up and made a big speech telling everyone you hoped they had a good time, but you had to leave early on an urgent union matter. Your own son's bar mitzvah. You're a good one to talk."

"At least I lived under the same roof as you, didn't I? I paid the bills. I didn't walk out. I didn't leave you and your sister and go live by myself. Your mother has a grandson she hardly ever sees. She cries herself to sleep about it…"

"Morris, *please!*"

"And meanwhile we have to pray every day for your sister to have a baby. Why you have one and she lost hers…"

"*Daddy!*" Becky screamed. Too late, Becky burst into tears, bolted from the chair, around to the hall and slammed the bedroom door shut. Molly took off after her, followed by Mickey, glaring back at them.

"Way to go, *both* of you," he said.

"You had to bring Aaron into this," Jamie said. "We were having a discussion about the strike, a simple discussion."

Jamie stared at his father, waiting, almost hoping for more. But Morris sat back in his chair. He played with his fork, squished a boiled potato.

"Let me just say…" Lou started to chime in to calm things down. But Morris glared at him. "OK, fine," Lou said and shut up.

Jamie wanted to say more, but anger had set up a roadblock between his brain and his mouth. His father had, as always, rendered him speechless with his seething, unyielding silence. Judgment had once more been passed with no allowance for appeal.

Morris pushed himself away from the table. He grabbed a newspaper from the counter and headed for his sanctuary, the bathroom. Lou continued eating with a pained look.

Jamie let awkward moments pass as if awaiting his own execution. Finally he stood and walked stiffly into the living room. He grabbed his jacket from the couch. He left, pausing for several seconds outside the front door. No one was coming to coax him back in. The only candidates were his mother, who was busy with Becky, and his uncle, who probably wanted to wring his neck for inferring that Steven was a grandstanding prima donna.

He was still seething as he switched lanes to pass a bus on Ocean Avenue. He pushed hard on the gearshift into fifth and was about to pump the accelerator to make the light at Church Avenue. But it turned yellow and so did Jamie. He hit the brake. His tires screeched. In his rear view mirror, Jamie saw the driver behind him gesturing and giving him the finger.

Jamie knew the guy had every right to be pissed, but he was in no mood for remorse. "Sue me, you have to wait a minute at the light," he said. Then he talked to the rearview mirror as if his father's face was in it.

"This union bullshit is your goddamned life, not mine. I didn't ask for it. I don't need it. I don't want any part of it."

The light turned green.

"That's right, you heard me," Jamie said. The offended driver behind him hit the horn. "And fuck you too," Jamie yelled. He drove through the intersection and continued his imaginary conversation until he was almost to Brooklyn Heights. He took a deep breath and realized how absurd it was to shout at no one.

He was almost home anyway, driving along the Brooklyn waterfront, the downtown Manhattan skyline he always found beautifully haunting and calming in twilight.

He got off the highway at Atlantic Avenue and turned left onto Hicks. He slowed on the narrow cobblestone street, turning right at a stop sign, nearly clipping a car parked in the crosswalk. He pulled into a spot a few inches too close to a hydrant. It was the best he was going to do at this time of evening. He figured the odds of getting a ticket were about fifty percent. He didn't care. He slammed the door so hard that the heads of a couple walking arm-in-arm on the other side of the street turned to stare. Jamie didn't look up, didn't care, preoccupied as he was with Morris' main claim to compassion: he'd slept under the same roof as his children.

"Good for you," Jamie mumbled. He wondered if his father thought he deserved a medal, a token of appreciation, like some commemorative union trinket for lasting fifty years on the job.

Day Three: Wednesday, November 9, 1994

CHAPTER SIXTEEN

Movement on the picket line outside the *Trib* had ground to a halt. A blustery wind blew off the river and a chilly noontime realization had set in. The paper had again made it to welcoming newsstands and into the hands of grateful commuters largely indifferent to the strikers' plight.

Through the window of the vending machines outside the building, their slots gummed up or glued, the headline "**54**" dominated the *Trib* front page. That was the number of seats the Republicans had seized from Democrats in routing them from control of the House of Representatives. Further mocking the vanquished party was the sub-head: **Dem's the breaks.**

Morris and Lou Kramer were the only picketing printers out early that day, taking up slack for the others—not surprising that so many were still in bed, given the collective lifetimes they had spent working deep into the night and sleeping in.

While eavesdropping on one of the young reporters nearby, Morris heard him whine, "Every day it gets out is another nail in our coffin." Lou wandered away toward Steven and a frail blonde who melted into a long black coat under a fur collar. Behind them stood a strapping black man, balancing a television mini-cam on his left shoulder while savoring the last bites of a candy bar. He dropped the wrapper to the ground and watched it blow away into the street.

All around, the strikers were red-faced, huddling to stay warm within the wooden blue police barricades. They stuffed hands into their pockets and sipped coffee from Styrofoam cups. They took long drags on cigarettes. The rumble of cars on the elevated roadway across the street forced them to shout to be heard. When the occasional passing motorist palmed a horn in support, the heads of the strikers turned. A few raised their arms in synchronized salute.

A sympathizer had surfaced from the city's teachers' union, promising that no self-respecting educator and supporter of organized labor would so much as look at a *Trib* front page as long as the rank-and-file stayed out. She shook Steven's hand and half kidded that the teachers were behind the Alliance despite what he had written about their lack of enthusiasm for summer-school hours.

Steven playfully changed the subject. "Have you met my father, Lou Kramer?" he said. "And this is Debbie Givens of NY1 News."

"Okay, I get it. I won't bring the summer school piece up again," the teachers' rep said, with a schoolgirl giggle. "I guess people are down, with the paper getting out and all."

Steven hunched his shoulders and shook his head. "Like I was telling Debbie on her show last night, it's early. We're just getting started. We're contacting advertisers, trying to get them to pull out. Our people are talking to the big newsstands about not taking the paper."

"Talk," Lou said. "Used to be that all you had to do was look a few of them in the eye, maybe torch a bundle of papers. They wouldn't touch it."

Steven wrapped an arm around his father's shoulder.

"The Mayor owes the publisher his firstborn for getting him elected," he said. "And he's got the cops—good union people themselves—practically working for management. So it's time for Plan B. We've got to unite labor all around the city. The other papers are not going to go after City Hall. They're rooting for us to get our asses kicked so they can do the same thing to their own unions when their contracts are up."

"The Mayor," Lou said, ruefully.

He excused himself and went back to Morris, who was still standing beside the *Trib* boxes. He had picked up a copy of the *Times* that had been set on the ground by one of the reporters. Morris opened it to the *Trib* strike story. It was on page four of the Metro section, below the fold.

STRIKERS SHADOW BOXES, TRIB LANDS PUNCHES

The headline sat over a story that stopped just short of declaring Leland Brady the winner of the fight by an early TKO.

Random samplings of the city's newsstands confirm that *Trib* sales were sharply curtailed on its first day of publishing during the strike and many vending machines were reported to have been tampered with. But the publisher Leland F. Brady was said to be jubilant over the newspaper's ability to produce roughly half the normal run of seven-hundred-fifty thousand, with a skeleton staff of management employees manning presses and other union positions. Maxwell Brady, the executive editor and the publisher's son, said more management staffing from Brady-owned newspapers in Ireland, Great Britain and Canada would be available by the end of the week. Union sources said its leaders were irritated by what they viewed as City Hall's favorable treatment of Mr. Brady, an ardent supporter of the Mayor.

Morris refolded the paper and jammed it into the armpit of his jacket. "What's Stevie saying this morning?" he said, as Lou blew into his left hand.

Louis Kramer's stubble of gray around his chin accentuated the darkened circles under his eyes. The tallest Kramer no longer elicited the praise he had once received for his lean youthful look. In the years following his wife's departure, he ate too little, smoked too much, slept like an octogenarian. His thick dark hair had surrendered to gray. He retired unceremoniously from his one-time passion, schoolyard handball.

"I left a message for him last night and asked him to call Jamie—see if he could, you know, talk some sense into him."

"I'm not talking about Jamie," Morris snapped. "I meant, what does Steve think about the other unions, about what they're going to try to do next?"

"He says the Alliance will go after the advertisers and they'll meet with the newsstand people—try to talk them into not taking the paper," said Lou.

Another honking car puttered by. This time, a window rolled down and out floated a thumb pointing south. After a prompt rebuttal of obscenities, the hand turned upside, thumb to middle finger.

"Yeah, you too, *asshole*," Lou said, waving in disgust. "Mo, remember the last big one, what was it, 78?" he said. "The drivers broke a few windows, glued a few locks, threatened a couple of dealers, and that was it. I don't understand this. I know they keep saying that Brady's got the Mayor protecting him, but how can the cops guard every newsstand and deli in New York?"

"They can't," Morris said. "But didn't you hear Brady on the news the other day? He said he would personally cover damages done to anyone selling the paper. Then the Mayor's going around saying the city will arrest and fine anyone who destroys property. They start fining people, it won't be chump change. Who has the money these days to deal with that? It's up to the unions to find another way."

"Have you called Colangelo?" Lou said.

Morris nodded grimly.

"Called, left a message," he said.

"And?"

"That was the other day, after Brady sent us the letter. Haven't heard a word."

"Damn," Lou murmured.

At the far corner of the building, several drivers milled about rather than picket the loading docks on the sunless side of the plant. They wore windbreakers and baseball caps. They drank coffee, smoked cigarettes and mostly ignored their fellow strikers.

"I overheard one of them say that some of the scabs Brady has got driving the trucks are the homeless," Lou said. "Bums—you believe that? This guy is saying he got in one guy's face last night as he was walking past the line, with the cops right there, and he says, 'You think you're working one day after we settle? That they won't put you right back out on the damn street?' He said the scab looked at him and said, `Motherfucker, I *lives* in the damn street!' The scab was laughing, like the whole thing is a complete goddamn joke."

Morris stared at the ground, shook his head.

"Those guys over there, we need to keep an eye on them too," he said. "They don't operate the way the rest of the unions do. Twenty-five years ago, I remember them coming in to see us one day saying they had had it with management stalling on this and that and wanted to go out and would we go out with them? You know what Jackie told them? 'You have the most corrupt, undemocratic and disloyal union in the city. You refuse to join the council of union leaders and now you're asking me to put my people out?' I thought Jackie was going to tell them to get the fuck out of his face, but I'll tell you something about that guy. He could lose it like anyone but when it came to tactics, he had more common sense than all the rest of these guys put together. He said, 'OK, tell you what. We'll give you three days to posture, make some noise, then three days of a slowdown, then another three days of a shutdown. Beyond that, I can't help you, so do what you have to do but understand there's a limit.' The point was, he knew there was nothing gained by telling them to take a hike. No point in pissing them or anybody off if you don't have to. There's no union in this business that can survive by itself forever. He'd say: 'I know we've got management by the balls right now. Tomorrow, who knows? You don't have the other guys owing you, sooner or later you'll wind up taking it in the you-know-where when you're not looking.' Jackie lived by that. You try to never cross someone else's line, no matter how bleak it looks. Because the only thing that counts is muscle. Not violence but muscle, the ability to keep everyone together when things get tough.

Because once this union goes one way and another union goes the other way, it's good for management, divide and conquer."

Morris paused, resuming in a more hushed tone.

"Those guys over there should realize—I say *should*, Louie, not that they do—that if this is the point where scab drivers can get the paper out, they're no better off than we are. We're all in this together until we figure out a way to hit this guy. And I know that we're taking the biggest risk with the lifetime guarantees. I know the guys are scared because they think this time there might be no way back in."

Lou nodded and figured this might be the perfect opportunity to mention that Sean Cox had woken him at the crack of dawn, sobbing like a baby on the phone. The doctor had found a lump in his wife's breast. The battery of tests was completed. The verdict was in: double mastectomy followed by weeks of chemotherapy. He was worried sick that he was going to lose his health insurance benefits if he stayed out.

"Mo, speaking of this, I've been meaning to…" But Morris, more in monologue than conversation, cut him off.

"I just feel it in my bones that going in would be the wrong thing, the easy way out. They get us in there and they know we're alone and this SOB Brady would smell fear. He doesn't need us. He knows that. I still think we're better off out here, sticking with what we know."

When his brother had finished, Lou intended to try to raise the Sean Cox situation again. But from around the corner he was facing he saw trouble advancing. It was Jamie—eyes narrowed, face taut.

"Mo, uh…"

He tugged at Morris' elbow and motioned for him to turn and face the more impending crisis. Too late. Jamie was upon them.

He smiled at his uncle. He looked down at his shoes and finally up at Morris.

"I wasn't sure you'd be here, but it's just as well," Jamie said. "I already told Steven this morning, but I'd rather you hear this from me."

His eyes returned to the shoes, which seemed dangerously close to his father's. He stepped back a half-step, inhaled cold air.

"I'm going back to work," he said. "I'm going in."

CHAPTER SEVENTEEN

The room was shrouded in gloom, its windows painted over a fire-engine red. The lone evidence of sun appeared through a spot where paint had peeled away. The half-dozen tables were stark, save the few empty beer bottles and ashtrays overflowing with cigarette butts. Eight bar stools sat unfilled.

Gerard Colangelo pushed open the front door to the storefront establishment known as Maria's. It was a few minutes after nine in the morning. Even the unlicensed joints in town couldn't stay open round the clock.

Colangelo had been huddling with a half-dozen of his drivers outside the *Trib* plant when a guy in a leather jacket, cigarette dangling from his lips, pulled over in a black Lincoln Town Car, rolled down the window and handed him a note. Colangelo finished chitchatting, slapped a few backs, shook a few hands and excused himself. He walked briskly along South Street under the highway, turning right up the narrow cobblestone side street near the trendy Seaport shopping district.

Inside the bar he found the man who had summoned him. He was dropping quarters into one of the two blackjack slot machines which hung on the far wall beside the pay phone.

"You know something? I don't think I've ever won a damn thing playing these things," said the lawyer Colangelo knew as Schmoo. The nickname pleased him more than Robert Sharfsein. Schmoo was Colangelo's link to the wise guys he worked with on the side.

The *arrangement*, as Schmoo liked to call it, provided his clients with daily bundles of newspapers to distribute and sell on their own. In return, Colangelo could count on a cut that doubled his salary and provided him the money to send his kids to a good Catholic school. He could also occasionally stuff a hundred-dollar bill in the pocket of a needy union brother.

A little trickledown—and it's not killing anyone, he rationalized.

Colangelo removed his coat, folded it over the back of a chair and sat down. "You're not winning on that thing," he said. "In all the years I've been coming in here, I've seen it pay off once, maybe twice—and no great fortune at that."

"Well, listen," Schmoo said. "This isn't exactly Trump Casino now, is it?"

He flushed one more quarter and gave up. He walked over to the table, his long coat open, letting Colangelo glimpse his expensive blue suit. A red tie with blue dots was draped around his neck, undone. Schmoo's office was downtown on lower Broadway, and he, much like Colangelo, drank a good deal at Maria's. It was small. It was private. A subtle transaction could be completed without attracting attention.

"So they steal a few quarters," Schmoo said. "Who doesn't?"

Colangelo nodded and lit a cigarette.

Schmoo started to slide into the chair opposite Colangelo but stopped about halfway down. He jerked his thumb in the direction of the vacant bar.

"You want a beer?" he said.

Colangelo held up his left hand.

"Never touch the stuff during a strike."

Colangelo resented Schmoo's thirty-something smile that came off to him as smug.

"Then I guess it is incumbent upon you to see that this one doesn't go on much longer," Schmoo said. He reached into his coat pocket and pulled out a *Trib*, laid it on the table—a transparent reminder the paper was being published and delivered, in spite of the walkout.

Colangelo took a quick drag, inhaling too much, causing him to cough up some congestion.

"I can always smoke myself to death," he said.

"Not as much fun," Schmoo said.

"I don't do this for fun," Colangelo said.

"Which brings me to why you *are* here, Gerry," Schmoo said. "The people upstairs are a little, frankly, concerned. They're anxious to know how long this might last. I think they'd like to be—you know—reassured."

Colangelo ran his left hand across his brow, then up through his glistening combed-back hair.

"Listen, we've never really had a situation like this where all the unions were out and the paper kept publishing. On the one hand, they've got the damn thing out today and the dealers are taking it. On the other, the *mooks* they got delivering it don't know the Bronx from Bushwick, they're late with it all over town and their sales have to be off at least a few hundred thousand."

"Which means?"

"Don't know. Right now, I'd say it's like an election that's too close to call. Brady thinks he's made it over the big hurdle by just getting the paper out. But it was probably losing some money before the strike and it must be bleeding by now, with the loss in circulation revenue. We figure that by next week the advertisers will start getting antsy. Some of them will want rebates. The reporters are planning to pressure them and maybe the big stores will decide to walk. When that happens, maybe Brady will be willing to sit down and bargain instead of just walking in with that union-busting redneck lawyer he's got working for him and throwing his disgraceful offer on the table."

Schmoo listened, nodding and drumming his fingers on the table. Colangelo resisted the urge to grab one and snap it like a Popsicle stick.

"And what if the drivers he's got working for him now start figuring out the routes—no disrespect but this isn't brain surgery—and by next week sales are back up? Then where's your leverage? What do you do when

Brady says, 'I'm doing almost as well without you as I was with you and I'm paying these idiots half what your people get?' Then you've gambled and lost everything for what, a few work rules that even you would probably admit are out of line for a business that's losing money?"

"Whoa, it's not that simple," Colangelo said. "First of all, Schmoo, do you know what this guy has been proposing? I'll tell you, he wants to take the manning process completely away from us. He wants the one-time right to examine every driver inside out to decide if that guy should keep his job. Then he wants to scrap the existing pay system, put in a new scale that reduces the hourly wage and have total control over overtime shifts. On top of that, those guys who walked off their posts last Sunday night to help out the disabled kid they fired? They're all out, no questions asked. Listen, it doesn't take a genius to figure out what this is. The minute we agree to something like that, he lets half our people go and starts hiring every fucking spook or third-world boat person in the tri-state area for sweatshop wages. Then he can make his butt-fucking buddy down at City Hall look like a Democrat because he helped create minority jobs. Meanwhile, Brady saves a bundle. This is not like the other times where we started here and they started there and we'd meet in the middle. This is how they negotiate: the redneck comes in and asks if we have anything new to propose. We say, 'Yes, certainly do,' and we lay out a deal that I'd have to say would not exactly taste like cotton fucking candy to my people. Then the redneck says, 'OK, we have to caucus,' and off he goes with his flunkies to have a circle jerk in the men's room. Then we sit around for an hour and a half, and then they send word with a secretary that our offer is unacceptable and that bargaining is adjourned, and they'll be in touch. That's the way it went for six freaking months up until Sunday night."

"So now you just sit back and wait?"

"Frankly, I don't know what else we can do unless we start taking out a few news dealers. But the Mayor's got the cops on alert, even though every one of them I see tells me they hate this shit. We go violent now, the arrests, fines and lawsuits start flying. We don't have the money to pay our people strike benefits much less the legal costs and bail if someone gets busted. Unless our friends want to start bankrolling us…"

"That's not happening, Gerry. They've already got enough problems on the legal front without getting involved in that. Look, I understand you're not in a good spot here. But you've also got to understand why our friends are so concerned. What do they get from your guys, about fifteen thousand papers a day?"

"Give or take," Colangelo said.

"So they take their bundles and distribute them with their people and get about—what?"

"Look, Schmoo, stop with the prosecution, this isn't a courtroom. You know what the numbers are."

"That's right, Gerry, and you do too. You're out less than one week and our friends are already down more than twenty-five grand. This thing goes on through a few more weeks and they miss a couple of Sundays at a buck a pop? That figure starts getting up near a hundred fifty thou. Now, no one's saying you got to go back today or tomorrow. It's not like anybody's going broke if you're out six weeks. But nobody wants to risk losing the franchise. This is a nice little four-to-five million-a-year business at stake here. Nice piece of change for them, a decent living for you. Is it worth risking everything you've built over this? I know that guys are going to lose their jobs. That happens. It's happening in every industry. But our friends want you to know they'll throw something back in to help out with some buyout money. For a nice, peaceful ending to this thing, they are willing to do a little something. No one's going to have to walk away empty handed."

Colangelo took a long drag of his cigarette and turned his face away from Schmoo's to exhale.

"I accept one of Brady's offers the way he's got it worded, and he could lay off more than half my people," he said. "They'd lynch me."

Schmoo wrapped one end of the undone tie around his neck, and, bug-eyed, pretended to gag. Colangelo stared at him with a poker face and wanted to throw the stiff right hand that helped him win twenty of his twenty-four amateur fights way back when.

"You think you're going to be responsible for putting these guys out of work but let me show you something," Schmoo said. He reached into the pocket lining of his suit jacket and pulled out a crisply folded newspaper clipping.

"Check this out."

Schmoo unfurled the story and laid it out on the table for Colangelo, jabbing an index finger on the first paragraph.

"They ran this last week on the business page of the *Times.* I read this shit. You really should too. You're the one running a newspaper union."

Colangelo checked his shirt pocket for his reading glasses, and realized he'd left them in the car back at the *Trib.* He hunched over the clipping, squinting:

> The internet's World Wide Web—that great repository of data—has yet to become the great market many have predicted it will be. But right now a number of innovative service-oriented companies are using the Web not to make money but to save some. Not nickels and dimes either, but possibly millions.
>
> For companies ranging from overnight package deliveries to banks, the Web is the place to offer technology-savvy customers a new convenience: automated customer service. In the process, these companies are finding that a Web Site is a lot cheaper than operating customer phone banks.

Colangelo looked up at the lawyer, baffled.

"OK, sounds good. Banking by computer. We already got cash machines. So in the not-too-distant future, we'll do—what?—order a new box of checks from home instead of making a call?"

Schmoo shook his head, as if he were pointing a gun across the table, about to make Colangelo plead for his life.

"Banks. Companies. The ability to *reduce* payroll and expenses by running their businesses electronically."

"So what?"

"Newspapers, Gerry. You don't get it? If customer service goes onto the computer, on this internet they keep saying is going to revolutionize everything, then why can't they put the newspaper on it too?"

"Schmoo, I never even heard of this internet until a couple of months ago and I don't know what the hell you are talking about. People paying their subscription bills by computer? What the hell does that have to do with what we're doing, with getting this bastard Brady to give us a fair shake?"

"It has everything to do with you, Gerry. *Everything.* I'd bet a year's salary they're already planning to make the same shit you deliver every day available on the computer. Because sooner or later, probably sooner with the way the technology is going, these people will figure out how much cheaper it will be to not have to cut down trees and pay for the newsprint or run printing presses or finance a fleet of trucks and drivers to produce a newspaper that can be delivered right into the home with the press of a button."

Colangelo tapped his foot and took a deep breath, going out of his way to appear unmoved.

"What are you going to do, take a computer on the A train?" Colangelo said. "Onto the crapper?"

The Fordham-educated lawyer shook his head at the contented smile across the table. He was almost convinced that Colangelo was utterly incapable of grasping what separated man from beast—an awareness of mortality.

"Let me put it this way," Schmoo said. "Ten, fifteen years ago, how many papers did the *Trib* sell on an average weekday? A million-something?"

"In that neighborhood, yeah."

"And now it's what—seven hundred thousand?"

"Give or take."

"So where do you think all those readers went? They died? They all moved to Florida? They started watching *Headline News?* How come nobody, especially their kids, automatically replaced them? Isn't that the way it always worked? Maybe you think it's fucking ridiculous to sit here now and predict that an electronic newspaper might be the future. That someday people will prefer to read off a computer screen what today they hold in their hand. But let me tell you something. My kid, he's in second grade. All he does is look at screens and punch buttons. He watches television with seventy-five different channels to choose from. He has video games with shit on it that I couldn't dream of when I was his age, playing *All-Star Baseball* with those numbered cards and the needle you flicked to spin. He's going to grow up with all of this and more to come, sitting in front of a screen and learning from it, and that's what he'll know. That's what he'll be comfortable with. Do you know what I'm saying?"

Lips pursed, stomach knotted, Colangelo said nothing.

"You are all dead men, Gerry. Dead men driving. You guys…the pressmen…the printers have been dying off for years. I can't tell you when, but it's possible that in the next fifteen-to-twenty, you'll be no better off than the printers are now. Sure, they'll keep publishing the paper because not everyone can afford a computer and the baby boomers grew up before all this shit and they won't be able to imagine not buying it on the commute in from Scarsdale. But don't kid yourself, the world is changing and today's kids are being conditioned to think that all they need to do to get what they want is to move their fingers. These kids don't think, *Oh, I like the feel of paper in my hands.* By the time my kid is in college, the newspaper will be a boring piece of worthless crap to him. Everything he does will be audio-visual. If what I read is true—and it's not like I'm reading this shit in the *National Enquirer*—when my kid is in high school he'll be jerking off in his bedroom while making eyes at some little cutie in California. And by the time these kids grow up computers will be part of everything they do and you'll be lucky to have a quarter of the readers you have now."

Schmoo paused again, as if he were Perry Mason badgering a witness into thinking the whole court was on to him and he might as well come clean.

"Gerry, you ultimately can't win this war. You know that. Or let me put it this way: You *should* know that. And you are absolutely crazy to personally stand up and take a bullet for some outdated principle and a bunch of guys who are going into the street soon, one way or another. You've got to survive as best you can, for however long the gravy train rolls. Get the best deal for however many of these people as you can. Our friends don't care about who's right and wrong. They just want this over soon. And like I said, they'll even help you a bit by tossing a few bucks to anyone going overboard."

"I don't get it, why?"

"Because they like the deal they have with you. It's good for them and it's good for you. And they don't like the sound of permanent replacement workers. They don't want to see these scabs wind up with taking every last job and then the whole arrangement is done and they have to start over. What I'm saying is they don't like change."

"What if I can't sell it to my guys?" Colangelo said.

"Then maybe *you* have to make a change. Then maybe our friends do make a deal with these scabs and you all wind up getting fucked."

Colangelo looked at the table, at the crumpled *Times* clipping. He had noticed the word internet appeared to be in every paragraph.

Schmoo stood up and folded his coat over his arm.

"And then you'll have lost the best gig you're ever going to have."

Like the master of the universe he believed himself to be, the lawyer strutted all the way to the front door, pushed through it without looking back. In his most sober monotone, he said: "Think about that for a couple of days and get back to me."

The door closed. Colangelo was motionless, transfixed by the swirling dust particles in the sun-lit center of the room. He rose slowly and walked robotically around the bar with the cheap wood paneling. He pulled a mug from behind the counter, positioned it under the spout and poured himself a draft.

"The hell with it," he said, the moratorium officially relaxed.

CHAPTER EIGHTEEN

Steven had been watching out for Jamie all morning. He spotted him right away, marching in the direction of Morris.

Jesus, he's actually going through with this.

He excused himself from the flirtatious teacher's union rep and hurried across the street where Debbie Givens and her cameraman were perched in the back of a white car with its hatchback open. Her legs weren't long enough to reach the ground.

"I think you're on," Steven said. Givens nodded enthusiastically. The cameraman wiped a smudge of chocolate from the corner of his mouth and stood up while ducking his head under the raised hatch to gather his equipment.

Givens followed Steven back across the street, in the direction of his father, uncle and cousin.

"Listen," Steven said, wheeling around and placing an arm on her shoulder. He moved in close enough to whisper in her ear. He could almost taste her makeup.

"No questions, just video, like we agreed."

"All I need are pictures and a little sound," she said, nodding. "We dub in the rest."

"Deal," said Steven. "And we're on for tonight?"

Givens edged even closer, so that her spray-tamed hair tickled his nose.

"Tonight," she said with a wink. "And maybe tomorrow morning if you're up for it."

She walked off without turning back, leaving him to his anticipation. He followed her in the direction of the developing story.

The sight of a television cameraman hustling toward the three Kramer men had piqued the interest of other strikers as well. A small crowd began to form around Jamie, Morris and Lou, though keeping its distance.

Morris was still holding the *Times*, impaled against his ribs by his elbow. His hands were tucked into his jacket. Lou instinctively stepped between father and son. Jamie looked at his uncle and said, "Steven didn't tell you this morning? I called and told him about what I was planning late last night."

"No, well, yeah, he mentioned to me early this morning that you were thinking about crossing," Lou said. He turned his head away from Morris, to speak confidentially. "But Jamie, look, I thought you were just pissed off about what happened at dinner. I wasn't going to say anything to your dad because I figured you'd get a good night's sleep and realize, you know, this is crazy."

He tried to steer Jamie toward the street, a few feet away from Morris. And better yet, a little farther from the front door.

"This will kill him, I'm telling you," Lou said. "It'll just about kill him, and especially if you cross this line out here in front of everyone."

"Uncle Lou, this is not about him. It's about me, what I need."

"You need to be out here with us, not up there," Lou said, gesturing with his head. "Jamie, come on, you want to be, you know, a *goddamned* scab?"

"I just want to be a guy with a job, a career, money in my pocket. Uncle Lou, we've lost already. The paper is out. People are buying it. The sportswriters are back to work and so are some of the others. You know what I'm saying? It's one thing to be out here if the paper's not being published. What are you going to do, stand out here forever? My father's got a couple of more years of working before he retires. He's at the end of his career. And neither of you has any idea what's going on with Karyn and Aaron right now. Not that he would give a crap anyway."

"Stevie's out. Do you think he thinks he's throwing away his career?"

Jamie shook his head. "We went through this last night. I'm not him. He's a columnist. He's a star. He can get a job anywhere. I've written one decent story in my life that got any attention—and everyone hated me for *that*. If I lose this job, what the hell do I send Karyn to support my son?"

Lou glanced back nervously at Morris. He noticed the gathering crowd. He looked around for Steven, for his son's help, his natural way with words. He'd been here a minute ago. Now where the hell had he gone off to?

"Jamie, you won't lose your job, I guarantee you, don't do this," Lou said. He couldn't think of anything more promising or persuasive. Jamie shook his uncle off, moved back toward his father.

"Dad…"

Morris' grayish eyes were on him but they were cold and distant, unresponsive and possibly homicidal. He read the panic on Lou's face, watched him grow frantic just as he did when they were kids and a crisis would erupt without warning when the old man was at home.

"Jamie…" Lou persisted, his hand on Jamie's shoulder again. He tried to pull him away. Jamie shook him off to face his father.

"Dad, this is something I just have to do, for me."

Jamie waited but elicited only more silence.

"For Aaron too. I just can't afford to be out of work. I heard they're already replacing reporters. If I don't go in now…"

"Jamie, they're just trying to *scare* you," Lou said from behind.

Morris said nothing. Jamie met his glare. For a fleeting moment, he thought his father's lower lip had trembled. Now they were pursed again, as tightly as if they'd been nailed shut.

Jamie thought of just walking off. The revolving door to the *Trib* lobby was no more than twenty feet away. He thought, *Enough of this, it's my decision, why should I have to explain anything to him or anyone else.*

So what was he waiting for? Permission? Good luck. Understanding? Forget it.

What was the point of this impromptu summit? He honestly couldn't say. But for reasons he was too panicked to discern, he had promised himself that he would do this publicly. Even if his father was guarding the building, he was determined to cross *like a man.*

Now he was rooted to his position, to his cause, even if it seemed so unnatural for him to finally have one.

Am I doing the right thing? Should I have talked this out with someone first?

Jamie had asked himself those questions on the way to the building. But he knew if he postponed the plan he would probably never execute it. He—or someone else—would talk him into a sense of inertia. He would be one more powerless union drone.

Fuck the union. He'd gone to bed and woke up thinking that. But even as he sat on the subway and steeled himself for what was to come, he realized he had not actually spoken those treasonous words until…

"Fuck the union, okay, Dad?"

"Jamie, come on!" Lou said.

It had come out spasmodically, a Tourette's moment, too fast and too late to recall.

"Is that what you want me to say?" Jamie said. "Is that what it will take for you to stop standing there and say one stinking word to me?"

Morris continued his commitment to a state of statuesque dispassion. His right hand, having slipped from his pocket while the newspaper remained trapped in the armpit, was slowly, unconsciously, balling itself into a fist.

"And fuck you too, Dad, okay?"

This time, the defiance was expressed in more of a whisper.

His eyes already welling with tears, Jamie felt the gaze of others upon him. Though the strikers had kept their distance and probably couldn't hear what was said, they still were witnessing a spectacle—the kind reporters had routinely covered from behind police lines, from the perimeter, straining for whatever nuggets of information they could extract.

Surely they had not heard the words, *fuck, you, too* and *Dad* that echoed around Morris and Jamie in the chilly morning air. The street was suddenly devoid of noise, of movement, as if all traffic on the highway had rubbernecked at the sight of the Kramer family dysfunction.

Who else was watching? When Jamie veered from his father's glare, glancing up at the third-floor windows of the *Trib* newsroom, he swore he could see eyes peering down at him.

Probably an illusion of sunlight, he thought. *Don't get paranoid now.*

He reminded himself to focus on what he'd come for. He had made his stand, his rehearsed speech, and punctuated it with an ample dose of adolescent rage. There apparently would be no response from Morris, professional or paternal, pitying or punitive. Sorry, time's up and here was the final Jeopardy question: who is about to become the first male Kramer to cross the forbidden family line?

Jamie supposed they were right about him. But as usual, not quite sure of himself, he left room for the possibility that they were all full of shit. And in the end, he thought: *Nothing else matters besides Aaron. That's who I'm worried about. That's why I'm standing here.*

He looked down at his left foot, tapping—or twitching—a steady beat against the ground. Move one step laterally and then go forward. The path to the door would be unimpeded. His left foot curled onto its toes. His shoulder leaned in that direction.

When he was a clerk hanging around the office late at night, a couple of crusty sports department holdovers from the halcyon era of boxing would invariably ramble on about axiomatic "hit-'em-when-they're-moving-forward" punches. Like Ali all those years ago against Sonny Liston up in some nowhere town in the middle of Maine. Hours later, when there was time to recount this sad episode, frame by frame, Jamie would consider the gravitational mystery, conclude that while he had leaned toward the door, his weight had indeed shifted, his body following the lead of his brain.

Absolutely, he was going in of his own volition—and not the way it would come to look to everyone on the street, as a humiliating run for cover.

When his eyes had left his father, Morris' right hand had been concealed. He never anticipated or even imagined the hand propelling itself until it was too late. It was upon Jamie's left cheek with the momentum of a punch-in-the-making before fist yielded to palm. Jamie got off lightly, perhaps because Morris had long ago vowed he would never cross the line his own father had too often gone hurtling across. He would never hit his child.

He couldn't stop himself this time.

How long had Jamie looked away? A second, maybe two, but that was enough. He glanced at his father out of the corner of his right eye, saw the newspaper fall, felt the sudden sting of the calloused fingers meeting his cheek. They swept across the bridge of his nose before he stumbled, tried to grab hold of Morris for support. Jamie flailed with his right hand and scratched his father with a fingernail above the left eye as he fell back. And down.

On his back, Jamie could feel his father's surge of satisfaction. Another union mission completed. Mutinous son halted, consigned to his rightful place, ceremoniously dumped on his impudent ass.

From this position, this angle, there was less reflection and, yes, those actually were faces pressing against the newsroom windows. Like the strikers in the street, they were witnesses to Jamie's rise against his old man—and swift fall. He sensed movement all around him now. He heard the murmurs. He looked up at the rage and maybe something else—sorrow, perhaps?—in the eyes of his father.

Sorrow for striking his son in a crowd, in broad daylight? Or for the biological role he had played in the production of this drama?

Tears spilled down Jamie's cheeks. There could be no bluffing anymore, if that's what he had been doing in the first place. No more cries for attention. No more options.

I've got to go. Got to go now.

Events were blurring into a progression of circumstances beyond his control. It was time to leave without saying another word. The way it had been when Jamie had arrived at the hospital two years ago, too late for the birth of his son. Karyn's aunt had delivered her request that he seek new lodging. That's when he had discovered the consequences of decisiveness and conviction.

You make your move. You live with the results.

He momentarily convinced himself: *I got what I came here for. I made him pay attention to me. I stood up to him. Now get up. Get up and walk through that door.*

Jamie put his palms to the ground and pushed himself up. He adjusted his glasses. He felt for the strap of his bag still attached to his right shoulder, just as it had been the night he regretfully took one for the team.

He forged his way forward. In an instant he was across the line, through the front door, away from his father, whose team he no longer wished to be on.

CHAPTER NINETEEN

The video camera stayed on Morris after Jamie had gone. Debbie Givens nudged her cameraman forward, as best she could a man who was almost a foot taller and more than a hundred pounds heavier.

The redness in Morris' face was gradually losing out to a more sickly pallor. Most of the strikers began to back away, return to the monotony of the line. With the crowd largely dispersed, Lou suddenly noticed the camera trained on his brother's face.

"What the hell are you doing with that?" he said.

Givens pinched the cameraman's jacket so hard that she could feel his love handle. "Stay with it," she whispered as Lou moved closer. "Stay with it, just stay…with…*it!*"

Lou held a hand up to the lens. The cameraman backed off but held the shot. For a moment it appeared that Lou was about to wrestle for possession of the equipment, but he spotted his son behind the blonde.

"Stevie, help me here."

Steven stepped forward, cautiously. "Come on, we don't want any problems," he said, without making clear who he was addressing the appeal to.

The cameraman scrunched his face, tilted his head.

"I thought you said…"

"It's all right, why don't you just go now?" Steven said. He turned back to Lou. "Dad, they're reporters, doing their job. Something like this happens in front of them…"

"You mean they're going to put this shit on TV?" Lou said.

"They were here to interview our people on the line," Steven said. "It's not their fault Jamie showed up and Uncle Mo had to smack him."

Lou stared at Steven, disappointed, trying to think of a response. He settled on, "Just get them the hell out of here before I…"

He turned back to his brother. Morris had bent down to pick up his newspaper and was busily rearranging the sections, refolding, frustrated by pages falling, nonetheless grateful to have something to do with his trembling hands.

"This damn *Times*," he said. "It's so clumsy you can't keep it in one piece."

"Mo, let's go," Lou said. He noticed the clotting above his brother's eye. Pointing a finger at his own brow, he added: "You've got a little blood there…"

"Don't worry about it."

Lou nodded. He glanced back at the crowd, sliding his arm around Morris' shoulder.

Morris said nothing, for once inclined to have Lou guide him. They walked toward the corner. It wasn't until they had turned, out of sight from the others, that Lou could bring himself to look Morris in the eyes.

Holy shit, his brother, the rock, the most grounded person he knew, was openly unmoored. Practically in tears.

"What the hell did I just do here? I hit him in front of the whole damned street."

"Mo, I heard what he said to you. It wasn't right."

"I never touched one of my kids. And there were times…not with Becky…but this one…*believe* me."

"I know, Mo," Lou said.

He patted his brother's shoulder, uncomfortable leaving his hand there and—really—with the entire role reversal. How many times had Morris sat with him in the kitchen as Lou unburdened himself of the fury and sorrow following one of his ex-wife's binges—binges that had left her vomiting in the bathroom in the wee morning hours? She'd stay bedridden into the mid-afternoon, cotton-mouthed and curled up in the fetal position, demanding ice water.

"What should I do with her, Mo?" Lou would beg his brother. "Please, tell me what to do?"

"She needs help, professional help," Mo would say.

But Marge would swear on her mother's life to reform. She would behave herself for a week or ten days, as much as a month, before slipping out again at night while Lou was at work and Steven was preoccupied. The pattern repeated itself until the night she never returned, not even to pack. She called drunk almost a year later from a bar in North Miami Beach. She told Lou to send her a particular dress and pair of shoes he had already tossed in the trash with the rest of her things.

"I always knew I couldn't hit him though," Morris said. "With my temper, after the way Dad would lose it with me. You know what I mean?"

"Yeah," Lou said. "Dad was pretty bad. I remember crying like a baby whenever he went after you. And he would come out with his belt hanging out of his hand and say, 'And you, little shit, act up, you get the same thing, understand?'"

Lou let the thought dangle. "Course, it was the booze. He never remembered any of it the next day."

"This kid, he always winds up doing the wrong thing," Morris said, picking up the conversation he seemed to be having more with himself. "Married a nice girl, Jewish girl. I don't know why they had to move all the way the hell out there but, okay, they have a baby, a house—what more did he need? And where does he wind up? By himself in that shithole of an apartment. The baby's up in the country. He's down here. I told Molly years ago when she wanted me to help him out at the paper. I said, 'This is not a good idea. Not with this one. He needs to go find something else, on his own.' She said, 'Do something for him, he needs a break.' And this is what I get back."

"Mo, it's not your fault. Jamie's not a bad kid. He's just …"

"He's thirty-whatever, Louie, that's the thing. He's no kid anymore. He's got one of his own…"

"He don't understand."

"What's there to understand? Can you tell me what the hell there is to understand? I mean, cross a goddamn picket line? *Our* line? His *own* line? Louie, I can't believe. How could he even think…?"

Morris shook his head, rubbed the throbbing temple above his left ear, a tension headache coming on. Lou's left hand remained on his shoulder. Morris lurched forward, too preoccupied by his son's betrayal to think about where they were going. But on their present path there was only one possible destination.

Lou pulled open the door to Kelly's and waited to let his brother in. He placed his hands gently on Morris' back to guide him to the rear. Even at this early afternoon hour, the possibility remote that any other printers would be there, Lou silently prayed their regular table was vacant.

"Ayy, guys, we just opened."

Kelly Murphy was always a welcome sight, but Morris had only eyes for the lone patron at the bar.

Gerry Colangelo, his back to Morris and Lou, was perched on a stool, unmistakable with his hair gleaming in the pale light. A half-empty draft was in front of him on the bar. Colangelo was too immersed in papers he was poring through to look up.

Lou again tried to prod his brother into the back, but Morris was unmovable.

"Not now," Lou whispered. "Mo, you shouldn't, not after what just happened."

Morris raised his left index finger.

"One sec," he said.

"Mo, please…"

Morris advanced to the bar, sat himself on the stool next to Colangelo. Lou waited, twenty feet away, unable to hear. Knowing Morris was not one inclined to drink at this time of day, Kelly sprayed Coke into a mug and set it in front of him. She looked up at Lou with a palm upturned. Lou shook his head. Tense and restless, he went to the bathroom, pushed his way into the stall. He dropped his pants and himself onto the cold toilet seat. The bathroom was as much a lifelong station of contemplative solitude for him as it was for Morris, the one good place where their drunken old man couldn't get at them. He closed his eyes and lowered his head into his hands.

"Fuck," he said.

Lou remained there for what seemed like an eternity, ten minutes in all. He knew he would have to jump at the first sound of commotion. But he heard none. An eerie silence prevailed. Curiosity overtook his fear. Maybe there was good news. Maybe he should join Morris at the bar, have a beer, order lunch. Maybe running into Colangelo would turn out to be a good thing, a distraction from Jamie. But when Lou got within view of the bar Kelly was alone, wiping it down.

"Back here, Louie."

The voice came from behind, in the printers' section of the bar. Lou looked up at Kelly. She shrugged, raised her eyebrows. Morris was pacing, holding his soda glass from the top by the fingertips.

"Where did Colangelo go?" Lou said.

"Picked up and left," Morris said.

"Did he say anything about what's going on?"

Morris didn't answer. He dropped into a chair by the table, motioning for Lou to join him. They faced each other silently. Lou Kramer waited for his brother to enlighten him, as he had his whole life.

"Mo, tell me, what happened?" he said.

Morris removed his hands from the glass and massaged his forehead. It struck Lou that his brother looked pale, exhausted and possibly defeated.

"Louie, put it this way—nothing," Morris said. "He said nothing. If he has a plan, I get the feeling that we're only going to find out about it by watching the news."

Lou decided this wasn't a good time to mention the segment Morris and Jamie had just apparently co-starred in back at the *Trib*. His brother would hear about it soon enough.

CHAPTER TWENTY

Jamie wasn't three feet out of the elevator when he spotted Pat Blaine balancing a cup of coffee in one hand with a Manhattan white pages telephone book in the other.

"New policy!" Blaine announced. It was the kind of theatrical greeting Jamie would expect from him on any normal Wednesday. "No more dialing information when you need a telephone number. From now on our fingers do the walking."

Jamie felt better about his own ruffled appearance when he saw how unkempt Blaine looked. Unshaven, suit rumpled, the knot of his tie coming apart. Jamie was mostly grateful that the first face he'd encountered was familiar and friendly. Blaine was a sore sight for his own sad, teary eyes.

"Who says?"

"Our blessed Lord, that's who," said Blaine. "Any information charges showing up on your phone extension will automatically be deducted from your paycheck and they won't be going into your pension plan." Blaine took a swig of the coffee and grimaced. "Do we still have a pension plan?" he asked.

"I'm just here to find out if I have a job, to tell you the truth," Jamie said. He wondered for a moment if Blaine was drunk.

"So you are, Kramer." Blaine's tone at least was gracious, almost avuncular.

"Did you see or hear about what just happened downstairs?" Jamie said.

"I've just spent the last half-hour in the can reading today's paper, which, I am obligated to report—because I am and will always be a reporter even if they call me a columnist—is about the only appropriate place to be reading the piece of crap that was delivered to the newsstand this morning."

"Never mind, then," Jamie said. They walked together through the double glass doors that led into the newsroom. They were, as usual during day hours, wide open despite Steven's and Robbins' insistence at the union meeting that the locks had been changed and the place was under heavy security.

"That's funny," Jamie said. "I thought…"

"What?"

"Never mind."

"That's the second time you've said that. You lose credibility when you repeat yourself," Blaine said.

"No, I just thought this place would be crawling with security—and especially with Brady's people," he said.

"Security costs money and he's going for the record lowest union-busting budget in the history of the printed word. He's got his lawyer to bust everyone's balls and his son in charge of the product."

"Maxwell Brady is editing the paper?"

"Absolutely, hands-on, at least until it's time to go hit the bar and Willis salvages whatever he can. Young Master Brady is promising to win us the Pulitzer for the best scab paper of all time."

They were inside the newsroom, Jamie trying to at least appear relaxed. His sweaty hands remained in his jacket pockets. The city room was quiet, eerily so. Cal Willis was at his usual station, four other editors clustered around him. There seemed to be no one else around.

It was still early in the newspaper day. Some of the editorial staff and especially the culture people were notoriously late getting started. The sportswriters seldom appeared unless it was the time of the month expense accounts were due. Still, even with the bulk of the union staff out on strike, there should have been more activity.

Blaine finished off the coffee with one long gulp, crumpled the cup and tossed it toward a wastepaper basket. He missed by a foot. He rested his free hand on Jamie's shoulder.

"Kramer, whatever the hell it is that you are doing in here, whatever made you walk through those doors downstairs, it's too late to second-guess yourself. You're here, pal. Deal with it."

"Pat, I've got my reasons," Jamie said. "You know, I have a kid…"

"You're here. I'm here. Somehow, we both got here."

Jamie bit his lower lip, looked down at the floor.

"Just do yourself a favor and don't read the damn paper," Blaine said.

"I haven't seen it since we went out. Have you written?"

Blaine shook his head, scratched his nose and stifled a yawn.

"Offered to write a column when you guys went out, but Cal said he didn't have room. Funny man. He told me to work on something *really* good. Not to rush it. He said, 'I don't have any room for your lousy effin column.' Cal is a great man—you know what I'm saying?"

"So who is writing?" Jamie said.

Blaine smiled and made a sweeping motion with his right arm, presenting the eerily serene newsroom.

"Behold," he said.

They parted near Willis' desk in the center of the room. Once there had been plaster and glass separating departments, but Willis had tired of having to stand, stretch his neck over partitions and shout to get a person's attention. He long ago had refused his own office along the back wall near Maxine Hancock's spacious digs and the paper's conference rooms.

"What's the use of going to work in an office and then when you get there you go into another one?" he'd said.

Jamie warily approached his desk. As if his eyes could peer through his forehead, Willis said: "You got anything good?" It took Jamie a moment to realize that Willis was talking to him.

"Does that mean I can work?" Jamie said.

"You got another effin reason for being here?"

Jamie shrugged. "I just thought, you know, maybe there's a process…"

"You report, we edit. That's the process."

Jamie was about to walk away to his desk for lack of anything else to say.

"And whom do we have here?"

Maxwell Brady stopped suddenly by Willis' desk. He was the body opposite of his father: wiry thin, prematurely gray, demonstrative and party-boy buoyant.

"Kramer," Willis said, nodding to Jamie.

"Mr. Brady," Jamie said, offering his right hand.

They had already been introduced but only in passing. On that occasion, Brady was on the way uptown to make a sloppy spectacle of himself for the benefit of the gossip columnists staking out the popular haunts—especially those from the *Sun*, which dubbed him Brady Boy.

"Kramer," Maxwell Brady said, nodding. "The great labor columnist crosses the picket line?"

"You're confusing me with my cousin," Jamie said. "He's still out."

"And you are…"

"Jamie. I'm a reporter. I just came back today, right now."

Maxwell Brady, his Groucho eyebrows suddenly at attention, pointed a finger.

"You're not the bloke who was just downstairs…"

"I was…I mean, I had to cross the line to get in."

Jamie stole a glance at Willis, who frowned and returned to his keyboard.

"My father and I, well, we had a thing."

"I heard a row from Lord Brady's office, so I took a peak out the window—saw the whole fracas. You were assaulted trying to report to work. *Appalling!* The bastards tried those tactics in Dublin and London, and we had them all arrested."

The notion of his father being led away in handcuffs was momentarily amusing, but Jamie reminded himself of why he'd crossed the line: he just wanted to be back at his desk, his computer screen, perhaps have another crack at his still-unpublished nursing home piece. He wanted his life back.

"Actually," he said, softly, "it was nothing. My dad, he's the head of the printers' union, and this is like life and death to him. I guess he just lost it."

Jamie looked away from his aspiring defender. Willis was punching computer keys and whistling a tune from his most beloved musical, *Les Miserables.* He liked to brag that as many actors that had played Jean Valjean, that's how many times he had seen the Broadway production.

"No big deal," Jamie said.

"You mean, you crossed the picket line right past your daddy and he took a poke at you?"

Jamie nodded, sheepishly.

"That is incredible. Willis, did you hear that?"

Willis didn't look up. Maxwell Brady pounded his palm on the desk and went cackling down the aisle, bounding in the direction of his father's office.

"Cal, where are all the new reporters they hired?" Jamie said.

"Hired?"

"People were saying that Brady brought in new people. He's been on television insisting that they're going to be permanent. Isn't that why the sports guys crossed?"

"The sports guys crossed because the basketball and hockey seasons just started and they didn't want to miss the damn buffet at the Garden. Otherwise, Brady hasn't hired anyone."

"But I was hearing from Steve and he said…"

"You just heard Maxwell Brady say a few things—would you believe anything that jackass said?"

"So who's writing the stories?"

Willis shook his head and threw up his hands.

"Who would you like to have writing them?" he said.

"What do you mean?"

"In case you forgot, Kramer, yesterday was Election Day. All we had to do to put out a paper was to put the results in it, use the wires. That's all we pretty much have to do every day. But if it's local news and quote-unquote staff reporters you're looking for, we're all over that too."

He lifted a *Trib* off his desk, turned the front page and skimmed a few more. "Okay, what's our big local story? We had a drug bust yesterday at Kennedy High School up in the Bronx by one of our new reporters, Sylvia Stallone."

Willis wheeled around to face a group of vacant desks.

"Ms. Stallone, say hello to Mr. Kramer, one of our regular general assignment people. Mr. Kramer started here as a copy boy and worked his way up." He turned back to Jamie. "Ms. Stallone joined us yesterday, a name Max Brady apparently found in the Brooklyn telephone book. A good fightin' name, he said, perfect for the crime beat."

Jamie took the newspaper from Willis and began thumbing through the front pages, scanning bylines. "Martin L. King…Robert Zimmerman… W.J. Clinton," he read out loud. "You mean to tell me that you guys just made up these ridiculous bylines and put them on stories in the paper?"

"Not we—him, Brady the younger. And keep it down, Kramer, you don't want to offend our new staff, do you? These people are very sensitive about their prose, especially Mr. Zimmerman over there. He writes protest songs in his spare time so we're letting him cover City Hall."

"This is crazy."

"Jamie, who would you like to be? You can actually be several people on the same day, write as many stories as you want. We just take them off the wire and rearrange a few paragraphs and sentences. You have a favorite athlete? Musician? Journalist? If you go with a journalist, make it a dead one. We don't need a lawsuit."

"I don't get it," Jamie said. "Why are the union people saying that real reporters are being hired to replace us? What's the point of making us all think we're about to be permanently replaced?"

"Because they assumed striking reporters would know it's a load of effin bull. But in the eyes of the rest of the city, it makes Brady look like he's trying to break the unions," Willis said. "The Alliance and other *Trib* unions need support from the teachers, hospital workers, sanitation—everywhere they can get it."

Willis held his palms up, in effect asking Jamie how the hell this hadn't been obvious to him. Jamie suddenly wished he were as invisible as Willis' new reporting staff. Willis and Blaine had been contractually obligated to do Brady's bidding but understood the mockery he—and by extension they—were making of the newspaper. They had little choice but to go along until the dispute was resolved. Jamie, on the other hand, was in the building because he had made a rash decision that, in lieu of what he'd just learned, was devoid of all common sense.

The words from Blaine—*Whatever it is you're doing here, you've got to deal with it*—had been fair warning.

Jamie was numbed by the realization that the sense of normalcy he was seeking did not exist, not in this building, not right now and perhaps never again. Walking toward the *Trib* from the subway station, he had imagined himself calling Karyn to say, "Cancel those plans, and let me speak to my boy." What a joke he had played on himself. Who was to be the fictionalized author of his next piece? Ronald McDonald? Or would Jamie proceed to make himself a bigger clown by putting his name in a newspaper that was now nothing more than a daily lampoon of itself?

He walked away from Willis' desk in the direction of his own. He sank into his chair, suddenly overwhelmed by the emptiness all around him. He closed his eyes, trying to stave off another cresting wave of emotion.

"You should have called me before you came in," Willis said, standing over him. He leaned over slightly, placed a hand on his shoulder. "You're a reporter, Jamie—did you forget that? All you had to do was pick up the telephone and find out what was going on. I would've told you not to bother. But you're here now, and I gather from what Max Brady was yapping about that you made it worse by coming in the front door."

Jamie looked up at Willis. He begged himself not to tear up, but he couldn't help it.

"People downstairs saw a lot more than me crossing the line," Jamie said. "They saw the *Big Apple Circus*. The question is: What the hell do I do now?"

Willis frowned, shook his head.

"Unless you are determined to be part of this, I'd say go home, have a drink. Don't talk to anyone. Get a good night's sleep and see what comes out of this in the next day or two. I can't tell you what it'll be, but we didn't create this, and we can't end it. Inside or out, we're just bystanders in a game of chicken."

Obediently, Jamie nodded. He rose from his seat and began a stiff walk up the aisle toward the double-glass doors.

"Kramer, one more thing."

Jamie turned back. Willis had the exasperated look of a disbelieving parent. He pointed an index finger toward the exit on the far side of the office. It was the one Jamie had used when he became an unwilling prop on the night the strike broke out.

"Will you use the effin side door?"

Day Four: Thursday, November 10, 1994

CHAPTER TWENTY-ONE

Another long fitful night came to a merciful end. Dawn arrived with Jamie still able to muster just a couple of hours of uninterrupted sleep.

His back was sore. His neck felt encased in cement. He lay motionless on his back, staring at the ceiling, asking himself, *What now?*

His crossing of the picket line had been executed with the simultaneously comic and tragic touch of slipping on a banana peel and falling in front of a speeding bus. He had alienated everyone important in his life, with the possible exceptions of Cal Willis and Patrick Blaine.

Steven wouldn't be making any more recruitment calls. Morris was possibly sitting *shivah*, mourning the loss of a striker more than a son. Even Molly might be furious with him at this point.

If the *Lonely Planet* travel guide Karyn had left for his viewing displeasure was the precursor to accepting the job at the invisible bookstore, what would Jamie have left with Aaron in effect out of his life?

My life sucks, kept running through his mind like a self-pitying mantra.

He had nowhere to go, nothing to do. What else to do besides isolate himself in his apartment, eat junk food and watch television until his vision faded to black?

One day down. And counting.

On the previous afternoon, Jamie had gratefully taken Willis' advice and slipped inconspicuously through the side door of the building. Back in

Brooklyn, he moved his car from the spot he'd left it in the previous night and found another one three spaces from his front door. It was a Monday no-parking zone, good for the next three days. Covered on that front, Jamie proceeded to shop as if the city was on Category Five hurricane alert. He purchased a pound and a half of sliced turkey and Swiss cheese, three large bags of chips, three six-packs of diet Coke. He stopped by the meat counter and bought a few hamburger patties, a dozen chicken wings and a large container of potato salad. He dropped two boxes of his favorite breakfast cereal, Special K, into the cart.

Two doors down, he propped his grocery bags against the front counter of the video store. He prowled the aisles and stacked videos against his body like a clerk taking inventory. Needy for companionship, he rounded up bad-ass hombres for a guys' night in. James Dean in *Rebel Without a Cause*; Al Pacino in *Dog Day Afternoon*; Robert DeNiro in *Taxi Driver*; and Dustin Hoffman in *Midnight Cowboy*. He passed on Sylvester Stallone's *Rambo* in a voluntary show of good taste.

Severed from the world outside his apartment, he settled in at home with the mad, misguided and misanthropic—the only real friends he believed he had left.

He avoided television for fear of strike news. He unplugged the telephone in the event his mother was moved to make another futile attempt to broker peace. He was hanging with Travis Bickle, with Ratso Rizzo. But even they were merely a temporary distraction from his misery. Not long after a dinner of the chicken and chips, Jamie shut off the television and lights.

Why didn't I think it through? Why did I go in?

Brief intervals of dozing were accompanied by dreams impossible to understand or recognize, ending when he'd snort himself awake and into that familiar moment of panic.

The worst insomniac hours for Jamie were always between midnight and three. After that, he was too exhausted to stress out over much—

which was probably why he could finally drift off. It was easier, naturally, contemplating sleep deprivation when there was nothing planned for the next day. But its emptiness was reassuring only in those wee hours. By daybreak, a plan of nothing seemed worse than having to do something— *anything*—in a state of fatigue.

He was repelled by the thought of Ratso, still cued in the machine, looking like death warmed over or like exactly how Jamie felt. If nothing else, he was inspired to shave and shower. His face still tingled with sensation—but was it from the collision with the *Trib* driver or from the sting of his father's open hand?

I've got to force myself to do something, he told himself. He decided on a run through the neighborhood.

He slipped into a pair of old basketball shorts with the official Lakers logo that reached only mid-thigh—out of fashion, thanks to those yappy Michigan players who reveled in being called the Fab Five. He yanked his favorite tattered Hunter College hoodie from the hook in the closet by the front door.

Jamie would have preferred exercising on a treadmill or stationary bicycle, but he couldn't afford the membership to the neighborhood health club. He and Karyn had belonged, but that was a family membership on two salaries. He had never thought of himself as much of a runner. His style could easily have been mistaken for accelerated walking. And he often paused to admire the neighborhood brownstones and tastefully-situated carriage houses along the quiet, tree-lined streets he missed so much during his brief and spectacularly unhappy stay in the suburbs.

"I love how different all the buildings are," he told Karyn one afternoon in the neighborhood soon after they met. The architecture contrasted so starkly from the numbing identicalness of the two-family brick row houses of his native outer Brooklyn. Sunday mornings they would stroll the Promenade, end-to-end, exiting at Montague Street for brunch before returning to the apartment. They would spread the papers on the area rug in front of the couch, sometimes making love amid the scatter of pages.

They would nap through mid-afternoon, grab a slice of pizza on Henry Street and catch a five o'clock movie at the neighborhood art house. The theater was old, almost decrepit. But it was local, artsy. It was decisively Brooklyn Heights, not mainstream Brooklyn.

Jamie relished those days. But when he began to feel nostalgic, he would ask himself, *Was it really the relationship or more a sense of self-discovery?* In the Heights, he felt like an explorer uncovering an invigorating new world, his stylish paradise.

He made himself run. *It'll be therapeutic.* He knew he could use some real counseling—if only he wasn't terrified of what he'd find out. His standard route took him from his apartment on Hicks Street over to Henry, down past the cinema. He turned left onto Poplar, over to Columbia Heights, closest to the river and down to the lower Promenade. He liked to treat himself to a waterfront view while working his way back. He always exited by the toddler playground onto Pierrepont Street, where he would occasionally run past Karyn's old friends. If they spotted him they would wave enthusiastically—as if he and Karyn were still together, and they were all part of the noble society of posh-Brooklyn sophisticates who had resisted the clarion call of the suburbs, the comfort and security of the two-car garage.

"Jamie…Jamie…"

Oh no, too late. Keep your head down. Maybe she'll give up.

He recognized the voice. It was Lucy, a redhead with soft, freckled skin and somber blue eyes. She had been a member of Karyn's book group and at some point had sent out cards to friends asking that they address her from then on as Lucinda. She and her attorney husband owned a spacious co-op on one of the neighborhood's most desirable blocks. In the time since Karyn and Jamie had left the Heights and he had returned, they had added a daughter and a golden retriever, both several months younger than Aaron.

From time-to-time he would run into Lucy/Lucinda and her husband. They always agreed that it had been *much too long* and they should all get together for a drink, a bite. Jamie knew before his smile had faded it was just congeniality. Jamie had enjoyed their company. But the foundation of these friendships was no different from those developed in high school, stitched together by a mutual interest—a family life they no longer had in common.

"Jamie…Jamie."

Slowing his pace, Jamie looked up, forced a smile and waved. He recognized the woman sitting with Lucy/Lucinda but couldn't recall her name. Only that her husband had once, at a couples-night-out dinner, corrected Jamie when he misidentified Neil Simon as Noel after raving about *Lost In Yonkers*.

Karyn couldn't get enough of Manhattan—the museums, the Broadway shows and the pricey restaurants that made Jamie cringe. On his salary, he was happier to go to the movies in the neighborhood and eat pizza. He could admit she had helped him expand his city horizons but that only made Karyn's sudden compulsion to leave more bewildering. Many nights when falling asleep was an hours-long process, Jamie's head filled with contemplations of paths not taken.

What if Karyn had not been trapped in that subway elevator—would it have made any difference? What if he'd argued that he was happy, truly happy, to be living in Brooklyn Heights and did not want to leave? What if Aaron had been born in a hospital downtown and Jamie had been by her side?

In those dead-of-night hypotheticals, he wondered: might they have lived happily ever after? In the light of day, he had to admit that their compatibility was always in question. It was possible that they were together only because he had needed to latch onto someone at that point in his life. So apparently had she.

Jamie was coming up on the entrance to the park. He wondered, *Should I go over and say hello?*

He wasn't in the mood for pleasantries. Fortunately, Lucy/Lucinda relieved him of the responsibility by yelling, "Say hi to Karyn" and resumed her conversation. Jamie continued his run, veering left onto Pierrepont Street. He turned right onto Henry, where he jogged the rest of the way to Montague. He completed the mile and a quarter run that left him, as planned, across the street from the newsstand.

Once again, the *Trib* was stacked alongside the *Times*, the *Sun* and the *Journal*. It was another blow to the unions, but no doubt also to Willis. Jamie could picture him in the back seat of a taxi, resisting the temptation to peruse his night's work. *Does he take a copy of the paper home? Can he even stand to look at it? W.J. Clinton…the least they could have done was come up with clever bylines that were not so damn obvious.*

But, he guessed, that was the point. Brady was trying to ridicule the reporters, assure them they could easily be replaced by absurdist fiction.

Maybe he's right. Maybe all our readers really want are crime and gossip with bold headline and big pictures. Like whatever this crap is they threw out there today…

FAMILY FEUD

Below the *Trib's* front-page headline was a blurred photo that was clear enough to distinguish the fingers of a hand brushing a cheek…glasses askew, tilting right…facial contortions…recoiling in astonishment…a newspaper, suspended in mid-air…a third man nearby, mouth agape, hands reaching out, fingers spread apart…the sub-head, which Jamie read like a first-grader carefully enunciating his first oral class presentation, as a dreaded realization began to set in:

TV Crewman Records Picket Drama Outside Trib

Jamie froze with two fingers pressed against the top copy of the *Times*. Bewilderment gave way to panic. A hand with long, feminine fingers sporting a glittering diamond ring and fire engine red nail polish reached from behind his waist—*"excuse me"*— to grab the copy of the *Times*. Jamie tried to apologize but was unable to speak.

It was him on the front page of the *Trib*. Him and his father and his Uncle Lou, starring in today's twisted tabloid tale, a "Family Feud" that was no standard mafia fare.

How could Willis have made this the wood? How could he have done this to me? No, he would never stoop so low. But who? And how?

Maxwell Brady!

Jamie recalled Brady's primal glee upon learning what had happened outside the building. How he had gone off cackling, no doubt straight to his father's office to share his scoop, to revel in another moment of comic striker futility.

But where the hell did this photo come from?

TV Crewman Records Picket Drama Outside Trib

He re-read the sub-head, lip-synched the photo credit, confirming the nightmare: "Courtesy of NY1."

Cable television…Debbie Givens…

This photo had to have been reproduced from a frozen screen image. And that meant the entire scene with his father had been captured on tape, rewound and rebroadcast, running like a train through the Kramer family every 30 minutes.

The caption with its own bold heading—**KRAMER VERSUS KRAMER**—was one long paragraph.

Trib printer Morris Kramer decks son, Jamie, a reporter returning to work, as the newspaper continued to publish without its striking workforce. The junior Kramer was knocked off his feet but quickly recovered and courageously advanced across the picket line—Full Story, Page 3.

Inside, surely there was another photo or two pilfered from TV, probably of Jamie on the ground. To complete the humiliation, there would be an expression of appreciation for Jamie from management—perhaps from Lord Brady himself.

Grabbed by the shirt collar like millions of tabloid gawkers before him, Jamie desperately wanted to turn the page, survey the full extent of the wreckage. Instead he made a closer inspection of the shadowy reprint. His father's hand obscured the left side of his face, which was angled just enough so that it was more of a profile. The clarity was further compromised by the process of reproducing it from television.

Still, he thought, *the damn thing was on television!* Jamie remembered that his parents at least did not have cable—he was always complaining about that to his mother. But what if Molly raced downstairs to Becky's apartment? Mickey insisted on having a box installed for the Knicks games. He could only imagine his mother watching—Becky at her side on the couch, weeping into a tissue pulled from a rapidly emptying box.

The vision of Molly's inconsolable misery produced deeper, labored breathing. *Have to get away from here.* He reached into his pants pocket for change, dropped the coins in the tray on the ledge of the open window. He lifted a *Times,* folded it against his side, under his arm, turned and walked away with an aimless leaden gait. He crossed to the north side of the street between cars stopped for the light.

He'd lost his appetite. *Just get home.* But he felt lightheaded, nauseous. He suddenly was bent over, vomiting into a perfectly situated trash basket.

The contents of the previous night's shut-in dinner—the wings, chips and cola—erupted with a fury. A pause for breath was followed by another round that splattered onto a mound of Burger King wrappers.

"You okay, mister?"

The inquiry—female voice, again—came from inside a car, stopped in traffic for the light at the corner. Jamie almost smiled at the absurdity of the question, but he refused to look up. He nodded like a drunk about to pass out more than a man trying to convince the unseen Samaritan that there was no need for alarm.

In fact, now that he had unburdened himself, the nausea was making its inevitable retreat. Jamie still held tight to the topsides of the basket, like a gnarled geriatric gripping his walker. The autumn breeze soothed the flush of his cheeks, as he took deep, desperate breaths. The third one finally registered the fetid contents of the trash basket, repelling him upwards.

An elderly woman, having watched Jamie purge, stood twenty feet away with a hand over her mouth. Jamie did her a favor by stepping into the street and walking alongside parked cars.

The street was largely empty, the lunchtime rush still a half-hour away. Jamie turned right at the corner of Hicks, walking unsteadily, past a smiling mother holding hands with her young son in a red Power Rangers costume.

Just a block and a half to go, keep moving. In the crosswalk, just a few doors from home, Jamie looked up to see a neighbor from the floor below him passing by. He dabbed at the corner of his mouth, wiping away, he hoped, the last vestiges of vomit. He smiled weakly and said hello. The distraction left him unprepared for the one-woman reception committee at the front of his building.

She was sitting in a hunch on the third step, hair characteristically tied back, hands resting on the edges of a newspaper folded on her lap.

Carla Delgado was smiling and sarcastic.

"Hey there, Mr. Celebrity?" she said. "Can I have your autograph?"

CHAPTER TWENTY-TWO

Morris boarded the downtown express bus, eschewing the faster subway ride from the nearest station at the Flatbush Avenue junction. With morning rush hour past, the bus was more likely to accommodate his preference for a window seat from which he could observe Brooklyn as it went by in an ambiguous blur. Better that than facing subway riders holding up the humiliating *Trib* front page.

Louie had warned him about what was coming the previous afternoon. He followed that up in the early morning with a piercing rant against the *Trib*. Morris' advice to Molly—not that she was in the mood to take any from him—was to avoid the newsstand altogether. Becky and Mickey had been out late and were gone to school early. Molly thus was spared the misery of rushing downstairs to watch her men lead the cable news cycle from the dinner hour late Wednesday afternoon and well into prime time.

How would Morris have recounted the event to Molly had it not been recorded and reported for public consumption? He wanted to believe he would have come clean. That he would have admitted losing control. That he had tried to wish away the inglorious act even as his fingers splayed across Jamie's face.

He just couldn't be sure that the version of the spectacle he would have shared with Molly would have matched his shame. So he didn't utter a word about it when he returned home. He retreated to the bedroom and tried to nap. But the telephone kept ringing and Morris' game plan became a moot issue. A flood of pitying calls reduced Molly to tears.

Infuriated as Morris was to learn just how much of his confrontation with Jamie had been broadcast, his immediate instincts were, however belatedly, to comfort his wife. She shooed him away, spurning all requests to let him explain.

"How could you do such a thing?" she kept saying. "Your own son!"

"He was disrespectful," Morris said.

"Why? Because he disagrees with you? He has a right to figure out his own life."

The tears streaming down her cheeks and the disgust in her eyes made Morris back off. Molly dialed Jamie's number without knowing what she would say.

He wasn't home or answering the phone. But the machine didn't pick up either. Molly busied herself with dinner and avoided eye contact with Morris. While she fiddled with dishes at the sink, he picked at her grilled chicken and baked potatoes. The silence continued, Morris feeling like a schoolboy sitting outside the principal's office.

Giving the final plate a cursory wipe, Molly coldly announced, "I'm going to bingo at the temple with Becky."

"Okay, call me when it's over," Morris said. "I'll pick you up."

"Don't bother, it's only a few blocks," she said. "We'll walk."

"You shouldn't—you know what's been going on around here late at night. They come up from behind and grab your purse. They've been writing about it in the weekly paper, been going on for weeks. Just call from the pay phone in the lobby."

On her way to the door, Molly said, "If anybody here needs to use the phone, it should be you calling your son."

She walked out before Morris could respond. He took a deep breath and leaned back on the sofa. He worked over a bowl of pistachio nuts, piling shells on the cushion alongside him. He tried but couldn't pay attention to a rerun of M*A*S*H. Alone, he could at least admit to himself something he could never say to Molly. Bad as he felt about what happened with Jamie, the day's most chilling event had been his brief conversation with Colangelo.

It was the agitation that Morris couldn't shake, the evasive body language. How Colangelo had drained his glass as soon as Morris and Lou materialized. Even Kelly Murphy had raised an inquisitive brow as Colangelo dashed for the door. It gnawed at Morris that Colangelo was withholding something strike-related.

While he mulled over the possibilities, none of them promising, the telephone rang. Morris feared it was another busybody calling to sympathize. He only answered because during a strike he believed it was his responsibility to be available twenty-four/seven.

"Tough guy, big fucking media star."

Morris instantly recognized the unflinching, gravelly voice—the Boston working-class accent that made his name sound more like *Maris*.

"You there, Mo?" Ryan said.

"Jackie…?"

"Yeah."

"Hello…how are you…what can I…?"

Morris was embarrassed by his stammering and by the immediate reference to what had happened with Jamie. But Jackie Ryan wasn't the type to begin an inquisition and Morris knew why. Across the years, he'd seen much worse during a strike—men bloodied, livelihoods battered, families broken. Morris knew that Ryan, more than anyone, would know how painful the subject had to be and why it needed to remain respectfully unaddressed. So he relaxed and they chatted amiably for several minutes about nothing union-related. Ryan did wedge in a few choice words for the baseball owners, a miserly fraternity if ever there was one, he said, for provoking a strike and depriving him and millions of hard-working Americans of their rightful Fall Classic.

"And just when your Yankees were looking pretty good," he said. "Poor bastard, Mattingly, I actually feel sorry for him. He'll never make the Series."

Ryan had resigned his post as the head of the printers' union in 1989. He needed the distraction after the death of the only woman he said he could love. Annie Ryan, an Irish immigrant and artist, had coaxed him into the Union Square area of Manhattan after they'd raised five children in a Long Island middle-class suburb. She died six months later.

Odd that Ryan was calling, Morris thought. When he relinquished his union post at age sixty-six, he declared himself utterly spent, eternally retired. He was determined to devote his remaining years to his children and grandchildren and surprising eclectic interests. Classic literature, for one—or so Morris recalled reading in a *New York Magazine* profile that circulated at the *Trib* on the morning after Ryan was feted by the city's labor establishment.

The bash was thrown at a posh center for artists in Manhattan in a Fifth Avenue brownstone. Delighted by the invitation that reached him at the *Trib* by messenger, Morris attended but felt underdressed and out of place. He left early, soon after the toast, and hadn't seen or spoken with Ryan since.

Incongruously upscale as the midtown setting was for a champion of the workingman, Morris had to admit that Ryan was no conventional union power broker. He was part street fighter, part Renaissance man, tall and slender with an oval-shaped face and elegantly groomed goatee. Ryan was a child of the depression who had beaten the demographic odds. His family had depended on assorted handouts after his father lost his factory job. His mother died two years later. Morris believed that only a man who had experienced such a life had the capacity to usher Local 11 through its cataclysmic upheaval. Only he who realized that change was inevitable could envision and prepare for what awaited the printers.

"Listen, Mo, I'd like you to come see me at my place in the city," Ryan said. "But only if you can work it into your schedule, of course."

Morris was curious but at the same time gratefully distracted. He woke early the next morning and left Molly sleeping and still seething, judging from how she was curled up at the far edge of the bed. An hour and fifteen minutes later, he disembarked the bus at Fourteenth and Broadway, across the street from Union Square. He began the four-block walk to a ten-story brick-faced building with a green canopy.

Morris hit the sixth-floor button, his stomach queasy as the slow-moving elevator squealed and shivered to a halt. Ryan greeted him at the apartment door with a cordless telephone pressed to his ear. His left arm hung limp at his side, as it had since he was sixteen—the result of being hit by a car while riding his bicycle. There was always pain on that side, he told Morris once. "It only doesn't hurt when I get the contract I want."

He appeared older than Morris remembered—more lined around the eyes, though still fit and alert.

"I can't fly out until Sunday," he said into the receiver. He head-motioned Morris inside the apartment and pointed him toward the living room through the entryway hall.

Ryan disappeared into the narrow kitchen, continuing with his travel plans. Morris stepped into a room teeming with bookcases, including one entire wall of built-in shelves. The furniture was old but preserved. An L-shaped couch in the middle was set around a glass top coffee table littered with newspapers, magazines, a couple of coffee mugs and a brown paper bag.

The sea blue blinds were nearly shut. The light in the room was dim, the air a bit stale. *A widower lives here*, Morris thought. He could almost smell the solitude.

Morris walked to the window to peek at the view but noticed a magazine cover, framed, lacquered and mounted on the nearby wall.

He couldn't help but feel a spasm of delight at the sight of the younger and already graying legend, "Labor Boss Jackie Ryan." All these years later it sounded too simple, a gross understatement, to call him that. Against a black backdrop was a long and slender work tool, resembling a machine gun at first glance. Upon closer inspection you saw it was a wrench that was wedged between the rolls of paper on a printing press. The headline ran across the top of the magazine cover, just below the white lettering that spelled out *TIME*.

POWER OF THE PRINTERS

"You remember that one, Mo?" Ryan said. He startled Morris, who had become engrossed with the artifact. "Annie had it framed."

"March 1, 1963," Morris said, reading the fine print. "The big one."

"First walkout in eighty years, a hundred and thirty-four goddamned days on the street," Ryan said. He was alongside Morris, patting his back with his good hand.

He chuckled and said, "The damn photographer bitched during the entire shoot. 'Did you have to shut down all seven goddamned papers? I got nothing to read on the subway.'"

"Seven dailies, can you imagine?" Morris said.

"We were the bad guys, of course," Ryan said. "They basically used this article to question our right to go out. The reporter threw that damn JFK quote right in my face. Said to me, 'How do you defend the strike when the President says it's gone on for too long and the unions have to understand the damage they are doing to the fabric of the city?' Imagine that, a good Irish Catholic boy from Boston, and that's what he had to say about the American labor movement. So I said, and the guy quoted me in the story, 'It pains me to say this but the President doesn't have all the facts.' I said, 'Would he ask that we throw ourselves and our modest middle-class lives at the mercy of the wealthy publishers who forced us into the street in the first place?'"

He might have been reciting a prayer from his days as an altar boy, given his clarity and certainty. But not for a moment did Morris doubt Ryan's recall or conviction. He too remembered how the Kennedy rebuke had stung the rank-and-file. It was JFK, for crying out loud.

"The reporter asked if I was using the strike as a springboard to get the national presidency of the ITU," Ryan said. "I laughed and said, '*Schmuck*, I make twenty grand a year running the Ones. You know what I'd make by going national? Maybe twenty-five if I held my breath.' Who knows? Maybe I insulted the guy. He wrote the story and said that we were hurting the movement. He made a big deal of the fact that we had put ten unions and twenty thousand people on the street and only fifteen or twenty percent of them were ours, as if publishers weren't trying to screw the other unions too. And then they blamed us when those four papers closed over the next few years, said we killed them with the strike. *Bullshit*. Television was already eating away at us. Everything was changing. We found work for a lot of the guys who lost their jobs when those papers went down."

"I just remember that winter, it seemed like it would go on forever," Morris said. "We had people in and out of our living room, rolled up on the floor in blankets because they had to put everything they had to the rent and then their electric would get turned off…"

"There was a guy who called me about eight or ten years later, told me he wanted to write a book on that strike," Ryan said. "He showed me this list he had compiled of all the news that occurred, day-by-day, while we were out. Most of it, you know, was Cold War stuff—Khrushchev threatening one thing, Kennedy another. But I also remember some of the other big stories— Willie Mays and Mickey Mantle both signing contracts that winter for a hundred grand. Can you imagine, with the coin these guys pull today?

"And the other thing—and you could look this up—is that the day we resumed publishing was April 1. April Fools' Day. I'll always remember that because in the middle of all the craziness, I was making the rounds to the plants, and someone at one of them says to me, 'Ayy, can you believe it, the Mets just got Duke Snider.' And I said, 'Get the fuck out. What is that, an April Fools' joke?' But the Mets actually did get Duke Snider on that day."

Morris was reminded how skillfully, how effortlessly, Ryan could steer the direction of a conversation. Jocularity aside, he was still dying to know why the hell he was standing in his apartment.

"Jackie, what is it you wanted to talk to me about?" But before Ryan could answer they were distracted by the flushing of a nearby toilet. Puzzled, Morris looked at Ryan, who smiled and said, "Mo, why don't you just sit down here and relax? I apologize for the mystery, pulling you away from the line and all. And please don't think that I'm trying to meddle. But there's someone here who needs to speak with you."

Morris sank into the sofa's soft cushions. Ryan, still standing, asked if he wanted something to drink. Morris shook his head just as a door closed in the back hall.

Footsteps moved closer. Morris really wanted it to be Colangelo, ready to reveal whatever he was hiding at Kelly's the previous day. Instead it was Sean Cox, one of his own *Trib* printers—grim-faced and disinclined to make eye contact. Cox greeted him with a nod of the head and a mumble.

Cox was average size, slender except for a small pot belly, with hooded eyes and craggy cheeks and peach-fuzz remnants of hair. His hands remained deep in the pockets of baggy blue jeans. He kept his distance, glancing nervously at Ryan.

"Mo," Ryan said, "before we start, I want you to know that this was my idea, not Sean's."

Ryan extended a hand for Sean to sit, following alongside, on the longer section of the L. Morris leaned forward, hands on his knees, still trying, unsuccessfully, to make eye contact with Sean.

"Mo, you know, Sean here and I go back a ways," Ryan said. Sean nodded, finally cracking a brief smile.

Actually, Morris didn't know. He certainly was curious how one of the rank-and-filers came to have a relationship with the big guy.

"He knew Annie in the old country," Ryan said. "They grew up together, same grade school and everything, in the south. Kilkenny City. When Sean came to New York—what was it, about the mid-60s?"

He patted Sean's knee and again Sean nodded, not bothering to provide the exact year. He was clearly comfortable with letting Ryan emcee.

"He came here with a travel card, you know?" Ryan said. "You could do that back then. They'd give you a card and you could go look for work abroad, anywhere you could get hired. Sean came to see me, waited for a couple of hours, at least, because I didn't know who the hell he was. You know, those days, everybody and his uncle thought I could put them to work, get them into a shop. Anyway, my secretary comes in and says, 'There's this nice man who's been waiting very patiently. He says he knows your wife. I invite Sean in and he tells me, yes, he knew Mrs. Ryan in Kilkenny, and he's here looking for work, preferably at one of the papers. Said he worked as a monotype operator in Ireland. I told him, 'That's a whole different ballgame from the newspaper business, my friend.' But I sent him downtown to a small shop on Varick Street. The next thing I know, he calls me and says he got on as a proofreader at the old *Daily Mirror.* He's got three shifts a week and within a couple of months it'll be five. He and his wife would like to take the Mrs. and me out to dinner as a thank-you. Annie was thrilled to see him again. So that's how Seanie and Marlene became our friends, and they even were part of a group tour we took to Ireland. Must've been in the early 80s, right?"

"About then, Jackie," Sean said.

"Have you ever been to Ireland, Mo?" Ryan said.

Not unless there was a town of the same name in the Catskills with a bungalow colony, Morris thought. That's where the Jews from the city went. That was the only vacation spot he had known as a child and later when Becky and Jamie were young.

In fact, the only plane ride he'd ever taken had landed him in Fort Lauderdale for the funeral of a favorite uncle, who a couple of times had rescued him as a teenager from striking range of his father's non-negotiable temper.

Taking Morris' silence for a no, Ryan continued. "You can imagine how many times I was there over the years, family and all. And where Sean here is from—it's a wonderland, just magnificent, right on the River Nore. You've got all the great old architecture and this incredible castle that was built on a bend in the river that gives you a view of what looks like the whole goddamn world on a clear day. It was built in like…"

Ryan cued Sean, who responded in his still formidable brogue: "I think it was early in the 13th century, Jackie."

Even if their relationship was primarily based on family ties, ancestral commonality, Sean had never spoken of it to Morris. The truth was that Morris had never mingled breezily with the printers. He never wanted to get too close, to owe them anything more than the pragmatism that best served their ability to earn. He'd always had Louie to network for him.

"Well, anyway, Mo, you know Sean, he's a good union man, always has been," Ryan said. "But he's got a personal problem that's pretty damned urgent, and I think it may also speak to a larger issue, the situation you're looking at with management right now."

Ryan placed a hand on Sean's shoulder, which prompted Cox to edge forward.

"It's Marlene, Mo. She's got breast cancer and it's pretty advanced. We just got the report back the end of last week. They said she needs a double mastectomy. They want her in the hospital right away. But we're on strike and in violation of our contract, which means the health insurance company could challenge the claim. I put her in now and they could hand me back the card and say, 'Sorry, how you going to pay for this?' I can't pay. I don't have that kind of money. But Marlene can't wait. So what do I do?"

Sean was looking directly at him now, no way for Morris to avoid seeing the tears. He felt like crying himself.

"Why didn't you just call me?" Morris said, realizing too late how that might have sounded to Ryan.

"I talked to Lou," Sean said. "He told me he would take care of it with you. But then the thing happened yesterday with your boy. Lou called me last night. He said, 'Sean, I tried to talk to Mo but you saw what happened today. Now's not the best time to deal with it. 'Give it a few days,' he said. 'Mo will deal with this.' But I'm telling you, the doctors are saying Marlene can't wait to have the surgery. The cancer could spread. Maybe it already has."

In the ensuing silence, Morris was instinctively wary of sounding insensitive. He waited, wondering if Ryan would intervene, but Ryan was holding back, content for the moment to play mediator in this hastily arranged bargaining session.

Did Ryan believe his job was to bring the sides together, let them negotiate terms and subtly lead them to the possibility of an agreement? *Probably not,* Morris thought. The Jackie Ryan he knew had to have something more substantial in mind because, ultimately, he was not one to conduct caucuses in pursuit of consensus.

"Are you saying that you want to go back in, Sean?" Morris said. He spoke softly, almost encouragingly.

"I never crossed a damned line in my life," Sean said defensively.

"I didn't say anything about crossing a picket line or our picket line," Morris said. "I'm just agreeing that the only way you and Marlene will be guaranteed your benefits is if we're—you're—back on the job."

Sean frowned. "I'm just saying that I don't know what to do, Mo. I thought Jackie might be able to make a suggestion. That's why I called him."

Morris took a deep breath and ran a hand through his hair. He said nothing because he knew Ryan was waiting for the most opportune moment.

"Tell me, Mo, where are you right now?" Ryan said. "Where do you see this one going?"

"You mean, with us or with everyone?" Morris said.

"Let's start with you and then we'll talk about, you know, the drivers," Ryan said.

Morris fidgeted. He noticed Sean dabbing at his eyes.

"Funny you should mention the drivers," Morris said more casually, regaining his composure. "I happened to run into Gerry Colangelo just yesterday at Kelly's. It was right after the thing with Jamie…my son."

"I'll bet he was thrilled to see you," Ryan said.

Morris harrumphed. "My brother and I walked in. He was at the bar. Louie goes to the bathroom and I sit down next to him and, granted, after what happened on the line, I probably didn't look like I was in the friendliest mood. But I said hello nicely. He nodded. I said, 'Gerry, just us talking. What's the latest? There any movement?'

"Now, I know he couldn't be too happy because they'd gotten the paper out for—what—the second day in a row. But the guy looked straight at me for fifteen seconds. He stared at me like I was a total stranger. He checked his watch, finished his drink in one gulp and said, 'Excuse me.' Then he got up and walked out."

"That was it?" Ryan said.

"Not even, *I'll call you*. And that's after I had left a message for him the day before."

"So you think he's up to something?"

"No idea," Morris said. "But I can tell you, Jackie, I never really trusted this guy in the first place."

Ryan gave him an affirmative nod. He leaned forward and lowered his voice, as if to take Morris into his confidence, as if Sean couldn't hear.

"I wouldn't worry too much about Colangelo and the drivers in this situation, Mo."

"But how is that possible? It's their strike, their lead in negotiations."

"I know that," Ryan said. "I know. But it looks to me like they've already lost control of it. They took everyone out, and now the paper's getting to the stands without them. They miscalculated what this guy Brady was willing to do and the cover he had from City Hall. In the process, they've given the prick—and I'm sorry to say he's from the same beautiful country as my wife, God rest her soul—a golden opportunity to do much more damage to the unions, even the ones that have contracts, like…"

"Us?"

"Especially you, Mo. And because you, my friend, have the most to lose here."

"You mean because they'll threaten us with our lifetime guarantees if we don't cross?" Morris said. "They already did. I got a letter from Brady a couple of days ago."

"No, I don't think it's that," Ryan said. "Firing people in a union that has a contract because they honored a picket line would be a reach and Brady probably knows it. There could be a long court fight and organized labor would get behind you. He doesn't want to go there. But my guess is that he's on to something else. I'd be willing to bet that he provoked the strike not primarily to get givebacks from the drivers but to put the paper through a financial crisis. You know, even with it on the stands, circulation drops during a strike in a union town like New York. Advertisers start screaming for reduced rates. Now, it's not like the *Trib* was wildly profitable in the first place. It's not the *Times* or the *Journal*. It's probably already in the red and the only reason Brady bought it was to make himself a big man over here. He's that type, just wants people to pay attention to him. If he loses readers but cuts production costs drastically, he's still better off. So I'd say he's hoping you guys stay out a few weeks and the next thing you know, he's claiming that he's losing his shirt and, then, well, he's got his nuclear strike."

Morris waited for the bad news.

"He declares bankruptcy for the *Trib* company."

"Okay," Morris said. "But how does that affect us? I mean, other than the paper being in bad financial shape."

Ryan hesitated, suddenly uncomfortable. He looked almost pained.

"Well, that's the part we didn't really anticipate when we negotiated the lifetime guarantees," he said. "Because even though we had papers closing, we figured that the survivors would be mainly profitable for years and years, especially with the staffing savings from automation. See, if Brady declared the *Trib* bankrupt, he wouldn't necessarily have to honor any of the existing union contracts when he comes out on the other side. And that means…"

Morris knew Ryan's pause meant for him to finish the thought.

"No more lifetime guarantees," Morris said.

"I'm sorry, Mo. That's how it is. The truth of it is that those guarantees have kept our people working through the last couple a decades. Without them, we know it would've been a bloodbath from the beginning. Not only would the jobs have been lost, but there would've been huge shortfalls into the pension and benefits fund to keep those checks going out to our retired men. At least the lifetime guarantees kept a lot of good men on, retrained them to use the computers. And I'd bet most of you jokers are pretty damned good."

He gave Sean a paternal squeeze of the knee.

"Am I right?"

Sean nodded.

"But you and I know, Mo, that they only need—what?—a dozen of you guys? Maybe two or three a shift?"

Morris wanted to dispute the number but remembered who he was talking to.

"Are you saying that it doesn't really matter what we do?" he said. "That if he does declare bankruptcy…"

"There will be no job protection because there will be no contract or any carryover provision," Ryan said. "They will be able to pick and choose which people they want. With the drivers desperate to work, there will be no one union they absolutely have to deal with, and, in the process, no union able to stand up and say, 'We don't work unless you give such-and-such a fair deal.' Not that we could ever really count on the drivers to be that union. I would say at this point that the best thing you can do for your people is get them back in the building. Back to doing the job better than anyone else Brady can pull in off the street."

Morris could see in Ryan's eyes how difficult it was for him to speak what once would have been heresy. But he also trusted in Ryan's judgment and believed that, grave as Sean's personal situation was, he would never act to accommodate the plight of one man over the welfare of the many.

"Sounds to me like you're saying we might as well go back in and hope this guy doesn't go nuclear," Morris said.

"Mo, I know the last thing you would want to do is cross another union's line and to put yourself at the mercy of management," Ryan said. "But what choice do you have when Colangelo, who is supposed to be your ally, won't even tell you what he's planning to do? Won't even have a drink with you at the bar? Does that sound like someone you want in your bunker?"

The question was rhetorical, not intended to draw a reply. Morris didn't have one. Instinctively, he turned away from Ryan's earnest gaze to Sean, who was nodding in the hopeful manner of a child begging a parent to ease up on the reins, let him take his chances in the cold, cruel world.

CHAPTER TWENTY-THREE

How did she do it? Jamie wondered.

How had Carla, establishing herself as a human roadblock between him and his front door, convinced him to abandon his retreat? Greeted him with a cheeriness that in the context of the day seemed flamboyantly insane?

How can she be getting me to take a walk with her when I barely have the energy to stand on my own two legs?

Of course, he had already borne witness to her astonishing levels of certitude, Carla being Carla, the monarch of *Trib* office management.

"Come on," she said, rising from the stoop. She stuffed the folded *Trib* into her shoulder bag as if it contained nothing that distinguished it from any other edition. She slipped her arm in Jamie's and began to guide him as she would a blind man.

"It's such a nice day."

He obliged her with one request. He had to run upstairs to exchange his running shorts for a pair of jeans and to vigorously wash his face and brush his teeth to rid himself of the residual stench of his purging into a rancid trash basket. To augment the cleanup, he suggested a tactical stop at a deli on Montague Street to purchase a roll of mints and carry away a container of coffee.

Given the opportunity, Carla ordered a sesame bagel, sternly coaching the pimply young man behind the counter on the size of a cream cheese smear.

"Not too much, I'm working on my figure," she said. She shot Jamie a *yeah-right* roll of the eyes. Svelte was never going to be part of Carla's portrait. In the black Chuck Taylor Converse high-tops she apparently believed matched every outfit she owned, she couldn't have been more than three inches over five feet. She obviously felt no compulsion to camouflage fifteen extra pounds with a pair of heels.

Buxom she could certainly get away with. Especially in the light, olive-colored scoop-neck sweater she wore that drooped halfway down her tight black skirt.

They left Brooklyn Heights and walked down the commercial strip of Court Street.

"So what got into you yesterday in the first place?" Carla said after a half-block of silence. "What was that whole thing about?"

Munching her bagel did not blur the directness of the question. Jamie gulped more coffee, contrived a glance across the street up at the marquee of the Cobble Hill cinema. Yup, *Forrest Gump* was still playing on both screens. He'd been meaning to see it but going to a movie alone reminded him of being, well, alone.

"It's a long story," he said.

"We'll take a long walk," Carla said.

He smiled, as if to concede that the extent of their time together was her call. The caffeine buzz was invigorating. He still felt like changing the subject.

"You have a destination in mind?"

"I do," Carla said. "You're walking me home."

Wherever that might be. Jamie had known that Carla lived in Brooklyn but was embarrassed to not know where. She had never been one to volunteer much about her personal life. But he never asked either.

There were numerous and distinct possibilities within walking distance. But as they were already approaching the end of Court Street, where the residential quiet of the Carroll Gardens neighborhood gave way to the shadows and clamor of the elevated Gowanus Expressway, Jamie gathered they couldn't be going too far.

"I live in Red Hook," Carla said, almost blurting it out. "The Red Hook Houses."

She took her last bite of bagel and pretended to be distracted by a woman going in the other direction, pushing a baby in a stroller.

Red Hook was just beyond the expressway, figuratively a world away from the quaintness and quiet of Brownstone Brooklyn. It was the rare urban waterfront community ignored by developers and the mighty forces of gentrification. The area was centrally dominated by the Red Hook Houses, one of the largest and most forbidding subsidized housing developments.

"Fine," Jamie said, nonchalantly.

They crossed warily under the expressway, breaking into a light jog as a car approached from a distance. *What the hell,* Jamie thought. It was broad daylight. He wasn't by himself. It wouldn't be his first venture into the projects.

Carla was uncharacteristically quiet as they walked up Van Brunt Street, a drab row of low-slung buildings, bodegas and assorted storefronts. Some were shuttered. Adult men with too many empty workday hours to fill lounged on steps, in doorways. They turned down a side street of row houses, several separated by burned-out shells or vacant lots. The redbrick buildings of the Red Hook Houses came into view.

"Did you grow up here?" Jamie asked.

"Not really," she said. "But in every other Brooklyn ghetto. Crown Heights, East New York, Bushwick—you know, all the same place."

"My father lived in East New York as a kid," Jamie said.

He begged himself not to identify any further and especially not to impress her with tales of his adolescent basketball adventures. That had been the late 70s, New York before the horrific crack wars.

Nearby as Brooklyn Heights was, Jamie had never stepped foot in Red Hook before. He was aware of its isolation, wedged as it was between the expressway, the waterfront and the Battery Tunnel to Manhattan. The downtown Brooklyn weeklies occasionally ran stories lamenting the spillover of crime into the more fashionable neighborhoods. The *Trib* had joined the rest of the city's media in sensationalizing the December 1992 murder of a school principal, shot to death in the Red Hook Houses in broad daylight.

Jamie happened to be just beginning his reporter's tryout at the time, too inexperienced to merit consideration for a role on a story that dominated the front page for the better part of a week.

"I was there the day Patrick Daly—the school principal—was killed," Carla said. It was as if she'd been reading his mind.

"You mean, like, right there?"

"No, not, like, right there. It was just before noon, I was upstairs, getting ready to leave for the office. I called in that morning and said I'd be a couple of hours late. I had to take care of something at home, Christmas stuff, because it was like the week before. I remember it was cold and rainy. We heard the shots, the screams. I looked out the window and saw a cop who had reached him first. When he saw that the guy had been shot in the chest, he ripped off his own shirt, stuck it into the wound to try to stop the bleeding."

Carla shook her head. Jamie turned to face her and wasn't sure if she was teary-eyed or squinting into the overhead sun.

"You know why he—the principal—was even there, right?"

No, actually, Jamie couldn't recall.

"He was looking for a kid who had been in a fight that day and had left the school in tears. That kid lived in the building across from mine. He saw the principal looking for him, ducked down behind a trashcan or something, saw the whole thing. The poor guy walked right into the crossfire between two gangs shooting at each other, stupid kids fighting over drugs. That's when they started calling Red Hook the crack capital of America. You remember how the media and the activists, Sharpton and those guys, started in that the murder wouldn't have been such a big deal if the victim hadn't been white?"

That much he remembered.

"They were right about that but guess what?" Carla said. "Most of the residents didn't care, at least not as much as they did about the white man who'd been killed. When they realized that it was the principal from the public school, they were just torn up. Everyone loved him. And it finally woke people up around here. They started to organize because they began to realize how cut off from the rest of Brooklyn they'd been and how the politicians didn't give a damn what was happening in Red Hook. No subway stop. No full-service bank. Now we've formed a tenant's association and we're trying to get people involved, at least get us a supermarket. Can you believe we don't have that either?"

"You can have the one around the corner from me," Jamie said. "You go there, you'd better bring a credit card or a loan application."

Carla smiled, thankfully not put-off by his attempt at levity. Based on the condition she found him in, maybe she considered her mission, if that's what this was, partially accomplished.

"Go into one of these bodegas we have around here, see what we pay for food because there are no big markets," she said. "See what they charge for a box of diapers."

"When was the last time that you had to buy diapers?" Jamie asked.

"Yesterday, in fact," she said, leaving him riddled in speculation as they crossed Richards Street. They turned down a ramp into the projects and toward a small courtyard between eight-story buildings that deprived the common area of mid-afternoon sun. A handful of women were spread out on the benches while young children on tricycles circled one another on broken pavement.

In the vestibule of the building opposite the one Carla was leading him to, Jamie noticed a handful of teenagers, two or three puffing away on cigarettes—or whatever—and flaunting their truancy.

"We live on the second floor so let's take the stairs," Carla said. She pushed through the door, into the empty and dimly lit lobby, past a wall of mailboxes. With Jamie following, she turned left in front of the building's one elevator.

The stairwell had a musty odor, spiked by the faint smell of urine. Illumination came from one bare bulb that someone had scrawled the number 69 on with blue marker. Candy wrappers and squashed aluminum cans, beer and cola, littered the floor. A couple of empty vials lay at the foot of the stairs. Jamie had never seen one before but instantly surmised they had to be containers used for crack cocaine.

He quietly followed Carla up the stairs and onto the second-floor landing. He trailed her to the apartment at the far end of the hall and waited behind her as she turned the key. The moment they stepped inside, the diaper mystery was solved.

"How's my sweet boy?" Carla said, doing a deep-knee bend. A toddler, playing on the carpeted floor of the living room, made a drunken-looking charge into her embrace.

The boy's skin was darker than Carla's. He wore an *I Luv N.Y.* T-shirt that sagged to his knees. His face had cracker crumbs fastened to various parts. He looked to be about the same age as Aaron, although Jamie had no recollection of Carla being pregnant. Turbulent as those months were for him, no question, was he really that unobservant?

"And who do we have here?" he said, lowering himself to one knee, beside her.

"Robbie is my sister's son," Carla said, inducing relief on Jamie's part. "He's staying with us."

"With you and your sister?"

"No, with me and my mom."

"Hello Robbie, nice to meet you," he said, reaching out to rub the boy's tummy.

Robbie looked at Jamie through eyes perfectly rounded and sparkling before running off with a piercing shriek.

"Nana," he cried. "Nana."

"Don't be offended," Carla said. "He's a little shy."

"None taken. I have one myself who barely acknowledged me until he was almost a year and a half. But there were circumstances..."

Jamie followed Carla into a small kitchen, where he was momentarily startled by the brightness of orange wallpaper. Robbie had disappeared down a narrow hall, in apparent search of his grandmother. Carla pulled a bottle of Coke from the refrigerator.

"This okay?"

"Great," Jamie said, seating himself. "So, you and your mother are taking care of Robbie for a while?"

Carla set a glass in front of him and filled it to the top.

"Depends on your definition of a while," she said, sitting. "I would say that until he finishes high school or something to that effect is a while—a long while. But less than forever."

"And your sister?"

"Gone."

"Living elsewhere?"

"Gone, as in dead."

"Geez, Carla," Jamie said. "I'm...sorry."

As in the street, Carla's eyes were suddenly vulnerable, belying her straightforward brevity.

"She died in childbirth—or at least that was the official medical explanation. But the truth is that she had AIDS and her immune system was weakened and basically shut down. Robbie was fine. *Is* fine. No traces of the virus, at least not now."

"What about his dad?" Jamie said. He hoped he didn't sound more like a reporter than a friend.

"The father?" Carla said, sneering. "If you want to call him that. He was the one who got Dolores sick in the first place. Never said a word about the fact that he was infected. Didn't stay around too long after she got pregnant either. Probably doesn't even know she passed, if the crackhead is even alive. Which I don't mind saying that he doesn't deserve to be."

"I don't blame you for feeling that way," Jamie said. "I'm sorry you had to go through all that. I had no idea."

"No one at the *Trib* did—well, no one except Cal," she said. "I have enough to deal with there, being a woman, Puerto Rican, not a reporter or a college graduate, and trying to get people's respect. And you know what? I can live without the sympathy—just not the respect. Can't do my job without that, so the only one who ever knew anything about what happened, who even knows about Robbie, is Cal. I needed him to know because Calvin Willis *is* the *Trib*. Without him, I don't know if that paper would ever come out. He knows, because he could always cover for me with Maxine when Dolores got sick. And then with Brady, after Robbie was born. He's there all the time, and he is the most trustworthy soul in that entire building."

"Agreed," Jamie said. "Though I'll be honest, I had to remind myself of that this morning after I saw the front page. The first thing I thought was, *Did Cal really do this?* But then I remembered that Max Brady had seen the commotion outside. When he heard the story, that it was a father-son thing, he thought it was absolutely hysterical. He probably told the old man and then Cal had no choice."

Carla suddenly reopened her inquiry.

"So, Jamie, why did you cross?" Only this time she looked directly at him and her hand reached across the table, almost to his. "Why couldn't you wait another day or two—let this play out? It will, you know. It always does."

He took a deep breath, slumped in his seat. Feeling relaxed, much to his surprise.

"Well, I got a little scared. But not of being out of work—at least I'd like to think not."

"Of what then?"

"Of losing my own little boy."

"Losing? How?"

"The day we went out, my ex tells me she might have a new job. In Seattle."

"Seattle, Washington?"

"That's what I said. The other side of the goddamn country," Jamie said. He hoped Carla—with a silver crucifix resting on her sweater—didn't take offense at his language. He doubted it.

"Because you're out of work for a couple of days?"

"Well, honestly, I don't know what she's thinking, if she panicked because of the strike or it's something else," Jamie said. "Her career, a guy—I have no idea. But maybe I was hoping that it was the strike. And if I just got back in the building, she would forget about going. Because there's nothing I can think of that would be worse than her taking him—Aaron—that far away. Not having to cross a picket line or put up with my father or even looking like an idiot on television and on the front page of the paper. Not after I screwed everything up."

"You mean when you missed the birth because of your story?"

Jamie shot her a furrowed look, wondering how she knew. He had never confided in colleagues, with the exception of his cousin. Had Steven blabbed his personal business all over the newsroom?

"I took the calls that day," Carla said. "Your wife's before she left for the hospital. And then her mother."

Jamie playfully slammed his palm against his temple.

"Duh," he said. "But it actually was her aunt."

"Okay, her aunt actually called from the hospital a couple of times, as I recall. I told her, 'Soon as we hear from him.' But I left the office early because Dolores was in the hospital at the time. I was always running here, there. I gave the message to the clerk."

Jamie couldn't remember the name of the kid who had ultimately delivered it when he'd called in. The tall one with the long blonde ponytail who had dropped out of Columbia Journalism School a couple of months after arriving from Des Moines. He'd bragged about how he'd told Willis in his interview, "I just want to be around a real fucking newsroom, not professors in love with the sound of their own voice."

Willis told him, "Watch your effin mouth. You're hired."

That night, Willis told Jamie, "I've got your replacement on the desk, the hayseed who's been working weekends part-time. Start your reporter's tryout next week." The kid stayed a few months before going home to Iowa, rumored to be in need of drug rehab. Jamie could still hear the Midwest twang from that afternoon call on the day of the real estate sting, him practically bursting to share with Willis how well it had gone.

"Whoever took the call wrote down that it's really important," the kid said. "Urgent." Jamie's heart sank. He berated himself for not thinking of calling home from the pay phone at the diner before all hell broke loose with the sting. He hung up and dialed but all he got was Karyn's tinny voice on the answering machine.

"So I took off like a bat out of hell from the diner," he said. "I was on the Belt Parkway in minutes. But then there was this traffic jam around Kennedy Airport. I was beside myself. Pounding the horn like *I* was going into childbirth. I eventually made it past the rubbernecking delay and across the Whitestone Bridge. I got home pretty fast after that. I parked at the curb, raced up the walk to find this note taped to the front door."

"What did it say?" Carla said.

"Two words, upper case," Jamie said. "AT HOSPITAL…"

"So she'd gone into labor while you were in Brooklyn?" Carla said.

"At that point, I still had no idea. I was at the house, and the lights were all out. It was raining and I was standing there trying to figure out what the hell was going on. I thought, *Could I have just forgotten our Lamaze class?* Even though things weren't that good between us, I hadn't missed a class. I mean, I'd kept thinking, *Maybe once the baby is born she will calm down and things will get better.* But I knew something more had to be up."

"How far was the hospital?" Carla said.

"About four miles north on the Saw Mill Parkway in Mount Kisco. I got there in about fifteen minutes, parked on the street by a meter. I sprinted like a madman into the lobby and up to the desk. I'm sweating, breathing, my heart is about to burst through my chest. I found out that Karyn had been admitted about three and a half hours earlier to the maternity ward. I didn't even wait for the elevator—I just ran up the stairs a couple of flights. I got to within about five feet of the room she was in and all of a sudden Karyn's Aunt Sandra came out, like she'd been notified by the front desk that I was coming.

"She stood between me and the door and said, 'Your son is down the hall in the nursery. He was touch-and-go for a while, but the doctor says he's going to be fine. He's all hooked up to monitors, but it looks worse than it is. Karyn said the two of you hadn't picked a name so she took the liberty since you weren't here. His name is Aaron.'

"I'm thinking, *Aaron?* Where the hell had that one come from? It had never come up. Karyn liked J names—Jared, Jason, Jeremy. She always claimed to like my name. I was standing there in a daze, and I remember the only thing I could think of was that Aaron rhymed with Karyn."

"Did they at least let you see him?" Carla said.

"Yeah, we walked over to the large nursery window, and Sandra tapped the glass and pointed. He was in an incubator that was connected to all these wires and machines. They were monitoring everything, apparently.

He had on one of those wool caps with a pom-pom. He was kicking the blanket like a wild man. And then the aunt—Sandra—said, without even looking at me, 'Karyn does not want to see you. She also would like you take your things from the house before she gets home.'"

"Wow, great timing there—what did you say?" Carla said.

"Nothing, really. It was all so surreal, really crazy in the context of the setting—I mean, who can imagine being shown your newborn son and being told to get out of your house in the next breath? I just stood there, kind of mesmerized by the sight of him. I was trying to come to grips with his name. Aaron. Aaron Kramer. I kept mouthing the name and didn't even realize that Aunt Sandra had gone back to be with Karyn. I stood by the window for a long time, must have been about forty-five minutes, just watching him. Then his eyes closed and the kicking from under the blanket stopped. Another new father came up alongside me and was waving to his baby. His parents or in-laws were there too. That kind of snapped me back to reality. Got me upset. I decided it was time for me to go."

"When did you call your parents and tell them they had a grandson?" Carla said.

"I actually did that in the lobby. I remember thinking I would hang up if my father answered because there was no way I could talk to him in that moment. But my mother picked up. I said, 'It's a boy.' And she said, 'A boy? You mean…oh my god…the baby…I'm a grandmother?'

"I said, 'Yeah, I'm at the hospital. The baby is fine but I missed the birth, my marriage is over and I don't know what I'm going to do next.' She didn't seem to hear what I was saying because she was so excited. She started asking grandma questions: 'How much did he weigh? What time was he born? How is Karyn? When can I see him?' I said, 'His name is Aaron. I don't know when you can see him. I don't know. I don't know.'

"Then it hit her. She said, 'Jamie, what did you say about your marriage?' I just said, 'Mom, I'm sorry. I have to go. I just have to go.' I hung up on her and drove back to the house, fell asleep on the couch. I never spent another night there. I stayed with Steven for a few days in the city and was back living in Brooklyn by the end of the week."

"And that's it?" Carla said.

"That's it, pretty much," Jamie said.

She looked at him incredulously, not quite stifling a laugh.

CHAPTER TWENTY-FOUR

Carla poured more Coke into Jamie's glass. Foam rose over the top and down the side, onto the table.

"God, I spill everything," she said. "I'm like the world's messiest person."

She didn't seem eager to grab a sponge from the sink to clean up the spill. After living with Karyn, who practically followed Jamie around the house with a dust buster when he carried food from the kitchen, he wanted to give her a hug.

"So you're really telling me that your marriage ended because you couldn't predict that your son would be born a few weeks early and you were working in the city?" Carla said.

"I could have—should have—checked in," Jamie said. "I got so wrapped up in the stupid story."

"And so what?" she said. "You were trying to make a living so you could, you know, feed the baby after he was born. How about the fact that soon as you heard you got off your butt and got yourself to the hospital and probably almost killed yourself driving like a maniac?"

"I guess," he said.

"Guess nothing," she said. She shook her head, more scornful now. "You want someone who fucked up, excuse my French? Go find Robbie's poor excuse for a father."

"I know, it's not like I committed a crime," Jamie said. "But it wasn't just the birth. There were other problems. Something happened to us as soon as we left the city. It was never the same. Maybe it was never that good. But even though the pregnancy was a surprise, nothing we planned, I was good with it, really. I just couldn't talk to her after that, couldn't get on the same page. All she seemed to care about were the colors for the baby's room, how long she intended to breastfeed, whether we should use those cloth diapers."

"*Eww*, pain in the ass," Carla said. "Did she?"

"For two or three months. But then she said he was going right through them and she cancelled the service. I think she realized the environment wasn't that great a priority when it was me picking up the cost for disposables."

Carla seemed humored by how the subject had come back around to diapers.

"I'll bet they're not charging white people in Westchester what I pay," she said, defiantly.

She lifted Jamie's half-full glass off the table without asking him and put it in the sink. Carla was still calling the shots. It was time to go.

"There's a car service across the street," she said. "We can get you back to your apartment, and I've got something that I need to do."

With a raised index finger, she signaled him to wait a moment while she consulted her mother in the bedroom.

"Is your mom okay?" Jamie asked after she returned, and they were in the hall. Carla locked the door behind her.

"She's fine, just a little shy, especially speaking English."

The driver was waiting in the tiny storefront for a fare. The car—weathered and muffler-challenged as it was—was parked out front. The engine convulsed so badly at the first red light that the driver had to slip into neutral and keep his foot on the gas to prevent a stall. Jamie shot Carla a crooked smile while they sat in the back seat. The driver cursed under his breath in Spanish after steering into traffic on the service road of the Brooklyn-Queens Expressway.

Carla suddenly leaned closer to Jamie and gave him a smack on the knee.

"I'll bet she never wanted a husband—just a house and a baby that she could have all to herself."

"Who?"

"Her, your wife."

"Ex-wife. We made it official about six months after Aaron was born."

"Yeah, okay. My theory is that she felt her clock ticking, she found a nice guy who probably believed her when she said the pregnancy was an accident."

"Well, she said…"

"Oh, I know what she said. But I'd bet you it was bullshit. Someone like her, with the whole suburban thing going on, it was no accident. She was probably calculating what day of her cycle it was even as you were sticking it in."

Jamie laughed, but he also felt his face redden.

"Did I embarrass you?" Carla said. "I'm sorry. I have a habit of saying whatever comes into my head. No filter." Her hand brushed his cheek and dropped to his shoulder, where it remained for a few seconds.

"Sometimes I did wonder if maybe marriage was what she wanted only because her mother had died and her father had remarried and moved to California," he said. "She had a hard time getting his attention after that. She was an only child, alone in New York except for her aunt."

Carla shrugged. "Who knows? Maybe she was just being greedy. Let me tell you, a lot of women think they want it all—career, man, house, kids. But when they get it, they can't handle it. Too many responsibilities, too many things going on, so they decide they have to choose. The career goes first, then the man. The baby is always the most important thing and of course you have to have the house."

"Is that right?" Jamie said. He nodded thoughtfully. "You're quite the expert. You must be related to Oprah."

The needling was Carla's cue to continue, but the driver swerved to change lanes and pass an idled truck. Propelled sideways, practically into Carla's lap, Jamie broke his momentum by clutching both her shoulders.

She smiled as he settled back in his seat. In the process of lurching and disentangling, her hand became clasped in his.

"Take me, for example," Carla said. "I have my mother to look after. She used to work cleaning apartments in neighborhoods like Park Slope and Carroll Gardens. But she started having problems with her back, and then Dolores passed, and now we have Robbie. So she watches him during the day, and I give her a break when I get home from work. I don't have room in my life for a man. And to be honest, I've gotten to the point where I don't need one."

Not sure if she was joking or not, Jamie nodded.

"Men require so much energy," she said. "Even the good ones are so damn needy. Like you, Jamie."

"So I'm a good one?"

"Yes."

"And how do you know that?"

"Because you're willing to believe that something might be your fault, even when it obviously isn't."

"And that's good?"

"That's good, very good. It shows you have a conscience."

The car turned off Atlantic Avenue onto Hicks Street. It rumbled to a red light at Montague.

"Most men, no matter what they do, will convince themselves they're justified in doing it," Carla said. "And newspaper reporters, they're usually the worst. Most of the guys I've known around the *Trib* would never have let themselves feel guilty about missing a baby being born. They would have gone on about deadline and how important the story was, like it was their moral duty."

"You don't think reporters are sincere about what they do?" Jamie said.

Carla rolled her eyes.

"*Puh-leeze*," she said.

"Come on, really?"

"No, actually, I don't," she said, her voice rising. "At least not in the way they'd like people to think. I'm not saying they aren't good people for the most part, or they don't take pride in their work or that newspapers aren't an important public service. I just think reporters act too much like they're not in it for the same reasons that people do most things."

"And that is?"

"You know, ego, money—to go to the bar afterward and hope that some babe believes they are important enough to screw them."

"Oh, yeah?" Jamie said. "And what about the babes with notepads?"

"Same thing," Carla said, laughing. "They just want to be respected in the morning."

"I see," Jamie said.

"Seriously, though. I always think it's freaking hilarious when newspaper guys accuse people—like politicians—of grandstanding for things, of only being committed to an issue because they want to advance their careers. What's the difference? Why does a newspaper columnist go all crazy about something and put on a big show? Isn't it to get noticed for the sake of his career? To get a big book deal? Isn't that ambition all the same thing?"

"And my cousin?" Jamie said.

"What about him?"

"You don't think he's genuine about the columns he writes? Even the ones he knows Brady probably won't put in the paper?"

"I guess he is," Carla said, sighing. "At least at the moment he's writing them."

Jamie shrugged. He was aroused by her cynicism but more so by the fact that her hand remained nestled in his.

"Don't be insulted, Jamie. I'm not trying to say that Steven or any of you guys aren't good people. Shit, my standards for men have never been too high, with some of the creeps I've experienced and what my sister got for her trouble. I guess what I'm trying to say is that I really think that you're one of the good ones, and it's too bad that you don't seem to have a clue."

As the driver pulled his car over in front of Jamie's building, she leaned forward and kissed him, so delicately that their lips barely touched. But she held it long enough for the tips of their tongues to meet.

"Pay the fare," Carla whispered. She turned to unlock the back-seat door on the driver's side.

"You're getting out? I thought you said you had something to do."

"I didn't say what exactly, now did I?" she said, giggling.

She pushed open the door and before stepping out to the sidewalk to wait, she flirtatiously looked back over her shoulder.

"Didn't you just say that you don't need a man?"

"There's what I need and what I want."

Jamie reached into his pocket, pulled out his keys and a mass of bills, mostly singles. He searched for the ten he believed and prayed he still had. He felt a tremor in his hand as he pushed the bill at the driver and told him to keep the change. Jamie unlocked the door and with one foot out of the car flushed the wrinkled singles in his pocket. He stood up and promptly dropped the keys in front of the rear wheel. He began to reach down but Carla tugged at his arm.

"Let him pull out first," she shrieked. She rapped on the window, motioning for the driver to go.

"How many times are you going to save me?" Jamie said.

"I'm just being selfish," Carla said. She bent to retrieve the keys before he could and dangled them in his face. "I wanted to make sure when we get upstairs that you have full use of both hands."

She turned to walk up the steps to the front door, once again leaving Jamie with no choice but to follow.

Day Five: Friday, November 11, 1994

CHAPTER TWENTY-FIVE

Jamie lay flat on his stomach, head barely touching the pillow. When his eyes opened to the day, he was groggy, dry-mouthed and disoriented. But also as content as he'd ever felt.

What time was it? What day was it? Something very nice had happened but Jamie couldn't quite recall what. Then it struck him. He had slept. He had fallen into a deep, peaceful slumber sometime during the night and it had gone gloriously uninterrupted. He dreamed about playing in a basketball game. The crowd was cheering. Cheerleaders lined one side of the court, wearing short skirts and Converse sneakers. They chanted his name as he dribbled around hapless defenders. One of them was his cousin, in a dark pinstriped suit instead of a basketball uniform. Steven's eyes widened as Jamie dribbled and dribbled, a one-man Globetrotting show.

Nobody could take the ball from him. He couldn't be stopped.

And *she* was watching.

He remembered now that Carla had been alongside him in bed—but not anymore. Where had she gone? Had it all been a dream?

Jamie lifted his head. He looked over to the far side of the rectangular room and there she was. Carla was sitting hunched and cross-legged on the uncovered wood floor, facing the far wall. She had taken the telephone from Jamie's desk and set it down next to her. She cupped a hand over her mouth and whispered into the receiver.

The band knotting her dark neck-length hair into a kinky ponytail stub had disappeared, surrendered to the sheets after they'd stepped into the apartment, and she'd pulled him to her by the strings of his sweatshirt. She informed him with the formality of a pre-recorded message, even as she worked the zipper of his jeans: "When the strike is over, this didn't happen."

Jamie compliantly nodded. They began to undress each other, the removal of each succeeding garment precipitating another urgent kiss that neither seemed capable of attaching time limits to. Her hands were fastened to the sides of his head like bookends, her back arched to allow him leverage in their embrace.

It took the better part of half an hour to navigate the hall connecting the studio's front to the bed in the living space. Carla was stripped to her panties and Converse. Jamie was shirtless and moving his feet like they were manacled, trying not to stumble over the jeans that were bunched around his ankles.

He had never considered her glamorous yet there was something about Carla, an aura of desirability that couldn't easily be described, defended or denied. In the office Jamie many times had trained an eye on her— discreetly, he hoped—as she made her rounds, dispensing memos from high command. She wore fruity colored knit sweaters and dark skirts that didn't quite hide the stoutness of her thighs.

They had taken a walk and wound up in bed, Jamie not quite fathoming this reversal of fortune, Carla's ambiguous terms notwithstanding. Had she committed herself to an affair for the duration of the strike? Declared their encounter a one-afternoon-night stand? Whatever her rules, whatever her game, he was playing. He was determined to waste not a single moment, to draw his serendipitous lottery payment in one lump sum and leave no part of her unexplored or untouched.

They took an extended timeout for an evening pizza delivery and a rewound viewing of *Midnight Cowboy*. The leisurely pace allowed him to climax three times—once pre pizza and twice post pizza—before they shut down not long after midnight. Exhausted, emotionally spent, Jamie surrendered to unconsciousness as if it had been medically induced.

He was so happy to have slept—almost as much as he had been able to have done so with Carla—that he wanted to let out a yelp. He suppressed it though when he saw her, swathed in sun, further illuminated by the bright yellow bath towel draped from her shoulders like a cape.

He was aroused in no particular order by the mere sight of her, by the unshakable memory of her unabashed willfulness, her throaty moans. He thought about reaching for his glasses on the night table—just recalling how Carla had gently removed them and placed them there was a turn-on.

Stay quiet, he told himself. *Do not interrupt this rare moment of absolute serenity.*

But Carla soon delicately replaced the receiver onto the telephone and Jamie was forced to deliver a rehearsed "Good morning." He knew he'd startled her by the spasm of her shoulder.

"Oh, God, I didn't know you were up," she said.

She half-turned but pulled the towel around to cover her breasts. Jamie found this sweetly innocent but paradoxically amusing considering her obvious keenness to the attention he had paid them.

"You're an early riser," he said. A glance at the digital clock on his night table indicated it was already past nine.

Carla stood and knotted one end of the towel inside the other, her preoccupation producing a rather inelegant walk to the sofa. She sat on the edge of the cushion. Her decorum and distance seemed to preclude the possibility of a morning reprise.

"I've got to get going soon," she confirmed. "Remember yesterday when I said that I had something to do?"

"This wasn't it?"

"Well, actually, no," she said, giggling, but in a distracted, almost anxious way. "I kind of got sidetracked here."

"I'd be happy to distract you again," Jamie said, feeling sanguinely and strangely bold. "It's not like you'd be missing work."

"That's the whole point. We're still out but the paper got out again and with more copies than yesterday, based on what Cal just told me."

"That was Willis?" Jamie sat up.

"I told you, we talk all the time. Probably not a day goes by where we don't, even when I'm not working."

"At least one of you takes an occasional day off," Jamie said.

"Cal takes days off," Carla said, rolling her eyes. "The first day they open the racetracks, Belmont and Aqueduct. And then there's Christmas, definitely Christmas. That's when he usually has dinner with us."

"You're that close?"

"He's like family, maybe me to him even more than him to me because the man is just about alone in the world. Only child, no close relatives, at least none he's ever spoken to me about. But I bet you don't know that Cal was married once."

"Wow, no, I didn't. What happened?"

"What usually happens in the newspaper business with people who become obsessed with it?" Carla said. She pursed her lips and widened her eyes, the way she habitually did to emphasize the rhetorical nature of her question.

"Well, you said he doesn't have any kids so he couldn't have missed their births," Jamie said.

She pretended to be exasperated by his continuing guilt about Aaron.

"I told you yesterday, what you did, that was nothing."

She was standing now, surveying the room. Jamie correctly guessed it was in search of her clothes. She zeroed in on the corridor leading to the front door and remembered where most of the disrobing had occurred.

"You missed out on an event," Carla said. "Cal missed out on a marriage."

"She left him?"

"The way he tells it, he got tired of explaining why he had to work late every night. He told me once he decided to leave as a favor because he didn't want her to spend the rest of her life waiting for him to come home. He said he sacrificed the relationship out of love."

"Strange way of showing it," Jamie said.

"I guess what he was saying was that he loved his job and the people he worked with more."

Jamie laughed. "He has a strange way of showing that too."

Her eyes narrowed in mock disapproval.

Jamie held both palms up. "Joking," he said. "You know Cal, the original grouch. But I know, more than most—he's got a huge heart." He chuckled and shook his head. "You should have seen his face when I showed up there the other day."

"He told me about that," Carla said. "He said he thought you might have a stroke when you realized what was actually going on. He felt bad for you. He likes you, Jamie, always has. He told me once that your housing story took a lot of guts."

She said it so matter-of-factly, yet so sincerely, that Jamie was moved to accept the compliment at face value. He experienced none of the usual dishonor that surged through him like a fever at the recollection of the experience.

"And you were right," she continued. "It was Brady who ordered Cal to make the thing with your father the wood. He felt horrible about it, but there was nothing he could do. He called me that night and said he was concerned about how you would take it."

"You can tell him not so well," Jamie said. He wondered if he should wait until she left the room to get out of bed, if nudity was permissible on the morning after considering the stated terms of their tryst.

"Anyway, when Cal told me about what Brady made him do and about how NY1 had gotten the whole thing on tape, I figured you could use some cheering up."

Jamie slowly lowered his head back onto the pillow. Implicit was the invitation for Carla to rejoin him, lift his spirits once more in the most dependable way known.

"Thank you," he said. "I'd say you succeeded."

She blushed, which surprised and delighted him, made him feel momentarily in control of the conversation.

"This," she said, quickly recovering, with a nod toward the bed, "wasn't actually part of my plan. It just happened. What I was hoping to do was talk you into coming back to the picket line."

"You're kidding," Jamie said.

Now he was caught off guard.

Advantage: Carla.

"No, actually, I'm not," she said. "And I'll tell you something else, from what I just heard from Cal, things could get pretty interesting out there real soon."

"I hope you're talking about a settlement."

"Well, not quite that," she said. "But, well, I'd better not say anything more. Cal would kill me."

Jamie's interest was piqued but the mere thought of facing the strikers made him want to sink back under the blanket and stay there. Carla's forgiveness, amorous as it was, was one thing. Absolution from the picket line in general and his father in particular was not something he was inclined to seek or bound to receive.

"Carla, I wish I could go back and change everything, even if it would be just to prevent the spectacle it turned into," he said. "But it happened. I did what I did. I can't go back."

"I don't see why not," she said, defiantly. "It's not like you're going to show up for work again, at least from what Cal told me. And if you're not in, then you're out. The one thing I know about a strike is that there is no in between."

"I think I may have invented my own private purgatory," Jamie said.

"Okay, so you made a mistake. You overreacted. Your father overreacted. You think he doesn't feel terrible about it and wouldn't want you to come back?"

"No comment."

"*Bullshit,* Jamie. Really, he'd shake your hand if you walked out there today. Everybody would and the whole thing would be forgotten. You know why? Because this is not about you and your father and what that asshole Brady put on his front page or what they showed on some stupid television channel. It's about the people who put their livelihoods on the line when they walked out on Monday, who have families and kids to feed and Catholic school tuitions to pay. And if they miss more than one paycheck, they're in deep, deep shit—you know what I'm saying?"

"I do, Carla, I do," Jamie said, sighing. "I made that same argument to my father and uncle the night before I crossed because I'm one of those people who can't afford to miss more than one paycheck, especially now. But all they could talk about was how good Steven looked in a suit and how he preached about moral responsibility at the rally. And I said, you know what, it was easy for him to do that. Most of us don't make his salary. And I'm at the point where I don't care if I sound jealous of him either. I know he's been doing a lot for the union, just like you have, and I respect that. But I also think this has been some kind of ego thing for him, a game he's been playing without any real risk. Because in his gut, he knows he can miss a few weeks and not blink an eye. He stood up there with Robbins, sounding so righteous and committed. But he pushed us into this, knowing he could afford it. And if things got really bad he could get another job in a heartbeat."

Carla started to reply, but her face darkened. She looked away and then stood up and marched abruptly from the room, down the hall. She went into the bathroom and shut the door.

"Nice going, asshole," Jamie mumbled. "You had to drag him into it. They've only been working together fifteen hours a day."

Jamie was exasperated with himself. He fell back onto the pillow but in an instant bolted from the bed and pulled open the bottom drawer of the nearby chest. He found a pair of sweatpants. He slipped them on and chased after her. He knocked on the bathroom door.

"Carla?"

"One second."

"I'm really sorry."

Jamie projected his voice in a deferential way. "I shouldn't have said those things about my cousin. It's not his fault."

The bathroom door opened. Carla appeared, teary eyed.

"You know what? Maybe it is in some ways Steven's fault," she said. "Maybe it's my fault and Robbins' fault too. Maybe the drivers overreacted and we all shouldn't have been so quick to follow them out. But that doesn't matter now. Because people can only make decisions based on what they think is right at that moment. We went out because we thought we needed to stick together. Working people have each other. That's all we'll ever have. We're no different at the *Trib* than the people in my neighborhood. No one wants to give us a damn thing if they don't have to. Yeah, I know the big shots get the attention and they make all the speeches. They're useful in that way to make noise for us. But we don't kid ourselves, Jamie. We really don't. We know who they are. We know they're not part of us, especially Steven."

"Why him...*especially?*"

Carla took a deep breath. She was back in her skirt but had only popped her head through the sweater without pulling it down over her bra. She reached up and clasped her hands around the back of his neck and held him in place, like a solemn parent about to break sad news to a child.

"You probably should hear this from Steven. But what the hell: Cal just told me that he quit."

Jamie stared at her, blankly.

"Cal quit?" he said.

"No," she said. "Your cousin, Steven. He called Brady yesterday morning and told him to go fuck himself. Cal said that from what he'd heard, pretty much in those words."

"I don't get it, to go where?"

"The *Sun*," Carla said. "Steven told Cal a couple of months ago that he had a standing offer, more money and a contract. Cal told me but didn't think Steven would really go. But I guess he thought it over and decided that it was better than being on strike."

"But he…we're only out a few days…how could he just pick up…?"

A complete, grammatical sentence apparently beyond him for the moment, Jamie waited for more information that Carla didn't have.

"All I know is what Cal told me, Jamie. I'm sorry. I really don't know what else to tell you. Except that I've got to get going because when people on the line hear that the guy who champions union workers didn't bother to stick it out with us, they'll start thinking the whole thing is about to collapse. And if I know Sandy Robbins, he's not going to make it his business to show up and calm everyone down."

She pulled the sweater below her waist, knelt to tie her sneaker laces. Jamie stood over her. Their nocturnal passion suddenly felt yesterday's news, microfilmed for their personal posterity.

Carla swept her jacket off the floor and carried it, crumpled, like a football.

"You okay?"

He nodded, unconvincingly.

"You look a little washed out, sort of like yesterday when I found you," she said, maternal Carla again.

"I just can't believe he would quit after he stood up there and helped them run us out into the street. It's just…it's just…you know?"

"I know," Carla whispered.

She kissed his cheek. "Come to the picket line. People—your father—will be happy to see you. Like I said, it could get really interesting in the next day or two."

Before he could reply, she was closing the door behind her and was gone.

CHAPTER TWENTY-SIX

Jamie worked the telephone keypad so furiously that he dialed a wrong number.

"Hey people, this is Megan, I'm not home, please leave a message. *Buh-bye.*"

He hung up, steadied himself and re-dialed. Steven picked up halfway through the third ring.

"You *quit?*" he said.

He had not rehearsed his opening line. He spit it out more as an accusation than as a question.

"Who is this?"

Jamie heard a backdrop voice, feminine.

"Hold on a sec," Steven said. He yelled out, "They're in the upper cabinet, closest to the refrigerator." Then he was back. "Sorry, who's this?"

"You know who."

"Jamie?"

"Yeah."

"How'd you find out?"

"Let's just say I got it from a source."

"It just became official yesterday," Steven said, groggily. "I would've called you today."

"To tell me you're a total hypocrite?"

Jamie was aggravated by his cousin's tranquility, his likening the betrayal to the purchase of a television set.

"Jamie, come on, give me the benefit of the doubt. I would have called you this morning as soon as..." He paused, before lowering his voice to a whisper. "As soon as my company left and I was alone."

"When I found out and from who isn't what I'm talking about, Steve," Jamie said. "I'm talking about the fact that you *fucking* quit."

"Hold on again. Let me get to another..."

Jamie heard a thump, the receiver dropping, followed by an exchange of hushed voices and muffled laughter. After a few seconds, another line picked up.

"I've got it," Steven said.

"Uh huh," said the female voice. Jamie would have bet his next paycheck, whenever that might be coming, that it belonged to a certain NY1 reporter.

The hardcore evidence was in front of him or at least reverberating in his ear. Debbie Givens being with Steven had confirmed his suspicions. The NY1 picket-line story had been a setup.

Now he was sure that it was Steven—the only one who knew of his intention to cross—who had sold him out.

Except he was unsure about which infidelity to be more furious about.

"Okay, we can talk," Steven said.

"What should it be first? How you stabbed me in the back—or the union?"

"*You?* How do you figure?"

"Was it worth it, Steve? Is that your definition of moral responsibility? Screw your cousin in order to get laid?"

Steven sighed.

"First of all, I didn't know—I didn't really think—that you were actually going to be that..."

"What, stupid?"

"Yeah, now that you put it that way. Stupid enough to go through with it. And I definitely had no way of knowing how it would go down—you standing there, baiting your father until…"

Again, he didn't have to complete the thought, actually say "your father had to give you a good crack in the mouth." He only had to let it linger to regain some footing.

"So, yeah, I told Debbie that you might cross, that there could be some shouting, a little picketline action she could use with her report. That's all."

"That's all? I confide in you and the first thing that comes to your mind is, 'How can I personally benefit?'"

Steven's self-assurance had returned, but Jamie was too angry to concede the high ground. He waited for a response. All he got was Steven exhaling.

"I guess that explains part two then," Jamie said. "I don't really have to ask why you would quit the *Trib* in the middle of a strike that you helped create. Because if this is your idea of moral responsibility, then what the hell would you know about loyalty?"

"Will you stop with the moral responsibility already?" There was a pause, another deep sigh. "I know, the timing sucks," Steven said. "I didn't plan it this way, okay? The *Sun*'s been after me for a while. They called a few months ago, offered a huge raise. I thought we talked about that, but I guess not. I considered it for a couple of days, but I kept thinking, *How do I leave a union position and sign a contract with a newspaper that doesn't even have a union—to write a labor column?* It would've looked terrible. I turned them down but then they called me again, the day after we went out. I went to see them the day of the rally."

"Now the suit and all makes sense," Jamie said, recalling Uncle Lou's bewilderment over Steve's rally attire.

"Isn't that what you usually wear to a job interview?"

"Never mind."

"So not only did they sweeten the offer, they said I could write a general column," Steven said. "Anything I want to write about. No restrictions. No more columns being vetted and killed by the freaking publisher. The only catch was that they wanted me to start, like, yesterday. I had twenty-four hours to give them an answer. So what was I supposed to do? Pass up a dream job, something I would never get from Brady, because of bad timing?"

"What happened to all that shit about kicking Brady's ass, running him out of town and getting back your paper?" Jamie said.

"Come on, Jamie. You know I was a little drunk that night. And I can't believe you of all people are getting on my case about this. You crossed the damn line yourself. All of a sudden you're Dennis Rivera?"

Steven paused, apparently to determine if Jamie would recognize the blatant name drop.

"If you're wondering, yes, I know Dennis Rivera is the head of the hospital workers, 1199," Jamie said. "You impressed?"

His bluff called, Steven rushed back on point. "Let's be realistic here. They're getting the paper out. This strike can't last much longer. Sooner or later, no matter how damn stubborn they are, the drivers will have to capitulate. The Alliance will be back in the building with a contract. Brady will try to screw everyone, just like they do everywhere. The *Sun*, the *Trib*—it's all the same."

Jamie couldn't quite believe the rationalization that was coming from his cousin's mouth. He couldn't fathom that Steven felt no quote-unquote moral responsibility to Carla and the rest of them, who—forget the picket line—could all yet wind up on the unemployment line.

"You really think there's no difference when one paper has no union and the other has one that's out in the street and you helped put it there?"

"I don't run the Alliance, Jamie," Steven said. "Yes, I stood up there with Robbins. Yes, I talked about the security cards being invalidated even when it was stretching the truth. That's what you do when you're trying to get people to commit to something that most of them don't really have the stomach for. And that's what their union leaders wanted. I didn't make anyone vote for Robbins. I didn't make anyone walk out. I'm a columnist—was a columnist—who wrote about labor issues. That's why Robbins asked me to participate. I didn't volunteer. I'm a journalist, not a labor leader. I write and report. I just want to work for whoever will let me do that."

"And what about all those people who don't have another job to go to?" Jamie said. He was determined to keep the argument going even when he knew he couldn't win. "How can you be so self-righteous?"

"I'm just being me," Steven said.

"You know what?" Jamie said. "That's your fucking problem and you don't know it."

He gently put the phone down, stared at it for several seconds in disbelief and nearly jumped out of his skin when it suddenly rang.

"What?" he said coldly. He was sure it was Steven hell-bent on getting in the last word.

There was a delay in the response. "Jamie?" It was a female voice. It was Karyn, taken aback by his tone.

"Sorry," Jamie stammered. "I had just hung up a second ago. You caught me by surprise."

"You okay?"

"Yeah, I guess. It's just this…actually, nothing, forget it."

"Look, I know I've been telling you that I didn't think it was a good idea that you come to Aaron's party today. I know I said it would make me uncomfortable and that would make him uneasy when I want him to have a good time with the kids. But I've been thinking about it and, you know, that really isn't fair. I shouldn't project what I'm feeling on him. He'd want you to be there. Can you come?"

In the blur of the past two days, Jamie hadn't even given a thought to the party or the birthday. Once again, a parental milestone was obscured by career-driven intrusions. But here was Karyn, surprising him, opening a door and inviting him in.

"What time?"

"About four, four-fifteen," she said. "A couple of the kids have an afternoon pre-school class. It'll probably go until about six, six-fifteen."

"You need me to bring anything?"

"No, we already have your gifts here, stacked up to the ceiling. Just bring yourself."

"You sure you'll be okay with it? The ex-husband polluting the air around all those married moms, the crazy guy from the TV news?"

It occurred to Jamie that Karyn may not have even seen the clip or the front page. She wasn't much of a tabloid reader and NY1 did not broadcast in the suburbs.

Why even go there? Apologize before…

"Don't start," she said, but with a more compliant tone that seemed to concede that perhaps she deserved it for excluding him in the first place.

"Actually, from what they keep telling me, a couple of them are in marriages that probably won't last much longer either," she said. "No, it'll be fine. Really, it's what's best for Aaron. He…we…really would like you to come."

"I'll be there," Jamie said. He was buoyed by the offer, Steven's disloyalty already behind him.

"Good. I'll tell him."

"Karyn?"

"Uh huh?"

"Thank you," he said.

He put down the phone and smiled.

CHAPTER TWENTY-SEVEN

Morris Kramer was impressed. After all these years, Jackie Ryan still had clout.

"How the hell did you get all these guys together in twenty-four hours?" he said.

Ryan pooh-poohed him with a shrug and a wave.

"Made a few calls, promised them lunch."

He opened the refrigerator and reached in to extract a mound of cold cuts. He slapped them onto a serving tray, separating them into three smaller stacks—the bologna, the turkey and the Swiss cheese. He lifted the tray with his functional arm and balanced it against his chest.

"Grab the bread and those jars of mustard and mayo."

Morris nodded and followed Ryan from the kitchen into the living room. The others were deep in debate about what ailed the Giants. They'd been crushed in Dallas the previous Sunday. An eternity ago, it seemed, when their newspaper was still union-produced.

"Six in a row they've lost," Leahy of the pressmen was saying. "Reeves is no Handley. But I watch this team every week, and I'll tell you something—he ain't Parcells either."

"What, every time something goes wrong, it has to be the coach's fault?" a voice from across the room bellowed. It was Parlinski of the mailers. "What'd Reeves win last year, eleven games? It's this Brown guy. You ever hear of a decent NFL quarterback from Duke?"

There was snickering all around as Ryan laid the food tray onto the glass-top table. He had earlier set out cokes and bottles of Budweiser, several of which were already drained.

Morris followed Ryan with the mustard and mayo and stepped back to take inventory. He counted six others in the room, which meant that all but one of the nine *Trib* striking unions was present and accounted for, excluding the drivers, who were not invited.

Just as Morris began by process of elimination to identify the absentee, here came Vaccaro of the photoengravers out of the bathroom, tightening his belt. He made a beeline for the beer.

So they had all agreed to come. Morris shouldn't have been surprised. He might have known that even in retirement, years removed from Jackie Ryan's last job action, no self-respecting union rep would spurn his invitation.

"Whoever comes, it's your show," Ryan had told Morris after kissing Sean Cox's cheek, godfather-like, and reminding him to give his love to the Missus. "I'll bring them here but I'm not going to say much, if anything. It has to come from you."

Morris nodded and thanked Ryan for his counsel. He rode the subway home, determined to reveal nothing about the plan, not even to Louie. His brother customarily checked in by telephone to discuss the day's events in that solicitous way that reminded him of the days he covered for Louie growing up. Cleaned up his messes, signed his school papers that were festooned in red before their old man got home after a long day at the shoe factory and drinking away too much of his paycheck.

Odd that Louie hadn't called though. Morris figured his brother was just trying to give him some space—which, in fact, he very much needed.

Alone, Morris hoped to settle himself and resolve what was spooking him more. Was it the magnitude of the assignment he had been given by Ryan or doubts about its objective? It was just as well that Molly had set a turkey sandwich out on the kitchen table and carried her own to the living room sofa. She clicked on the television and all but posted a do-not-disturb sign.

Morris couldn't remember the last time she was mad enough to cold-cut him for dinner. Not that he cared. He had little appetite, even for a slice of the strawberry cheesecake Becky had baked for the aborted family dinner earlier in the week. Normally he could eat half the cake in one sitting but it sat untouched on the bottom shelf of the refrigerator. For once in his life, he could have used the calories. He'd lost some weight but not in the good way. He'd noticed it more in his face these days—wane and balding was not his best look.

He'd gone to bed early on Thursday night to rehearse his talking points silently, in solitude. The clock on the night table flipped to 8:21 when his head touched down on the pillow. He ignored the ringing telephone, letting Molly answer, grateful the call wasn't for him. He tried to focus on how he would begin, but was haunted by the warning that he best be prepared for a worst-case scenario, bordering on charges of betrayal.

"Some of these guys may be friends of Colangelo's and if they're not, they're probably afraid of him," Ryan had said. "Can you convince them that they've got to move first before Colangelo cuts a deal behind their backs? If he does and the drivers get back inside the building first, the rest of you are probably screwed."

Morris fell asleep before ten. He dreamed they had all returned to work only to discover the *Trib* had been converted to one of those brightly lighted supermarkets, and he had been ordered by Brady to man the deli counter.

Small wonder he had no interest in the cold cuts the others immediately set upon. Morris cracked open a diet Coke and watched them smother their sandwiches with mayo or mustard.

He stepped back behind the couch and waited, nodding and smiling when the others acknowledged him. He still had misgivings about the mission. What if he'd misread Colangelo's furtive behavior in the bar? What had it proved? For all he knew, Colangelo had just come from discovering his wife screwing the damned electrician.

Even with Ryan's blessing, the notion of advising them to cross another union's line seemed to be radical at best, heretical at worst. Morris never fancied himself a groundbreaker, let alone a speechmaker. He did know he was going to have to make a good case, and one—as Ryan had stressed— that could include no mention of the bankruptcy issue.

Any mention of the printers' job guarantees would provide an opening for the others to pounce. They would accuse him of scheming to use them as a shield to protect the printers at the expense of others.

He wished Ryan would start the meeting already. But he seemed to be in no particular hurry. He was on the far side of the room, directly under the framed *Time* cover, huddled with Sandy Robbins.

Morris studied Ryan, watched him as he nodded and put his hand firmly on the smaller man's shoulder. It was a gesture of confidentiality but also of subtle control. That was part of Ryan's genius, the leadership qualities that made others normally accustomed to having their way defer to him, even in seeming partnership.

Morris gulped more Coke, the can nearly empty but his throat still scratchy. Watching Ryan, he couldn't help but let the doubts out of their prison, synaptic insurgents prowling for trouble.

Has he been straight with me? Is it in everyone's interests to isolate the drivers? Is this one last opportunity for Jackie to protect the printers to compensate for his bankruptcy miscalculation and by extension his legacy? Jesus, listen to me. I sound like a damn schoolboy. And who the hell am I to question Jackie Ryan? A scoundrel like Brady was likely to exploit weakness wherever he would find it. Colangelo at this very moment might be shaking hands with Brady's labor lawyer, putting the finishing touches on a contract. Jackie knows what he's doing.

Morris watched Ryan and Robbins closely. They had the body language of men in cahoots. Ryan caught Morris' bemused stare and sent back an assuring nod. He walked to the center of the room. The others grew quiet.

Morris remained behind the couch. Ryan laid a half-sandwich in a napkin onto the table and took a couple of steps back.

"Gentlemen," he began. "Let me first thank you for coming, especially on such short notice and in the middle of a job action. You know, I experienced a few of these unfortunate situations myself…"

He paused, seemingly to let them behold the man who had once frustrated the President of the United States and a labor-friendly one at that.

"I know how many things must be pulling at you in so many directions. But before we go further, I'd like you to know that while I called you all here, it was only because Mo Kramer asked."

Ryan acknowledged Morris with a finger-point. The others half-turned to nod. Morris pursed his lips and forced a smile. His stomach was so knotted he had to fight the urge to excuse himself to go sit on the toilet.

"Mo thought that my apartment, being downtown, would be a good meeting place. I have no idea what he wants to say, but I will tell you that I've known him for many years. He worked closely with me, and I've always considered him one of the most dedicated members of the Ones."

Ryan realized his indulgence. No one had referred to the printers' union that way in years. He gave himself a mock smack upside the head.

"That's the problem with getting old," he said. "You start forgetting what damn year it is."

The others chuckled uneasily. Morris wondered if they suspected Ryan of having a senior moment. Like Willie Mays—another giant of New York when Ryan was a star—falling down in center field as he played out a glorious career with the Mets.

"Anyway, let's not waste more time. I know Mo is very anxious to speak with you."

No denying that. As Morris made his way forward, passing Ryan, he paused to grab a beer. Maybe the alcohol would relax him. At the very least the bottle would give him something to hold onto.

He twisted off the cap, took a more sustained pull than he had intended. The cold beer was soothing. From the rear of the couch, the position Morris had just vacated, Ryan nodded in support.

"Like Jackie said, I want to thank all of you for coming," Morris began. "You know me. Well, most of you do. And you know I've never been one to make speeches." He coughed twice and took another sip. "My nephew Steven is probably the best in the family at that."

"Speak of the devil," Leahy of the pressmen said. He was only audible enough to only get Morris' attention.

"Mike?"

"You mentioned your nephew. The word on the line last night was that he's going to work for the *Sun*. That true?"

Morris looked at Leahy with his head angled sideways in the manner of an uncomprehending dog.

"I'm just saying that's what a couple of my guys told me," Leahy said. He turned to the others, providing them an opportunity to chime in that they had heard likewise. "I stopped by the line late last night, and they said some of the Alliance people were pretty ticked off."

"Mike, I don't know what you're talking about," Morris said. "If that were true, my brother Louie, well, I'm sure I would have heard."

But they hadn't spoken since early Thursday morning when Louie had called in a rage over the *Trib's* front page. Had he found this out later? Was that why he hadn't checked in?

"Mo, I'm sorry you're hearing it here, but your nephew did resign yesterday," Sandy Robbins said. He rose from his seat on the short side of the sofa. "I heard it from Cal Willis, who, as you all know, is inside putting out the paper."

Morris blinked several times, involuntarily. He could feel the trickle of perspiration on his brow.

"I can't believe Louie didn't tell me. I honestly don't know what to say," he said.

"What is there?" Robbins said. "It happens. Maybe your brother is a little embarrassed. I will admit the Alliance was surprised because it was the guy who writes about labor, and he was working so hard for us. But it's not the first time a star reporter or columnist has picked up in the middle of a strike and gone to the competition. That's part of the business. And I don't think that's really why we're here."

Did he have to remind them? Uneasy as Morris had been about the meeting, now he had to process this unsettling news. It was unfathomable to him that Steven would leave the *Trib* at all, much less during a strike. And how the hell was he supposed to convince these men to trust his instincts when he had no idea what was going on inside his own family?

"I think we all know that this is a very different kind of situation for us, given that Brady has City Hall working with him and he's getting the paper out," Robbins said.

He had made his way front and center, inviting himself to co-moderate. Morris wasn't objecting. In fact, he wouldn't have minded falling through a trap door, where, upon landing, he would hope to locate a telephone to call his brother to find out what the hell was going on.

"One way or another, we can't allow this to continue much longer," Robbins said.

"Nobody wants it to, Sandy, but what's your point?" Leahy said.

Even in a loose-fitting flannel shirt, Leahy's muscular torso was striking, almost menacing. His self-appointment as group spokesman was more the result of a membership that was larger than any *Trib* union with the exception of the drivers and Robbins's Alliance of white-collar professionals.

"Why don't we just let Mo make his?" Robbins said.

Leahy sat back, momentarily chastened. Robbins had at least managed to give Morris the chance to regain his equilibrium. He appreciated that. Just the same, he wanted to speak his piece and get the hell out.

"I have reason to suspect that the drivers may be about to cut their own deal to get back in the building," Morris said. "I can't give you exact information. All I can tell you is that I ran into Colangelo in the bar the other day and when I asked him—just us talking—if anything was happening, he didn't so much as give me an answer. Just looked at me for a few seconds, finished his drink and walked out."

"Which proves what?" Parlinski said.

"Nothing, I know," Morris said. "But it was the way he reacted to the question, like I had no business asking. To be honest with you, it was uncalled for, under the circumstances. It pissed me off and made me suspicious. I have a right to know what's going on. We all do when we're out supporting his line."

"As far as I know, you guys are the only ones out who do have a contract," Leahy said. "Is it possible that you're reading more into what happened because of the risk?"

Before Morris could respond, Robbins stepped in front of him, glowering at Leahy, who was twice his size. Morris had to admit the little man had balls.

"I don't think Mo was reading anything into it and I believe he's right—Colangelo is up to something," he said.

"And why is that?" Leahy said.

"Because we have reporters, people who make it their business to find out information like this, and they are telling us the same thing," Robbins said. "We're hearing that Gerry is under tremendous pressure to make a deal. My guess is because scabs are doing their jobs, which isn't the case for the rest of us. We know they're going to need us when this is over but if the scab drivers get the routes down, well, you do the math and figure out how much Brady can save if he keeps them on and they work for the shit pay he's giving them now."

"They'll never keep scabs," Leahy said.

"Really? And how much do you know about Lord Brady, Mike? How much have you looked into what he's done with his union shops overseas the last half-dozen years? And while we're on the subject, let me ask you this: if Brady cuts a deal with the drivers, and it doesn't give him the savings he wants, where do you think he goes looking for it next? Does he say, okay, I know you're all still out there and even though I can publish the paper and have my regular drivers back to deliver it to every newsstand, I really want to be fair with the rest of you? Can we just sit around and wait for that to happen?"

Robbins had control of the room, as if Morris had disappeared. It was an intervention so thorough and timely that Morris suspected it had all been rehearsed. *Had he and Jackie anticipated Leahy's hostility and calculated on there being an opening for Robbins to step in? Was he even telling the truth about what the reporters had heard?*

So many unanswered questions for Morris to ponder as he tried to listen, maintain his focus. But the voices grew indistinguishable and distant. He was steps away, but they might as well have been in the apartment next door. He became lost in his own internal debate, absorbed in an effort to separate speculation from fact and fact from fiction.

He had initially felt a surge of that old-time electricity when Ryan had called. He believed he would be emboldened by his old mentor's unexpected involvement, energized by the opportunity to ride shotgun again. But the issues were suddenly more complex, bewildering even. They were so upside down and inside out that Morris began to wonder if they ever were really as straightforward as he had always remembered them.

Never had he questioned the time consumed by his union calling, the sacrifices made. In a self-congratulatory manner, Morris had never much dwelt on money, on material consumption. Predictability suited him fine. More than a few times over the years he had told Molly, "All I care about is being able to pay the mortgage, put food on the table for all of us, have a little left over for a ballgame or a movie or one of the Broadway musicals you like to see. All I ask for me and the guys is some security for when we get old. Don't we deserve that for the years we put in?"

He'd always had an unshakeable faith in union efficacy against the management position that anyone, with the introduction of the latest technological triumph, was expendable and only employable due to a dollop of corporate mercy. But now the *Trib* was publishing without him while the union brotherhood and his own family were fraying.

Louie obviously couldn't bring himself to break the news about Steven, and how the hell was he supposed to deal with Jamie, if only to square things with Molly? *And who the hell knows where this meeting is going and what Jackie and Robbins are up to?*

He still didn't quite have an answer when it mercifully ended without a clear consensus. Leahy stormed out of the apartment. Parlinski shook his finger at Robbins and told him he'd better be careful. The others trailed, albeit with less vehemence. That left Morris, Robbins and Ryan, who pounded Morris' back and gushed, "You did great, just great."

Robbins nodded enthusiastically, almost obediently. Morris' opinion of his own performance was quite the contrary—though, surprisingly enough, without great regret.

"You said what you had to about Colangelo, laid it right out there with no bullshit," Ryan said.

Robbins finished chugging a beer. His face was flush with excitement. He held a palm up for Ryan, who had to reach down to give him his high five.

"Leahy fucking couldn't believe it when I told him the Alliance is going back in tonight with or without them," Robbins said. "But my guess is that no matter how much of a noncommittal asshole he was, he'll swallow his pride and take his people back. He'll follow *us* this time, not Colangelo. The last thing he wants is to be left outside and to tempt Brady to start hiring scabs to replace them too."

"But what if he and the rest of them won't go in?" Morris said.

Robbins and Ryan exchanged cat-canary glances, confirming what Morris had guessed earlier. They were partners in this dog-and-pony show. Maybe now they would let him in on their deal.

"Doesn't really matter," Robbins said. "It would be nice if they—we—all went back together for the sake of unity. But to be perfectly honest, if they don't, they don't. The important thing is for you to go back and to put out the paper tonight. And we'll be in there with you because we don't want you to have to cross by yourself."

Still baffled, Morris turned to Ryan, who motioned for Robbins to continue.

Instead, Robbins grabbed his arm and took a step toward the door.

"Let's get a cab downtown," he said. "You'll see what I'm saying."

Morris allowed Robbins to lead him out of the apartment. Ryan followed but stopped at the door. He patted Morris on the back one last time and watched them walk to the elevator. Morris looked back to see him shut the door with a contented smile.

CHAPTER TWENTY-EIGHT

Jamie drove to Pleasantville for Aaron's party rather than take the train. It was pragmatic planning, the possibility of having to make a hasty getaway.

Yes, he was pleased—thrilled even—that Karyn had changed her mind and asked him to come. But he didn't know any of her suburban friends. He anticipated being the only man and didn't know how long he could stand it.

He arrived fifteen minutes late and steadied himself for the grand entrance he had hoped to avoid—all eyes upon the notorious ex. The front door to the glass-enclosed porch was open, as was the inside door to the living room. Aaron was the first to spot him. He toddled more steadily, or so it seemed to Jamie, than he had just days before. He wore snapped blue jeans and a sweatshirt of his favorite color—*ellow*—and already had an *ellow* cone-shaped birthday hat strapped under his chin.

"*Dah-dee, dah-dee,*" Aaron squealed. The greeting was so spontaneous, so genuine, that Jamie wondered if a two-year-old was capable of sensing his father's apprehension. *Bless him*, he thought, *in any event.*

The room was crowded with shrieking children and mothers chatting in clusters of two and three. They made no pretense of sizing Jamie up as Aaron led him into the dining room to the lavishly prepared party table.

"*Dah-dee sit hee-uh,*" Aaron said. He pointed to one of the metal folding chairs. On a paper plate sat one of Aaron's letter blocks, the green one with the letter D.

As it turned out, this was right next to the setting with the *ellow* block with the A facing up. Aaron held up his arms for Jamie to lift him. Airborne, he put his hands around Jamie's neck and laid his head on his father's shoulder.

"Happy birthday, sweetie," Jamie said, hugging Aaron back, tight as he could squeeze a two-year-old without bruising a vertebra.

Jamie turned away from the rapt audience in the living room. Only Karyn, who appeared through the open entry from the kitchen, could see that Jamie's eyes were shut tight.

"He's been waiting for you," she said, tousling strands of Aaron's hair that flowed from under the birthday cap, irresistibly curling down the back of his neck.

Where else could the mothers of Pleasantville break the monotony of another day in suburbia by encountering such family poignancy? *What a sight we must be,* Jamie thought.

But who cared? Not Jamie, not at this moment, with Aaron in his arms. His ivory soft skin was chocolate-scented by the Hershey's kiss that was part in his mouth, part on his fingers and in the process of being transferred to the shoulder of Jamie's light brown corduroy jacket.

All in all, Jamie felt more socially empowered than he would have imagined. He even enjoyed the conversation with the assembled moms. He smiled and shook hands as they announced themselves as the mother of Alex or Emily, Julie or Charlie; shared precise dates of their arrival in town; explained why they had left the Upper West Side or Park Slope or a spacious co-op in Yonkers convenient to Bronxville village shopping and restaurants; how life in P-Ville, as they called it, had been a difficult adjustment but, once made, was simpler, healthier.

"Like living in the 1950s," said Missy, mother of Mason, a lanky woman with a graying Princess Di hairstyle.

Jamie lit the candles for Aaron and helped blow them out. He cut and served—at the request of the mothers, especially the adult portions—very thin slices of vanilla ice cream cake. He tried to memorize the names of the children and volunteered to be the blindfolded scary monster in the backyard twilight chase. All the while he managed to resist the temptation to worry that these magnificent hours were not *merely* Karyn's parting gift to him on the way to removing Aaron from his life.

As dinnertime approached, the mothers began checking their watches, casually remarking how they had meals to prepare, dogs to feed, husbands to be home for. Their kids were overstimulated, getting cranky. They had missed their afternoon naps.

"Can you stay and help clean up?" Karyn asked Jamie, matter-of-factly. "This place is a mess. I'm getting ill just looking at it."

This is rich, Jamie thought. *For all the time I was living with this woman, she drove me crazy with her compulsive need to clean up. Now we're divorced, and I'm delighted she asked.*

Karyn's first task was to clear the table of cups and plates containing liquids or cake and roll the paper tablecloth with all of its gooey contents into one disposable mass. Jamie lugged the big garbage bag outside and deposited it into a trashcan.

Next he emptied the cardboard boxes of the few uneaten pizza slices, wrapped them in tin foil for refrigeration. He folded the boxes so they too could fit into the garbage bins. He gathered all the wrapping paper and ribbons strewn about the living room from the gift-opening ceremony (Aaron had absolutely cleaned up in the puzzle and book department) and stuffed them into two shopping bags. He stacked everything into piles and carried them up to Aaron's room.

All the while Karyn tidied up the dining room and kitchen. Aaron pretended to help, organizing and reorganizing the toys. But when the vacuum cleaner came out, his face turned ashen and he took off in the direction of the stairs.

"He hates it, can't stand the noise," Karyn said. "Maybe you can take him upstairs."

Flashing back to the misery of his childhood visits to the *Trib* composing room, Jamie felt a surge of kinship. Morris had made him feel like a weirdo or a wimp for hating that place. But he was just a kid, a few years older than Aaron, *for chrissakes*. Jamie could at least understand how a little boy could be frightened of noise.

"I think I know where he gets that from," he said.

Karyn cupped one hand around a side of her mouth and whispered, "Check his diaper."

He reached Aaron after he had climbed and crawled his way to the third step of the carpeted stairs, lifted him from behind.

"How about you and I go up and read a book while Mommy finishes down here?" Jamie said.

Jamie tickled Aaron under the armpits as he carried him up to the second-floor landing. He pressed his nose into his backside to confirm Karyn's suspicion. He laid Aaron down on the blue bedroom carpet he remembered as immaculate when inherited from the previous owner. Now it was stained beyond hope after two years of regurgitated milk and unrestrained urination.

The rug grossed Karyn out so much that she regularly asked Jamie for the money for a new one. He resisted, insisting it would be ruined within weeks. "At least wait until he's potty trained. And even then maybe a while until you know he won't have accidents."

She backed down, for once, and strategically fastened room fresheners to the walls to reduce the smell.

Jamie pulled a diaper from the changing table that Aaron had plainly outgrown. He reached into the plastic container for a handful of wipes.

During the months Karyn was making her ecological statement by going with cloth, Jamie dreaded changing his son's diaper. He could never get enough experience during his visits and feared he would botch the folding and that Karyn would return to eventually find Aaron a feces-stained mess.

"*Dah-dee 'tay hee-uh*," Aaron said as Jamie pried apart his legs and slipped the clean diaper under his bottom.

He snapped Aaron's jeans together at the waist and lifted him onto his feet. Aaron lurched to the books that were neatly stacked on the shelf on top of the toy bin, not quite able to reach them.

"Let's see what we have," Jamie said, doing a deep knee bend and selecting a handful.

Books in hand, he plopped down on the carpet, inspecting the titles. He leaned back against the sideboard of the bed Aaron had already been sleeping in for three weeks since he rebelled against naptime by vaulting over the crib bars and into his startled mother's arms. Jamie knew because Karyn called him that night and told him she had purchased a bed on credit and would let him know when payment was due.

Aaron lowered himself into the nest formed by Jamie's crossed ankles and grabbed for the top book.

"*Dis one, dah-dee*," Aaron said.

"*Slombo The Gross?*"

"*Lombo geen*," Aaron said, giggling and pointing to the colorful cover.

"Good choice, Aaron," Jamie said, skipping pages to the beginning of the story. "Right over by the dump, just behind the dirty part of the highway, lives a truly disgusting guy…"

"Who write, *dah-dee?*"

"Write?"

"Mommy say."

"Oh, right," Jamie said, reminded that Karyn always followed bookstore etiquette.

"*Slombo The Gross*, by Rodney A. Greenblatt."

The author was apparently an Aaron favorite. After Slombo he chose another Greenblatt offering, *Uncle Wizzmo's New Used Car*, followed by *Sam Goes Trucking* by Henry Horenstein, in which a father wakes his son at dawn to accompany him in an eighteen-wheeler as he hauls his load across the interstate.

Jamie suspected that this book—filled as it was with photos and explanations of how to hitch a trailer to a cab, pump air in the tires and fill the tank with diesel fuel—was published with the purpose of inducing sleep without having to medicate the child. It seemed to work effectively on adults too, given Jamie's sudden craving for a nap of his own.

Sure enough, just as the fish were about to be unloaded by forklift, Aaron unleashed a mighty yawn. His chin sank into his chest.

"Looks like it may be time for sleeping," Karyn said. She stood in the doorway, clutching Aaron's favorite stuffed animal, a light brown, floppy-eared dog he called Ruffy.

"*Dah-dee* read," Aaron insisted.

"What if Daddy reads you *Goodnight Moon?*" Karyn said. "But you have to be in bed."

She handed Aaron his stuffed animal, lifted him from Jamie's lap and deposited him gently onto the sheet. She unfurled the quilt that was neatly folded at the edge of the bed and draped it over his body.

Jamie untied his sneakers and slipped them off. He climbed onto the bed from the far end and wedged himself between Aaron and the protective guard. Karyn handed him the copy of *Goodnight Moon*, purchased by Karyn soon after she had quit her job in the city and began working at the bookstore.

"Ready?" Jamie said, turning to Aaron, who nodded.

"*Goodnight Moon*," Jamie began. Aaron held tightly to Ruffy under his right armpit. He scratched his nose with his free hand, looking earnestly at his father.

"By Margaret Wise Brown. Pictures by Clement Hurd."

Aaron's eyes were already half-closed. He rubbed them with balled-up hands. Jamie caressed his soft cheeks.

He read the rest of the story without further input from Aaron. He reached the last page and finished—*"Goodnight noises everywhere"*—in a soft, theatrical whisper.

Karyn rose from her perch at the edge of the bed and put a finger to her lips. She cautioned Jamie to dismount as quietly as possible. He lifted his sneakers from the carpet and pinched them together to carry downstairs. He and Karyn stared lovingly at Aaron, their shoulders nearly touching. They reveled in tandem, almost a family.

Just as Karyn hit the light switch, Aaron's head made an impeccably timed rise from the pillow.

"Dah-dee?"

"Yes, Aaron?"

"You seep hee-uh."

Jamie bit his lip and seized up.

"I'm just going downstairs with Mommy for a little while," he said. "Daddy loves you very much."

As they descended the stairs, Karyn first, she said, without turning, "You're welcome to stay, you know. I can make up the bed in the guest room or even put some blankets and pillows on the carpet next to Aaron."

Outside, a gusty rainstorm was emptying trees of their more stubborn contents, providing the perfect excuse to take Karyn up on her offer. But as much as Jamie could feel in his bones how thrilled Aaron would be to climb out of bed, jump on his father for the first time in his two-year-old life, he worried about misleading him.

"I'm afraid he'll get the wrong idea about where his father stays," Jamie said. "And then what happens if…well, you know, this job you've been talking about…?"

"I know," Karyn said. "We do have to talk."

They sat facing each other at the small table stationed against the wall, working on a pot of coffee she had brewed. Jamie couldn't help but wonder if this was the real reason she had invited him to the party.

Two hours later, exhausted to the point of lightheadedness, he glanced at his watch. He said it was getting late and that he thought it would be better for him to leave.

"You look so sad," she told him at the door. "Don't be. This doesn't have to be the end of the world."

"I'm just a little tired," he said. "And I have a lot to think about."

"But this—today, I mean—was good, wasn't it?"

"Yes, it was good," he said. "It was really good."

She gave him a hug, stiff to the point of being formal. He appreciated the gesture.

Jamie turned and walked to the car. He was indifferent to the pelting rain, grateful and suddenly buoyed by the blurring newsreel his life had become. He needed to think. He told himself, *The drive back to the city will do me good.*

The wind picked up on the darkened parkway. He'd hated this road from the time he began using it. He felt fortunate to have survived more than a few late-night drives going in the other direction without falling asleep at the wheel.

On one frightening occasion just weeks after they'd moved in from Brooklyn, Jamie found himself in a snowstorm that got worse the farther north he drove, not another car in sight. The traction was treacherous, only glimpses of the broken white line visible enough to guide him through the more curvy patches.

Jamie shelved his agnosticism that night and prayed for a safe pathway home. The main town roads were plowed but accumulations on his narrow street turned the walk from the driveway to the back door into an artic hike. Karyn had tacked a note onto the refrigerator to inform him that the boiler had shut down. She had called the oil company and been promised a repairman by mid-morning.

She was asleep upstairs under a stack of blankets with a verticality that rivaled the snowdrifts outside. Jamie slipped out of his clothes and under the blankets. He couldn't stop himself from wondering out loud why the hell they had ever left Brooklyn. He mixed in an F-bomb for good measure.

Like a zombie rising from the dead, Karyn turned and glowered, the whites of her eyes giving her a ghostly look in the darkness.

"Why didn't you take the train when you knew it was going to snow?" she shouted. "That's all you talked about when we bought the house: *walking distance to the station, you can read the paper, you can take a nap.* So don't you dare blame me!"

Looking back, he could see how their relationship had devolved to being all about blame as soon as they'd left Brooklyn. He held her responsible for dragging him to the suburbs. She resented him for not rising above his relocation misery for the sake of their unborn child. Jamie's missing Aaron's birth was proof to her that he never wanted the baby. He'd spent two years trying to prove her wrong. Maybe he had finally succeeded.

He tapped the eject button and yanked a Jackson Browne cassette from the mouth of the car's cassette player. He dropped it into the passenger seat. He was in the mood for something more up-tempo, less self-pitying. He reached over to the passenger seat for the tape he had pulled from the glove compartment before starting the car. He slid it through the slot and fast-forwarded from the middle of the album, approximating where he needed to stop.

He tapped his left foot lightly against the clutch to George Harrison's opening guitar riff to his favorite Traveling Wilburys' tune.

Well it's all right, riding around in the breeze
Well it's all right, if you live the life you please...

The cassette, having loosened from its spool, popped out of the slot. Jamie yanked it out and dropped it onto the passenger seat. He wished he had the money to spring for a new car with a compact disc player. In his apartment, vinyl was still retro hip. Here in the car, cassettes were so fragile, so 1980s.

The radio automatically switched on, tuned to the all-news station, a male anchor's resonant voice.

"It's ten-thirty, and here are the top stories. The five-day strike at the Trib has ended for all but one of the newspaper's nine unions returning this evening to produce tomorrow's editions, the drivers being the lone holdout…"

The radio shockwave was followed by a torrent of wind-blown rain drenching the windshield. Temporarily blinded, Jamie gripped the wheel tight but violated the Drivers Ed manual by hitting the brake as he splashed through a puddle. The car skidded, veering right. He tapped the brake again but remembered another fundamental rule—to ease off the pedal and steer into the skid. He brought the car to a crooked halt on the shoulder.

The engine stalled.

He took a deep breath and closed his eyes for a second before he realized he was sitting at a ninety degree angle, the rear of the car still in the right lane. He saw headlights coming in the driver's side view mirror. He needed to move fast. He depressed the clutch, turned the key to re-start the engine, exhaled when it turned over. He straightened the wheels and maneuvered out of the right lane.

The approaching car slowed for the puddle and rolled past to where Jamie was parked. The driver rubbernecked to see if there was any problem before speeding on.

While the car idled, Jamie's thoughts raced at breakneck speed. On the radio, a reporter was reading a statement by Leland Brady welcoming the returning unions back to work. He conveyed his "sincerest wishes" that they would finally agree to engage in contract negotiations that would address the need for concessions, ensuring "long-term financial viability of the newspaper."

Of course the unions were welcomed now that he had all but one back—with their strike leverage scratched like a losing lottery ticket.

Eight unions, including his own and more notably his father's, had crossed the drivers' picket line. None of this made any sense to Jamie, who could only ask himself what was the point of striking in the first place? What on earth had they accomplished by returning to work without a deal?

He pumped his brake as a safety precaution and steered the car back into the right lane. Anger surged through him. He wanted to howl at the moon but settled for yelling, "Are you fucking kidding me?"

There was one positive development in the end of the strike. Jamie was no longer the only Kramer male to have crossed a picket line. But why on earth had he needed to humiliate himself two days before everyone returned?

The only person Jamie wanted answers from more than his traitorous cousin was his hypocrite father.

CHAPTER TWENTY-NINE

The rain had turned into a foggy mist by the time Jamie crossed the Triboro Bridge and headed south on the FDR Drive. He had heard no new details of the strike's conclusion when the news cycle restarted on the Deegan Expressway in the Bronx, the shuttered Yankee Stadium still visible in his driver's side view mirror.

He couldn't wait to get downtown and find out just what had happened. He cursed under his breath when traffic slowed for an accident near Forty-Second Street.

Finally downtown, he blew through a stop sign at the South Street exit. The strike news aired again, this time with a reporter on scene. He described a large police presence to control the drivers, the last striking union.

As Jamie approached the building, he could see for himself: barricades lined both sides of the street. Dozens of cops were wandering around in bunches. They were stationed opposite the front entrance, warily minding the handful of drivers milling in the vicinity of the door. Jamie rolled by to the corner of South and Catherine. An officer motioned for him to proceed straight through the intersection. He slowed and looked right to the loading docks along the side of the building. There, inside more barricades on the far side of the street, was a long picket line with more clusters of drivers and cops. Abandoned by the other unions, they were out in force and no doubt spoiling for a fight.

Jamie accelerated down South Street. He parked three blocks away under the highway. He walked back at a brisk pace, mindful of the fact that no matter where he entered the building, he was likely to encounter harassment. To the drivers, anyone who walked into the building was technically a scab, but this time Jamie had his own agenda.

I could give a shit what they think.

Holding court at the corner was Gerry Colangelo, his back to Jamie but unmistakably identifiable by his slicked-back hair. He wore a blue windbreaker with *Deliverers* scripted across the back. Next to him was the ubiquitous Debbie Givens. *They deserve each other,* Jamie thought. He shook his head in disgust as he walked past. He made his way toward the front door where a dozen more drivers were cordoned off twenty feet away.

They lit into Jamie the moment they saw him advancing, fresh meat for a pack of wolves. One of the cops turned to determine the cause of the commotion, the eruption of profanity. He pointed his nightstick, first at Jamie and then at the entrance to the building.

In his own pissed-off mood, Jamie looked directly at the faces made partially visible by the street lamp, indistinguishable as they were in contortions of anger. Not the time or place for mischief, he knew. He couldn't resist. He flashed a two-fingered peace sign. The drivers responded with solitary middle fingers and the corresponding four-letter epithet.

"Go ahead, knock yourselves out," he mumbled.

With the *Trib* staff already in the building, it made strategic sense that the majority of drivers would be by the loading docks, leaving the other entrances sparsely covered. They were getting ready for the trucks to roll. But Jamie could care less about the drivers. They weren't why he was here.

He pushed through the revolving door and rode the elevator to the fourth floor. He headed straight down a narrow corridor leading from the newsroom. Left turn at the vending machines leading to another musty smelling straightaway and dead-ending at a metallic green door with a small, rectangular window. The only means of identification was a strip of adhesive tape with the word "reflex" printed in smudged black marker. This was where his father worked.

During his early days at the *Trib*, clerking overtime one night, Jamie had taken an unplanned detour to this door while grabbing a candy bar. He peeked through the window and was surprised by the sterility of the room, so disparate from his recollection of the old composing room pandemonium.

There were a few desks with bulky computer equipment. A couple of bigger machines stacked against the far wall, three or four of the workstations manned, though no trace of his father or uncle. They might have been on break, returning within minutes. But Jamie left without asking and to this day had no idea what actual service the transitioned printers contributed to the production of the paper.

"We move pages," Morris had grumbled when Jamie had asked— whatever that meant.

He never understood why his father had to be so evasive even when the line of questioning was exceedingly benign. He once asked his mother, "Is he that way with everyone or just me?" She laughed. "I learned to figure out what he's saying even when he won't say anything. Don't take it personally." Jamie did anyway.

For him, meaningful conversation with his father was painful even before the cold war caused by the dissolution of his marriage and his real estate story. After that it was near impossible.

How naïve Jamie had been to so much as harbor a fantasy that his picket line provocation could have ended in any other way than it had. *This time it'll be different*, he assured himself, believing—and perhaps hoping—that Morris would have gently tried to dissuade him the way Uncle Lou had. *Should have known better, he's always been so high and mighty. But let's see what he going to say now.*

Jamie told himself that he didn't have to wallow in self-pity anymore or swallow more strike sanctimony after what Steven had done. His father and uncle had also caved with no discernible cause, downgraded their job action from military strike to extended fire drill.

Jamie only wanted to have his say now, the last word on all the empty rhetoric.

I deserve this, he told himself. *I owe this to myself.*

CHAPTER THIRTY

Morris was hunched over his desk, leaning left to spare his keyboard the residue of the seeded roll he was biting into. His back was to the door when the rap at the window came.

A holdout crumb fastened to his upper lip, he looked up to find Sean Cox—at the station opposite him—pointing a finger. His owlish eyes were barely visible above the computer screen.

"Looks like your boy, Mo," Sean said.

Morris swiveled around and, sure enough, there was Jamie's face framed in the window.

"Oh, brother," he mumbled, rising from his chair. Carrying his roll, he pulled the door open.

"What are you doing here?"

"Good to see you too, Dad."

In the ensuing and awkward silence, it struck Jamie that his father looked thinner, paler, in need of a shave. There was a small Band-Aid strip obscuring his left eyebrow. In his haggard state, he could see a more striking resemblance to Uncle Lou.

"I need to say something," Jamie said.

Morris shook his head, determined to forego another scene, but he spread his hands apart in reluctant concession. He took a deep breath and thought of Molly.

"Ok, fine," he said. "But don't you have work to do?"

"No," Jamie said. "I didn't come here to work."

"Then what are you doing here?"

"Well, I see that you're working," Jamie said.

"Yeah, the strike's over. We all came back."

"Not the drivers. Some of them would have lynched me outside a few minutes ago if the cops had let them."

"It's complicated," Morris said. "There's extenuating circumstances."

"Really?" Jamie said. "I thought you're not supposed to cross a picket line under any circumstances. That's what I heard for the last thirty some-odd years."

"Jamie, look, I'm not going to discuss this with you—not here or anywhere," Morris said. "So if you're not here to work, go home and come back tomorrow for your shift."

Jamie shook his head.

"I don't think so, Dad. I'm not coming back."

"Not coming back where?"

"Here to work," Jamie said. "I'm done."

"What do you mean, done? They didn't fire anyone."

"No, I didn't mean to suggest that I was fired," Jamie said. "I didn't even know the strike was over until I heard it on the radio driving in from Aaron's birthday party."

"So, what then?"

"So I'm quitting," Jamie said.

"Steve got you in at the *Sun*?" Morris said.

Another insult, posed as a query. Would the man ever stop?

"I'm not going to the *Sun* or to any other newspaper. I'm just quitting."

"To do what?"

"It's a long story. Do you want to hear it or is this not the time?"

Morris didn't immediately respond. But after a few seconds he offered a compliant nod, which Jamie interpreted as a triumph. He almost could have walked away satisfied without saying another word.

"I'm quitting the newspaper business, leaving New York," Jamie said. "Karyn has a job offer. Some guy she knew in college is starting a company and wants to make her an executive with a good salary and benefits. The problem is that the company is not being launched here."

"Where?"

"Out west."

"Jersey?"

The hilarity of his father's response almost made Jamie crack up.

"No, not exactly," he said.

"Then where?"

"Seattle."

Morris looked at him, with skepticism bordering on disbelief, as if Jamie was trying to annoy him by making up nonsense.

Jamie, meanwhile, wondered if Morris even had a geographic clue.

"That's crazy," Morris said.

"That's pretty much what I said when Karyn first told me," Jamie said. "I've known about it for a few days, actually since the beginning of the strike. I've been agonizing over her taking Aaron away ever since. I thought maybe if I went back to work the other day, she would look at things a little differently. Maybe she'd realize how far she'd be going. But the strike really got her thinking about money, which she—we—don't have much of. She's worried about Aaron's future, college and everything. I started thinking maybe I should be too. Because Karyn works part-time in a bookstore and me, I don't make enough here to save a penny. The annual union raise is—what?—like twenty-five bucks before taxes? We sat for two hours tonight and the more she talked about it, the less sense it made for me to try and talk her out of it. Then right in the middle of it, this guy happens to call and says he needs to know if she's still interested. She says she is but she tells him how difficult it will be to move Aaron three thousand miles from his father, which I was naturally happy to hear. But the next thing I know she's crying, and the guy is telling her he understands. Suddenly he's asking about me, what I do and then she's handing me the phone. I start talking to this guy about the newspaper business, how readership has been declining and how many people are predicting that it's going to get a lot worse in the coming years. Just like that, he's asking me if I would also be interested in moving out to Seattle to work for him."

"And do what?"

Jamie could only respond with a reluctant shrug.

"He said he would meet with me to discuss it after Karyn and I made up our minds that we'd both be willing to go," Jamie said. "All I know is that it's a new company that's going to sell books. On the computer, this internet thing everybody's talking about."

"Who's everybody? What's an internet?"

Again short on specifics, Jamie evaded the questions.

"I know it sounds a little far-fetched. But Karyn says he's some kind of Wall Street whiz, has money to burn and is sinking millions into this venture. So, what the hell, I said I'd do it. What do I have to lose that's more important than Aaron? Where am I going here? Do I love this job so much and am I so good at it, that I can't try something else? Let's face it: I only got in here in the first place because of you and maybe Uncle Lou. When I heard on the radio that the strike was over, I felt like I don't even care anymore. I don't even want to come back."

"So you and Karyn are back together?"

"No, that's not what I'm saying. Not as a couple, just, you know, for Aaron. We're going to do what's best for him and—who knows?—maybe that will turn out to be good for me."

"So that's it?"

"That's what?"

"What you came here to tell me. You're picking up and moving to...?"

"Seattle, yeah."

Jamie lied with such a straight face he actually surprised himself. That wasn't what he'd come to say. He'd accepted no such unidentified position with the invisible bookstore. He hadn't so much as pondered the question of resigning his job and moving to Seattle.

The call and the offer were real enough. But all Jamie had done was promise Karyn that he would think about it. He made no promise beyond giving her friend an answer within twenty-four hours.

"It would be great for Aaron to have both of us out there," Karyn had told him. She also said she was going to go no matter what Jamie did. "I know that's a lot of pressure on you, Jamie," she said. "But I need to do this."

If nothing else, Jamie could see that he had gotten his father's attention, even if he had to stretch the truth to do it.

For the moment, anyway, the benefit of telling Morris that he was quitting the *Trib* had given Jamie leverage, a feeling of liberation. *I can do this*, he thought. *I can pick up and move across the country, if that's what I decide to do. Maybe that's the only way he'll ever respect me—if I get the hell out of here.*

Their roles were reversed now on a multitude of levels, even across the labor divide. That brought Jamie back to the original point of his coming here: to confront his father with his own contradiction, lash out at him for betraying the principles that had overrridden everything—and everyone—in his life.

"Just one more thing, about what happened the other day," Jamie said.

Morris stared at him, tight-lipped and solemn, with eyes that looked tired of coping.

"I'm sorry for embarrassing you on the picket line," Jamie said. "Like I said, I had this thing with Karyn hanging over my head, all this pressure."

Jamie broke eye contact, looking down at the wrinkled neck in the opening of Morris' shirt collar. The words had come unrehearsed and unfamiliar, as if they'd been smuggled into his mouth by a subversive part of his brain. But in the context of this intriguing new dynamic, it was what he suddenly felt. While setting the conditions, on some unconscious level he could recognize the senselessness of taunting or gloating or punishing a man who seemed so…so…*sad*.

"That's it, I've said what I needed to," Jamie said. "I'll be going."

He almost wanted to tease Morris, to tell him, *And you can't do anything to stop me.*

Jamie was half a dozen steps down the corridor when Morris did do something to stop him.

"Hold on," he said. "I want to show you something."

Jamie half-turned, looked back at his father, hesitated and cautiously retraced his steps. Morris pushed the door open and held it for him. He followed Jamie inside and motioned for him to pull up a chair from the vacant desk nearby.

"I know what you're probably thinking, about us coming back to work," Morris said. He lowered his voice. "Believe me, there's good reason."

Morris comically pecked at the keyboard with stiff index fingers. Jamie had to admit that his own typing skills, developed informally on the job, weren't much better.

"This stuff we do here, it's nothing like the old days," Morris said, making small talk, eyes on the screen. "Do you remember the composing room?"

Not happily, Jamie thought. "A little bit, mostly the noise," he said.

"The couple of times I brought you in, you hated it. It was a lot different than this…"

Jamie beheld the spartan surroundings, two other once-upon-a-time printers parked at terminals and another on the telephone with one leg splayed over the side of his desk.

"You never did explain just what it is you do," he said.

"Nothing too much," Morris said. "We, uh, you know…"

"Move pages, yes. But what does that actually mean?"

Morris turned to him and nodded. "This is kind of like the traffic station for the paper. The editors make up the pages with the stories and photos and send them here. Then we tag them for the guys who operate actual presses—the pressmen—so they can identify the pages, know which ones go to the city edition and which ones are meant for Brooklyn, for Queens, etcetera."

He punched a couple of keys and a *Trib* front page appeared.

TRIB UNIONS CROSS DRIVERS

"This is tomorrow's first-edition wood," Morris said. "It's already gone to press. But now we get the changes, the re-plates, for the later editions. The basic stuff most nights would be a ballgame in sports—you know, the updated sports scores, maybe a late-night shooting in the Bronx. When the new page comes to me, I put a star over here on the top right corner. This way the pressmen know that this page has to be re-set for the late city. Two stars for last city edition, a circle for the sports final. That's the last one we do every night."

The circle was the edition that was sold most days on the stands in Brooklyn Heights. Jamie had counted on it religiously for the late Lakers box scores from the West Coast.

"The pressmen, they only know to look for the stars or the circle. They don't know one story from another. They don't know or even look at what's on the page. So if we don't let them know with the markers, they'll just leave what's already in the paper."

"How do you keep track in here who's supposed to send out which page?"

"The other guys mainly check the pages to make sure the ads are in the right place, that all the holes are filled," Morris said. "But all the pages come through this machine right here. It's the only one that can change the edition markings and send the pages downstairs."

"Why only one?"

"It's the way the system is set up, so that only the foreman can authorize a re-plate. That way there's no confusion, no mistakes, once the pages get down to the presses."

Jamie understood he was sitting with the man in charge, if that was the point. It didn't seem to be, given the tone of Morris's voice. It was soft and almost solicitous.

He turned to Jamie and dropped his head so that it was below the top of the computer screen. His whisper made Jamie lean uncomfortably closer to the stubble on the side of Morris' face.

"The other guys aren't involved with what I'm about to show you. They don't have to be so keep your voice down and don't make a big deal about it. And you can't walk out of here and let anyone know. Another hour, it won't make any difference. But for now this has got to stay between us."

Jamie nodded, clueless as to what Morris was getting at. He played along as Morris pecked away at a couple more keys. Another *Trib* front page appeared, with a bold-faced headline that was as big as any he'd seen.

HO MY LORD!

Under which, in smaller typeface, was the explanatory sub-head:

FEDS SAY *Trib* CAPTAIN BRADY HAS HOOKERS ON BOARD

"What the hell…?" Jamie looked at his father, who shushed him and motioned for him to read on.

Trib publisher and conservative values champion Leland Brady, known for entertaining the city's power elite with flamboyant parties on board the customized yacht named for his wife, has had ongoing dealings with a woman soon to be charged by the U.S. government with running a highbrow prostitution ring, the *Trib* has exclusively learned.

Ruth Ann Hollender, known to high-rolling clients by the pseudonym Ms. Annie, has told federal investigators that Brady has been a steady client for the last year and a half and has often had call-girls visit aboard the Vanessa Queen, typically docked off a South Street pier, a short distance from the *Trib* building.

Hollender has long advertised her business as a legal escort service but investigation sources say other clients, offered immunity from prosecution by the feds after being confronted with bank records and wiretapped conversations, have admitted to paying as much as five hundred dollars an hour for sex romps. The feds have also wiretapped conversations between Hollender and Brady, as well as his son, Maxwell, executive editor of the *Trib*.

Law enforcement sources also say some of the women may be underage immigrants from Eastern European republics recently freed of Soviet rule and that further charges could be forthcoming.

Brady's name and contact telephone number were on the client list provided to authorities by Hollender, whose name has also frequently appeared on guest lists for bashes thrown by Brady in the two years since he purchased the *Trib* from former publisher Maxine Hancock.

Story continued on Page 3.

"You want to see the jump?"

At the moment, Jamie was still trying to fathom the five astonishing paragraphs on the front, alongside of which was a photo of Brady's yacht and the caption: **LOVE BOAT?** He pointed to the sub-head, having finally noticed the clever reversal of the H and O in the large-print headline—Ho as a derivative of whore.

"This is incredible," Jamie whispered. "Where did this come from?"

"From the newsroom, like every other story," Morris said. "Like I said, my job is just to make sure the re-plate gets tagged so the pressmen know what they're looking for. This is the new front for the late city. It closes at eleven-thirty, on the presses by midnight."

Morris checked his watch again. It was a couple of minutes past eleven. "It's got to go soon, in fact."

"This is really going into the paper?"

Morris again motioned for Jamie to come closer.

"This is why we came back in tonight. They couldn't put it in the first edition because Brady is around most of the day and the son checks the first couple of pages when it comes off the press, and then supposedly disappears for the night. It had to be a re-plate to get this in and since they had management people or some guys from one of Brady's papers in Canada working in here during the strike, they needed one of us—me—back on the job. Otherwise..."

"But how does putting a story like this help? Brady will go nuts. He'll fire everyone."

"What I was told by your guy Robbins is that they think it'll disgrace him so much that he'll have to sell, even if he somehow beats the rap. They say there are a couple of big shots who want to buy the paper, especially some Canadian real-estate guy. Tell you the truth, I don't know if what they're doing is a smart move or not, but I do know this guy Brady was up to no good. He's screwing with all of us, and nobody wants to work for him. So when they asked me if I would help, I said I would."

Jamie nodded his approval, strange as it was that Morris seemed to be asking for it. He re-read the story, taking note that it contained no byline. He'd actually forgotten that Brady was married, but now did recall a profile in *New York Magazine* about the socialite wife who stayed behind at a Surrey .estate, who was said to have developed a dislike for America while spending a year studying abroad. She was quoted as saying she would visit from time to time, but that she had her own cultural and philanthropic interests in Ireland and England, as well as several grandchildren from a previous marriage, while Lord Brady had his newspaper to attend to in New York.

Among other more rapscallion endeavors, apparently.

The story's jump on page three contained only a few paragraphs alongside a photo of the alleged madam. She was a pretty woman with styled medium-length brown hair. Her age was difficult to ascertain due to oversize sunglasses perched on a sliver of a nose. She wore a spaghetti-strap blouse that paid homage to her full breasts. Jamie read on, but there was little additional information, no other names mentioned. The juiciest material was crammed onto the front page. Given the surreptitious haste in which it was no doubt prepared, understandably so.

But by whom? There had only been those fictionalized bylines in the strike paper, no reporters, with the exception of..."

Cal is a great man—you know what I'm saying? I've been telling him that I'm working on something for thirty years. Once in a while, I actually deliver more than the usual crap. In this business, that's all it takes...

Blaine—who else? This had to come from him. I should have known that Blaine was biding his time.

Carla was close to Willis and had known something was brewing that morning. The story was ready. That's what she had been tempted to tell him. That was the forthcoming development she had tried to lure him back to the picket line with.

Blaine obviously had the law enforcement sources telling him that Brady had been snared in a sting. Carla had the names of the guests stored in her computer. She easily could have given Willis access to her files from outside the building. There had to be countless city power brokers—perhaps even the Mayor—on those lists to make the story even juicier. But Willis and Blaine obviously had one target in mind: the rogue publisher who had made a mockery of their newsroom.

Jamie didn't have to be much of a sleuth or even a quasi-competent reporter to figure this one out. But neither would Brady. What if Brady admitted his sin and cited human frailty like some television evangelist caught with his pants down? What if he begged forgiveness in the eyes of God, his wife and his advertisers? What if he denied the alleged impropriety and dismissed the story as the hatchet job of embittered and easily identified old-timers still pining for the past? And marched into the newsroom, police in tow, and had Willis and Blaine—hardcore lifers from the halcyon days of print tabloid supremacy—escorted into the street?

"Dad, have you thought about what could happen if Brady follows the story's trail to you?" Jamie said. "I mean, won't it be pretty obvious that you had something to do with it?"

Morris shrugged. "Sometimes you don't think, you just do," he said.

"But you guys went through all this just on the chance that he'll have to sell the paper and the next guy will be better?"

"That's the unknown," Morris said. "The feeling was that we needed to do something. Maybe on some level we're just kidding ourselves—who knows? But Brady has shown no respect for the people who have put a lot of years in here, who have sacrificed a lot for the paper. We don't ask for much. But the one thing we do deserve—and demand—is respect."

Jamie nodded. He mumbled, "That took balls."

"What'd you say?" Morris said, eye on the screen.

"No, nothing," Jamie said.

For so many years he had resented his father's immersion in his work, his being tethered to the union. Now here he was getting all emotional about the stand Morris had taken. Jamie couldn't help but feel pride. He had come here wanting to taunt him, but now he wished he could do something to help him. Blaine and Willis as well.

He could picture them sitting at a bar somewhere, planning the counterattack, going after Brady with the only weapon they had left—the journalism itself. In his mental snapshot, Willis was looking over the story, marking it up. Blaine was lighting a cigarette and taking a long, contented drag.

Risk versus reward. Jamie seemed to have an opportunity to play that game now. He wanted to believe he had the courage.

"I need to get this page and the jump to the pressroom," Morris said.

Jamie put a hand on his shoulder.

"Can you wait a minute?"

He picked up the telephone on Morris' desk and dialed Cal Willis' extension.

Day Six: Saturday, November 12, 1994

CHAPTER THIRTY-ONE

Kelly Murphy's clear blue eyes dazzled like flash photography in the dim pub lighting. They fronted a winning bartending persona that could not be acquired, imitated or taught.

"Happy work night, guys," she said, setting down long-necked Buds and dismissing the twenty Morris pushed at her. "This round's on me."

"How're you and the husband going to pay off that mortgage on the Island if you keep buying rounds?" Morris said.

He extended an elbow onto the bar and let the soggy twenty sit.

"Mo, you know if I pay for a couple, I get the twenty anyway."

Kelly winked as she breezily moved away, whisking an empty shot glass and a scatter of dollar bills from a nearby setting.

"You guys want to look at something else maybe?"

The television mounted high in the far corner was tuned to a replay of the Knicks game from the Garden earlier in the night.

"The news, that would be good," Morris said. He turned to Jamie and said, "Unless you prefer…"

Jamie appreciated the acknowledgment of his basketball fixation. He had heard the Knicks had won while he was driving down from Pleasantville.

"Fine by me," he said. He knew Morris would have preferred a blank screen to the game.

"One of the guys told me the drivers were ready to riot when the trucks were loaded with the first edition, but there are so many cops out there tonight," Morris said.

"No riot, no reporting," Jamie said, repeating one of the many Willisisms permanently lodged in his brain. "But I guess the strike did end today so they'll have to show something on the news."

It was half past midnight. Twenty-four hours earlier, Jamie had had Carla in his arms, stroking her thigh as their conversation faded to half-conscious whispers. He still couldn't get over how well he'd slept.

It already seemed like days ago. But here he was, with Morris at the bar, after newly forged connections with Carla and even Karyn had completed a trifecta of the implausibly unforeseen.

In the spirit of détente, Jamie and Morris hunkered down at a neutral site. Some of the printers, Louie included, were at their customary table. The first wave of editors and reporters following the completion of the last edition were celebrating their return to the ranks of the employed in the renovated section behind the far wall.

"Uncle Lou's here, I see," Jamie said.

"He worked this afternoon, the first shift after we went back in," Morris said. "I guess he's been hanging around all night. He's still a little, you know…"

Morris pursed his lips and nodded in admission that Steven was a subject better left alone on this impromptu father-and-son night out. The mood was as awkward as it was amicable, Jamie and Morris not unlike one-time neighbors bumping into each other years later at the mall. The pace of their drinking—both were more typically inclined to nurse a beer until it was warm—was accelerated.

They nibbled at a bowl of pretzels. They stared vacantly at the television screen as one crime scene blurred with another. Jamie experienced a pleasant buzz from the beer and conjured up the tender image of Aaron curled in the fetal position, Ruffy nestled against his chest.

"You heard about your sister?"

His meditation interrupted, Jamie shrugged.

"You didn't hear the news?"

"What news?"

"That she's pregnant?"

Jamie's jaw dropped so quickly that a piece of pretzel nearly dislodged from his mouth.

"No shit! That's *great*, unreal. When did they find out?"

Morris christened the second beer with a pronounced gulp, foam spilling over the bottle mouth and down the side. En route to the bathroom, Louie gave them a wave, his sheepish smile unmasking his embarrassment about Steven. A couple of city room editors strolled past, their journalistic antenna pulsating at the sight of Morris and Jamie.

"She called from the doctor early this morning, beside herself. You should have heard your mother after she got the news, crying like a baby."

"Wow. I mean, they've been trying so long."

"The thing is, she's pregnant but we're not sure if it's, you know, a done deal."

"Dad, you are or you aren't," Jamie chided playfully.

"I know but this procedure they did, now what the hell is it called, in-vee-something…"

"In vitro fertilization?"

"Yeah, that's it."

"I didn't even know they were still seeing the specialist," Jamie said. "The last time I spoke to Mickey, he said that they couldn't take it anymore."

Morris fidgeted on his stool, slid his beer bottle forward and back on the bar. He lifted a pretzel from the bowl and bit off one side.

"I didn't know they were doing it either," he said. "This thing has been dragging on so long that I think Becky got to the point where she only wanted your mother to know. They talk all day. I think Becky even calls her during her lunch break at school. I only found out today that she had an in at some clinic in Manhattan because of that guy on the block."

"Which guy?"

"The one you wrote about, the doctor. You know, the black guy. He hooked them up with some big specialist, a guy he'd worked with as an intern."

"Thad Greene? No kidding."

Morris' phrasing—"the black guy"—was at least a step up from the Yiddish pejorative. It was still an unpleasant reminder that Thad and family hadn't exactly gotten the benefit of the doubt from his father or anyone else on the street. But at least, Jamie reasoned, the Greenes had made some social progress since Jamie's real estate intervention. This made him feel good, certainly better than he had in the days following the publication of his story.

"I didn't know he worked at Brookdale Medical until your mother told me today," Morris said. "To be honest, I didn't even know he was a doctor."

Many times, Molly had recounted to Jamie during occasional spells of motherhood nostalgia that Brookdale had been named Beth-El not long after Jamie was born there. The hospital sat at the edge of the Brownsville section, long abandoned by blue-collar Italians and Jews, and subsequently blighted by poverty, crime and sometime later a young street thug named Mike Tyson.

Hence the fear that neighboring Canarsie had embarked on a similarly downward spiral and the overreaction on Ninety-Fifth Street, among others, to any freshly minted household of color. Tyson and associates could be holed up in any one of them.

"Your sister did some research and found out the specialist was some miracle worker in the field," Morris said. "They told her the wait for him to do this procedure would take a while but the next day—this was sometime last month, I guess—they got a call and were told there was a cancellation.

The other night at the house, when I said that thing about you having a baby and her not—and I apologize for that—she was waiting for the results, probably all stressed out. But your mother called me today…"

He checked his watch and corrected himself.

"Yesterday now, I mean. And then there was a meeting about ending the strike, and I had to rush straight down to the paper. Your mother was so excited she forgot how mad she was about what happened—you know, with us. She said Becky and Mickey even took the day off from school and were planning to take the doctor and his wife out to dinner last night."

"The Greenes, you mean?"

Morris nodded. "To thank them for the contact and all."

What great irony, Jamie thought. As much as anyone, the *schvartzer* had assisted in the conception of a second grandchild. Thad Greene had solved the Kramer family's worst source of misery. Jamie couldn't have written a better and more paradoxically gratifying postscript to the story.

"There's also the possibility of twins, because of this treatment," Morris said. "They'll find out soon. But—and this is what I meant before about her being completely pregnant, what Mickey told Mom when your sister was taking a nap—there could also be higher odds of a miscarriage. She's pregnant, but Mickey is worried that if it doesn't hold, it'll be even worse than usual for her. Becky's floating on a cloud, she's so damn happy. Of course, you know your mother. She didn't want to hear it. She'd be shopping for clothes already if Mickey didn't tell her not to get too far ahead of herself."

Jamie could understand Mickey's apprehension, having experienced Karyn's life-altering fears of miscarriage—no caffeine, commuting and, above all, canoodling. Becky would no doubt be equally vigilant.

"If anyone has a right to be happy under any circumstances, I'd say it's Becky, you know?" Jamie said. "She's been through so much. And there's no point in expecting the worst. She's pregnant. She's going to have a baby. I'm going to be an uncle."

He thought about how Molly would react when he told her that Karyn was taking Aaron to Seattle and how she would carry on if he really did decide to go with them. He wasn't ready to make that decision yet. He pushed those thoughts away.

"It'll be great for Mom to have a newborn downstairs," Jamie said.

He raised his beer a couple of inches off the bar and waited for Morris to respond.

"To Becky," Jamie said.

"Becky."

Their bottles touched. On the television screen, NY1 was reporting on the return of the eight *Trib* unions, trucks carrying away the first edition, steered by scabs with a sizable police escort. There were close ups of the drivers' faces contorted in anger and eggs splattering against the side of the trucks. Debbie Givens interviewed an exhausted-looking Gerry Colangelo.

Morris harrumphed and stuffed more pretzels into his mouth. They sat in silence. The bar had filled, every seat taken. Kelly became a whirlwind of drink-serving activity.

"Listen," Morris said, still chewing, eyes fixed on the screen, now filled by the five-day forecast. "I should tell you—and this is all just talk so far, everything is so new—but it could be that we, your mother and me, actually won't be living in the same house as Becky and Mickey by the time the baby comes."

"Why not?"

"Well, first of all, we didn't—we don't—have plans, not yet. But your mother said the first thing your sister said after she got home from the doctor today was that she doesn't want to raise the baby in Brooklyn. She has her eye on the Island, always has. She says she's not bringing her child into the world in a cramped two-bedroom apartment. Your mother said they could have the upstairs, which is a little bigger, but then Becky started going on about a yard, a playroom, the whole suburban thing. She said she and Mickey could get teaching jobs out there. Like you said, she's waited a long time, suffered a lot. She should get what she wants. They've got some money saved for the down payment and she says she wants to buy something before the baby's born, have the room and everything set up. Your mother's already worked up about that. But it got me to thinking that maybe this is also a chance for us to look ahead, make some changes. Maybe take a look around out there too."

"You, move to Long Island?"

Jamie couldn't believe what he was hearing. Whenever relatives or friends, Jamie included, left the city for some nowhere hamlet, Morris would visit reluctantly and immediately pronounce the place as uninhabitable. He would brag that he was born in Brooklyn, would die in Brooklyn and would only be caught dead and buried on Long Island because union membership entitled him and Molly a cemetery plot in Suffolk County.

And only because, at that point, the lack of a legitimate kosher deli and a properly baked bagel would probably be easier to ignore.

"You're going to commute all the way downtown from out there?"

Morris shrugged. "For a while, maybe a year or two, but I'll be sixty-five in a couple of months. I can collect full pension and social security in another year. And who the hell knows what's really going to happen around here?"

He leaned closer to Jamie. "Maybe after tonight, I wind up getting shit-canned altogether."

To Jamie, Morris without a job, this job, was unfathomable. What would he do? Who would he be?

"Well, technically, couldn't you just say that you are not in the position to make editorial decisions?" Jamie said. "All you did was to send the re-plate to the pressroom, just like you do every night. You did your job."

"I've been doing it, whatever it was, for a long time. And you know what? Even after they brought in the computers, I always thought I'd stick around, that I'd be the last one of us to go unless they had to carry me out, feet first. But this whole thing, with all the crap that's gone on the last few days, I'm not so sure anymore. I've been thinking a little. The time comes for everyone to make a change."

"I'll drink to that," Jamie said. The beer seemed to be making him braver about the possibility of Seattle. But he was also uncomfortable with his father's reflective angst and was happy to have re-routed the conversation back to him.

"This thing in Seattle," Morris said. "People are really going to buy books on a computer?"

Jamie didn't want to make his own skepticism too obvious. He preferred for Morris to believe he was making a responsible decision, if and when he ever got around to making it.

"I have to say this guy was really convincing," Jamie said. "He made a strong case that a lot is going to change in the next few years. He also didn't exactly paint a pretty picture for the future of the newspaper."

"Ah, they've been talking about the death of newspapers for years since they put the news on TV," Morris said. "I remember they used to say there'd be no more radio."

"But look at how many papers have folded in the last fifteen, twenty years," Jamie said. "And he's not saying the news is dying, just that people may eventually be getting it and a lot of other things on a computer."

Morris flapped his hand. "And what else are they going to do on it? Scramble their eggs? Walk their dogs? Try on their clothes?"

"I'll be honest with you, I'm not sure I get it either," Jamie said. "But changes happen. *You* should know that. What you just showed me upstairs, the job you do now compared to the old days—how is that different from what this guy is saying?"

Morris' silence conceded the point. His eyes reflected the long tumultuous week. He took a deep nasal breath before exhaling.

"Listen, whatever happens…"

Jamie waited, the pregnancy of the pause drifting into a second trimester.

"If Becky...well, if she has the baby, and she and Mickey are living in the same house, or we both wind up moving to the Island, your mother, she's not going to love that one more than Aaron. That's not her way."

There was conviction in his voice, a sincerity Jamie could not recall coming from his father, at least on any subject that directly concerned him. Then again, he had broached the subject speaking on behalf of Molly.

"So you'll visit, bring him back here to see her? Because when you tell her what you're planning, she's going to think she'll never see that kid again. And that'll get her really upset."

Jamie was moved, nearly compelled to affirmatively respond with physical affection. He began to feel like he'd backed himself into a corner. This was certainly no time to confess that the move, at least his part of it, was at best still based on a foundation of whimsy.

"Brooklyn is home," he said. "And even if it winds up being on Long Island, I'll make sure Mom—you guys—get to see Aaron. I'll make sure he knows his cousin."

He felt a twinge of regret, a moment of self-recrimination about the timing of his semi-fabricated disclosure. Yet the longer he sat on the barstool, and not coincidently the more beer he drank, the more he began to believe he could really make the leap. He could pick up and move to a city he only knew for its spritzing, space needle and basketball's SuperSonics.

Seattle? Sure. Why not? What the hell. He could do it. What was left besides a sudden onset of fear-driven inertia to keep him here?

Then the front door opened and into the bar walked Cal Willis, with Carla marching right behind him.

Jamie straightened up on his stool. His eyes followed her as she strolled across the room, right past him without so much as a smile, a wink or a glance.

CHAPTER THIRTY-TWO

She couldn't have missed him. He didn't see how. Jamie and Morris, perched at the far end of the bar, opposite the front door, were in Carla's direct line of vision.

The snub—if that's what it was—deflated Jamie. He wondered, *Couldn't she have just winked? Smiled? Raised an acknowledging eyebrow? Was she embarrassed by having spent the night with him? Or was this her way of restating her terms?*

In any event, here he was, trying again to figure her out. Jamie was never much good at deconstructing women in general but Carla was a special case, something entirely different. By now he should have known it was nearly impossible to know what she would say or do next.

"I need to take a piss," Morris announced, breaking Jamie's concentration. He lowered himself from the bar stool and headed to the men's room.

Sports highlights filled the television screen. Patrick Ewing was being interviewed following the Knicks' victory, so doused in perspiration that he looked like he could use an umbrella. Around the bar, *Trib* reporters and editors were toasting their return to work, sharing their own theories on what had happened to get them back in the building. Jamie refused an offer for another round—he had promised Morris a ride home and the two beers were already taking their toll on his late-night acuity. His plan was to grab a few hours' sleep in his old bedroom and drop in downstairs in the morning to give his sister and brother-in-law a congratulatory hug.

On the way back from the bathroom, Morris bumped into one of the printers and stopped to chat. When Lou joined them, Jamie wondered if his father was consoling his uncle about Steven or informing him that they were about to be the only remaining Kramers at the *Trib*. Ah, *Steven*. Jamie couldn't seem to summon the anger he'd unleashed on the telephone. He actually hadn't so much as considered his cousin since he'd become preoccupied with his own potential life makeover. *Strange*, Jamie thought. Before the strike, he wouldn't have contemplated this decision without consulting Steven. But why would he bother at this point?

Carla—now there was someone to confide in with the candor she deserved. She would listen. She would care.

Damn, this is stupid. Jamie slid off the bar stool, turned around and bumped into her.

"*Whoa*, stranger," Carla said. She fended him off with two hands, Jamie close enough for a blast of spearmint. It reminded him of the first night of the strike when he'd regained consciousness with his head on her thigh.

"I was coming to say hello," he said. "Saw you walk in a few minutes ago."

"I saw you too," she said. "I wasn't ignoring you, if that's what you were thinking. It just looked like you and your dad were burying the hatchet. And it's about time!"

Jamie nodded, impassively. He had somehow failed to consider that as a reason. But he also didn't want to let on to her that he had taken her blow-by as a snub.

"We're trying," he said. "It's a start, I guess."

"Didn't I say that he'd be happy to see you and welcome you?"

"Well, actually…"

"I meant for tonight. I already heard you're not coming back to work."

Jamie shook his head, pretending to be surprised that she already knew about what he'd told Willis.

"Cal doesn't waste any time, does he?" he said.

"I told you—no secrets, like family."

Her dimpled smile made her seem less the woman on a mission than she was when she had found him half-conscious outside the *Trib*. Of course, now that he shared a few of her secrets—a mother to support, a child to rear, a sister to mourn—he could also understand why the strike's conclusion, complicated as it was, would make her more relaxed, more playful. And, yes, he could see in her eyes a touch of sheepishness. He took it as her recognition that their night together had meant something to her too.

Jamie wanted to tell her how much he wanted to be with her again. But it was more than lust that he felt. "I just want you to know that I really admire your character and strength," he said. "I wish I had half of it."

"You have more than you think," she said. "But like I told you the other day—you don't have a clue. Maybe you'll find one in Seattle."

"So Cal told you where I'm moving?"

"He just said west. It wasn't hard to figure out exactly where."

"Just a short six-plus hours plane ride away, in case you'd care to come visit," he said.

"Seattle? Oh, sure. Love to. But I'm guessing that little Robbie may have to be in college before I have the time and maybe the money to get out there. You'll keep a light on for me in the window?"

"Well, we'll see how long I can actually last out there myself or if I can go through with it at all," Jamie said. It was as close to the truth as he was going to get.

"You've got a job, I hear. That should help," Carla said.

"I've been told that, except I'm not really sure what it is. I suppose as long as they tell me I don't have to join a union and go on strike, I'll be okay."

She playfully punched him on the shoulder.

"I don't get it," she said. "This one didn't bring enough excitement into your life? You didn't have any fun?" She feigned a pout. Before Jamie could abort his response, he felt himself blush.

How many times could she knock him off stride? Seemingly, whenever she had the time and the urge.

"The last part, definitely," he said.

"Good, because it was fun for me too," she said, nudging him again, this time a light elbow to the ribs.

He was tempted to lean over and kiss her, though the cheek would have to do in the current setting. He had just about summoned the nerve when they were distracted by shouting nearby.

"TURN IT UP!"

"SOUND, QUICK!"

In an instant, Kelly found the remote and pointed it above her shoulder at the television, her thumb frantically working the volume button. On the screen, Debbie Givens was hoisting a copy of the *Trib*, running an index finger across the front page as the camera closed in on the tawdry sub-head:

FEDS SAY *Trib* CAPTAIN BRADY HAS HOOKERS ON BOARD

There it was, just as Morris had previewed for Jamie upstairs. The bar crowd at first was dumbfounded by the report before erupting in pandemonium. The story had clearly, and somewhat miraculously, been safeguarded right up to publication.

"...Nobody from the *Trib* has yet explained how this incredible story managed to land on the front page of Leland Brady's own newspaper. Sources tell me that the publisher left the building earlier this evening, accompanied by his son Maxwell, after presses rolled with the first edition. Which, as I said, had a very different front-page story..."

Jamie turned back to Carla, whose shit-eating grin confirmed that she had been party to the scheme all along—Carla and Cal and of course

Patrick Blaine, who had proved once and for all and even under the most outlandish conditions that there was no one better at the tabloid game.

"Another TV exclusive for our gal Givens," Carla said.

"I don't understand why she would have this one alone though," Jamie said.

"Because Cal and…"

"Blaine?"

"What makes you think *he* had anything to do with this?"

Of course he was involved, had to have been, but Carla was apparently not going to let on, not even to Jamie. She had almost slipped but Blaine had his contract and Carla had her limits on what she would divulge.

"Cal didn't want the other television people around," she said. "Too much risk of it getting out early enough for Brady to find out and do something to stop it. The other stations were here earlier, but they all left after the first edition. We just needed someone to put it on air in case something went wrong with the trucks getting out. We told Givens that if she hung around, she could count on something really good."

"*Good* doesn't begin to describe this story," Jamie said. "I guess the couple of years she spent in our newsroom paid off big-time. She'll wind up on the network."

Carla nodded and suddenly stepped forward and placed her hands on Jamie's shoulders. She lifted up on her toes, leaned forward and pressed her moist lips gently against his cheek. She held them there purposefully, before whispering in his ear.

"You're going to be better than okay, no matter where you end up, Jamie. You just have to believe in yourself."

Did she know that he still didn't know what he was actually going to do? Was she sending him an obsequious message, leaving the light on for *him* to stay behind and be with her? Before Jamie could respond, before his heart could resume beating at anywhere near its normal rate, she turned and retreated to the back. Jamie watched her disappear around the wall. He ran a finger across the spot of his cheek she had kissed.

The NY1 report on the *Trib* ended, but Kelly's was bursting with the kind of energy that seizes a newsroom at one of those moments when the unforeseen erupts and brings change to the world. In the midst of the clamor, Jamie turned back to the bar to find Morris nudging the twenty a few inches forward, leaving it all just as Kelly had predicted.

"The story is out—mission accomplished," he said. "I guess we can get the hell out of here. It's been a long day."

Amen to that, Jamie thought. He zippered his jacket, shoved his hands into the side pockets and followed his father outside.

"I just want to go in the building to pick up a paper," Morris said.

"Get me one too," he said as Morris stepped away into the street.

Jamie stayed behind, looking up at the starless, perfect sky. He closed his eyes and let the light-falling rain freshen his face.

CHAPTER THIRTY-THREE

Morris took his sweet time inside while Jamie waited in the street, imagining his father being hailed as the conquering working man's hero. Not that Morris was likely to enthusiastically admit to being the conduit of the story that exposed Lord Brady. He was never the self-promoting type, scoffing whenever Uncle Lou claimed he had single-handedly preserved their printers' shop during the post-Ryan years without proper credit. But in the aftermath of Brady's heavy-handedness and the front page that humiliated Morris and family, Jamie wondered if his father would have the urge to take an overdue bow.

Jamie had to wince at the implausibility of Morris retiring to doting grandfather-hood, of spoon-feeding a toddler in a highchair and making inane baby talk. Since he could remember, Molly had told domestic tales of Morris' revulsion to child-rearing. "All he had to do was get a whiff of a dirty diaper, and he'd grab the newspaper and run for the bathroom," she'd say.

For all Jamie knew, that's where Morris was now though he didn't mind the delay. There was no rush getting to Brooklyn. After being inside the bar for a couple of hours, the night air was invigorating. Jamie watched with growing curiosity the proceedings across the street at the loading docks. The trucks were being loaded with bundles, being readied for what was destined to be a memorable delivery.

At the front of the drivers' picket line, Givens and her cameraman had Gerry Colangelo backed against the wall for interrogation. Jamie was especially pleased to see Pat Blaine nearby—his notepad open, cigarette dangling, eyeing the clusters of drivers. A handful surrounded one guy holding a last edition, contributing boisterous and unabashed commentary to the inspection of the front-page blockbuster:

"Look at the rack on Ms. Annie."

"How come we never got any pussy in our benefits package?"

Jamie stepped into the street, leaning a shoulder against a red Volvo with a badly dented rear end. From this position he could see the back of the trucks being shuttered. Bodies were stirring. Something was happening. Cops were moving toward the side door and the platform, reinforcing the barricades between the trucks and the picket line. The door opened, bringing forward a burst of replacement drivers scurrying for the trucks. They flicked away cigarette butts, the brims of their baseball caps pulled so low that they couldn't have noticed the striking drivers paying them no mind, preoccupied as they were with Brady and Ms. Annie.

The replacement drivers wasted no time getting behind the wheels and their engines started. The disorderly procession was so punctual and rehearsed they might easily have passed for actors on a movie set. Without delay, the first truck inched forward as the police moved alongside, forming a traffic lane with a cordon of blue on two sides. One officer, stationed in the intersection, summoned the lead truck forward with his nightstick.

He couldn't see the black limousine coming his way, speeding on South Street and swerving left as it entered the intersection. It narrowly missed the startled officer and came to a halt in front of the lead truck, inches from its front bumper.

Within seconds, the limousine was surrounded by a half-dozen screaming cops. The officer who had nearly been run down hustled over, wielding his nightstick, crashing it against and shattering the left taillight. Pat Blaine hurried across to where Jamie had stepped forward to watch the spectacle unfold.

"You've got the best view here, Kramer. And believe me when I tell you, this is going to be good."

Within seconds the driver was out of the limousine, handcuffed and bent over the hood. An officer approached the back door, pulled it open with his left hand while his right was poised on his holster. A foot in a fire-engine red slipper set down in the street, followed by another, and finally a hulking figure in a silk white robe with an embroidered B over the left breast. He emerged from the car and rose mechanically yet majestically. Much taller than the officer, he looked over the mass of law enforcement.

"Everyone needs to just be calm." Leland Brady said.

The officers looked at each other in bewilderment, thinking—*the audacity of this fat fuck in his expensive bathrobe, an accessory to the near dismemberment of a police officer!*

One of them turned back to Brady and said, "Sir, I'm going to have to ask you to step away from the vehicle."

Brady smiled benevolently, like an amused CEO deigning to enlighten the company's new night watchman who didn't recognize him and who, by the end of the shift, would be folding a check for two weeks' severance into his wallet.

"My good man, I own this newspaper and every one of these trucks, and I forbid them from moving another inch."

The officers shrugged. Two approached Brady, each grabbing an arm, and escorted him to the sidewalk. They were no more than thirty feet from where Blaine, Jamie and now Givens and her cameraman were standing.

Blaine nudged Jamie with an elbow. He pointed to the cameraman, then to Brady. He raised his index finger to the side of his head and simulated the pulling of a trigger.

"I must speak to the Mayor," Brady said. His voice had doubt in it now, a high pitch, more pleading than demanding. His hands were pulled behind his back. His face was contorted with anger at the outrageous reality of his impending arrest.

"I've got news for ya, pal," the cop on Brady's right flank said. "The Mayor gave us the order to make sure these trucks get through."

"You don't understand. I can settle this if I can just call him, if I can use the telephone inside the vehicle."

Blaine chortled. "What do you think, Kramer? Hizzoner still wants to hear from the Lord now our story is out and that camera is rolling?"

"About that story, Pat…"

Blaine took a long drag on his cigarette before dropping and extinguishing it with the toe of his shoe.

"Damn brilliant reporting," he said. "What we do best in this business."

Blaine fiddled inside his coat pocket for another smoke, nestled it above his left ear and flipped his notebook shut. He held his palm up.

"You can't write a fucking thing when it's wet, you know what I mean? Got to keep your eyes open and make sure it all gets in here." He tapped an index finger against the side of his head. He winked, shot Jamie a crooked, knowing smile and turned to follow the cops as they led the intruders away.

The handcuffed Lord unleashed a torrent of profanity as he was forced into the back of a squad car. An officer backed the limousine from the intersection, parking it in front of Kelly's before radioing for a city towing service to impound it. The *Trib* delivery truck finally was allowed to turn onto South Street. A dozen of the striking drivers, assembled at the corner, waved the truck on, chanting "Go…go…go."

"Strikers cheering scabs—who would ever have thought they'd see this?" Jamie said, shaking his head. Debbie Givens called out to him, "Jamie, I need to talk to you but I have to…"

She gestured to the cheering drivers and hustled back across the street with her cameraman, enjoying the defining night of her professional life.

Coming in the opposite direction, straight for Jamie, was Morris. He had two late editions folded in the armpit of his jacket.

"What just happened?"

"You didn't see?"

"I had to go to the crapper and as I was coming out I heard a commotion."

Jamie shook his head, lamenting his father's horrendous timing. So that's where he'd gotten it from.

CHAPTER THIRTY-FOUR

A block and a half south of the *Trib*, with only their long shadows for company, Jamie and Morris could still hear the striking drivers whooping it up. They were celebrating Brady's sudden ignominy while forgetting the possibility that the spectacle they had just witnessed might under a certain set of circumstances also foretell their demise. For all they knew, the paper could fold.

Jamie filled Morris in. The oral version was somehow less believable than having watched it happen.

"They just handcuffed him and took him away?" Morris said. "They didn't even check him for identification?"

The rain was falling harder, not quite a downpour. Fortunately, they had the elevated highway for cover.

They reached his car as the interior light went out in another that had just passed by. It rolled into a spot across the street from where Jamie had parked.

Jamie unlocked the driver's door, reached across the front seat to lift up the latch on the passenger side. "It's open."

"Jamie?"

The voice, unmistakably familiar, came from the street. Jamie stood on his toes and peered over the roof of his car to see who it was.

"Is that you, Jamie?"

Morris turned upon hearing the voice a second time.

"It's me, Steve." Steven appeared out of the shadows and stood face-to-face with Morris. "Uncle Mo, hey," Steven said. He gave Morris a pat on the shoulder.

"What are you doing out here?" Morris said. He seemed flustered by the unexpected appearance of his nephew.

"I was uptown, out with a couple of old friends from Columbia, and just as I got home, I got a call from my editor," Steven said. "He said there was something on the news about Brady and the *Trib*, and I should get down here as fast as I could. But I didn't hear anything on the radio other than the strike being over. What the heck's going on?"

Jamie thought his cousin looked haggard, a bit frantic. His *Trib* press credential dangled from his neck. Steven apparently had been sent out into the night on assignment by his new boss before he could so much as be formally documented as a *Sun* employee.

Should he break the news to Steven that he was too late? That he was, on the scandalous subject of Lord Brady and the *Trib*, not one but two exclusives behind his good friend, Deb Givens?

Jamie didn't get the chance. Morris, who was carrying the two late editions, offered one to Steven.

"There you go, Stevie. It's all on the front page. Right here…in your cousin's story."

Steven took the copy and held it out for inspection, squinting to read in the darkness. He mouthed the headlines and hastily scanned the first couple of paragraphs. He looked up at Jamie, all bug-eyed.

"You got this?"

"Well, yeah, that *is* my byline, isn't it?"

"How…where?"

Jamie shrugged. "You know, I had a source. With you gone, someone had to put the Lord in his place."

A cheap shot, yes, especially in the context of the journalistic untruth.

Willis had grunted his approval when Jamie called from Morris' office to repeat the fabrication he had told his father about having already accepted a job in Seattle.

"You leave the story without a byline, Brady will draw the obvious conclusion," Jamie told Willis. "If Brady somehow survives this…"

Jamie got what he wanted—his name on the story—without even having to mention Blaine's name.

What was one more little lie in a newspaper already contaminated with numerous byline fictions and other deceitful manipulations in the name of the ethereal Lord? Jamie convinced Willis to allow his final act as a member of the Fourth Estate to be—at best—one of mercy for and appreciation of the man who actually reported it.

At worst, it was an indulgent but understandable claiming of revenge for the Brady-engineered humiliation of Jamie and his father.

The unexpected payoff—and one Jamie surely could guiltlessly relish—was the fading sight of his cousin, the defected mercenary, literally chasing a story with Jamie's name on it, already being delivered to outlets everywhere.

CHAPTER THIRTY-FIVE

"How many miles you have on this thing?"

"A hundred and nineteen thousand, plus," Jamie told Morris. He dropped into second gear and turned right onto the narrow ramp leading to the Brooklyn Bridge. "The odometer stopped about a year ago, but these Toyotas apparently run forever."

"What are you going to do with it?"

His announced plans being formulated minute-by-minute, Jamie had had no reason to consider the car or much else in the way of his unremarkable collection of worldly possessions.

"I don't know. I guess I'll have to figure out something."

"Maybe Becky and Mickey would take it as a second car if they're going to move to the Island," Morris said.

"I'll ask them," Jamie said. He was still riding the high of his *exclusive* but every tick of the clock brought him closer to a decision he was beginning to dread having to make.

He couldn't remember the last time he had been at the wheel with his father alongside him. They were so accustomed to steering their lives away from one another, trying to avoid head-on confrontation and mainly succeeding in disallowing the possibility of meaningful connection.

During Jamie's junior year of high school, Morris had tried to teach him to drive after he had passed his written test for a learner's permit.

The mentorship ended by mutual consent after less than an hour. Morris was painfully intolerant of Jamie's difficulty holding a lane, among other fundamental flaws of teenage judgment.

Molly took one look at her son's face when they walked into the apartment and immediately realized it had been a very bad idea. Her husband was so unforgiving in the passenger seat that she refused to renew her license when it expired in the early 70s. She engineered a raid on her underwear drawer—her reserve fund for the rare extravagance that Morris was bound to dismiss as unnecessary and wasteful—and purchased lessons for Jamie at a driving school.

"What will you do for a car out there?" Morris said.

"I don't know. If the job's in the city, maybe I'll be able to afford to live downtown. It's got to be cheaper than New York, right?"

"What the hell would I know about Seattle?" Morris said.

"Well, I'm just saying. It might be nice not to have to worry about a car, the insurance, and parking, after the last few years in Brooklyn Heights."

Morris snickered, shook his head. "You never could park the damn car. What was it, five road tests you failed?"

More than disapproving, it seemed to Jamie that Morris was just bantering, being playful. At least that was the way he was taking it, in the spirit of the night. On top of that, impossible as his father had been as an instructor, it was true that measuring distance for Jamie had always been an imprecise science, putting it kindly. The body of the Toyota bore its share of incriminating evidence.

"Actually, it was six tests failed and it wasn't just the parking that did me in. I got everything wrong on those tests, probably broke records for points deducted. I remember on one of them, I stalled out trying to back up and froze when the guy said to re-start the car. He told me to switch seats and didn't even let me finish. Another one I screwed up the parallel and he said, 'Forget it, just make the damn broken U.' But I was so flustered that I tried to pull out with the car in reverse, backed up at an angle and knocked over a garbage can. This guy sitting on the porch of his house came running out like a madman. That was it. The instructor said not to come back until I took more lessons, as many as they'd give me."

"You went to the driving school, I remember," Morris said. "Your mother sent you, not me. Those guys were such crooks."

"I actually only went to them two or three times," Jamie said, sheepishly. "Then Uncle Lou took me out—he made me promise not to tell you. He felt sorry for me and was pretty cool about it, even after I put a couple of small scratches on his car trying to parallel. He just kept making me do it again and again and after a couple of hours I got better, or at least good enough to pass. The next time I took the test—lucky seven. I got close enough to the curb, sticking out a bit, and the instructor—same guy who wouldn't let me finish that time—shook his head and said, 'Okay, good enough, just stay off my damn street.' Probably the longest year of my life, but I finally did pass."

Jamie shot Morris a sideways glance. Morris was staring straight ahead, but Jamie could see that his lips were moving. He appeared to be talking to himself.

"What'd you say?"

"What?"

"You just said something, didn't you?"

"Nah, nothing."

But Jamie, no question, had heard him say *something*.

Without the training to take notes shorthand, Jamie had always struggled to keep up with his interview subjects. He would furiously scribble while trying to sustain a semblance of eye contact and continuity. Soon as the person was out of view, he would finish the incomplete sentences with what he remembered or at least what he believed he had heard. In silent confessionals, he would admit his quotes were sometimes only reasonable facsimiles of what had actually been said. But what the hell, no one had ever challenged his veracity. In the grand scheme of things, what difference did it make? He never had knowingly changed the context of a quote. He did his best. He went with what he had.

"You sure you didn't say something?" he asked Morris.

"Yeah. I mean, no, I was just thinking."

Okay, have it your way, Jamie thought. But since the printers were technically under the editorial umbrella, and he officially was still in the employ of the *Trib*, still a reporter, it occurred to him that the last interpretative call on the conversation was his.

"That's right, kid, you passed."

That's what Jamie had thought he'd heard Morris say. That's what he was going with.

They rode over the bridge, Jamie for once enjoying the silence between them. He clicked the windshield wiper setting to off, the rain having slowed again to a barely perceptible drizzle. The traction was still slippery on the bridge's metal grating. That always made him uncomfortable so he clutched the wheel with both hands and steered the car into the right lane to exit into Brooklyn under a sign with a curved arrow that read: 278 West.

He drew a deep breath, exhaling slowly as the light up ahead, around the bend off the exit ramp, blinked green to yellow. Jamie started to go but quickly jammed on the brake. Just as abruptly—as if the machine had taken control of him—his foot boldly switched pedals. He went down heavy on the gas, jerking the car forward, through the red light, upshifting into third.

He was heartened, delighted even, by his rashness, this recklessness— the sudden willingness to move forward after his long history of playing it safe or spinning his wheels. He had surprised himself and someone else too.

Out of the corner of his eye, he couldn't help but notice his father lurching forward, hands extended on the dashboard to break his momentum. Startled, wide-eyed and perhaps momentarily frightened, Morris turned and gave him a look.

CHAPTER THIRTY-SIX

It was half past two when Jamie and Morris walked into the apartment. Molly was still up, sitting at the kitchen table looking exhausted. She wore a red bathrobe and, between sips of coffee, chewed on a fingernail.

Morris had phoned her from the office and said they were about to be on their way. When Jamie stepped into the kitchen, she hurried over and hugged him.

"Are you hungry?" she said out of habit.

"No, Ma," he said. "I'm just beat. It's been a long day."

"I made up the bed in your room," she said. "You heard about Becky?"

"Dad told me. Such great news—can't wait to see her. "

"A blessing," Molly said. "Now I'll have two grandchildren."

She kissed his cheek and went into the bathroom. Morris handed him his copy of the *Trib*.

"Show your mother," he said. "She'll get a kick out of it." Morris went off to bed. Jamie went into the adjacent bedroom—his old room—and shut the door.

On the drive home, Morris had asked him when he intended to tell Molly about the plans to move to Seattle. Jamie alibied that he didn't want to upset her at such a late hour. The next day would come soon enough. But that also meant he would need to actually make a decision because Morris would be expecting him to tell his mother *something*. The question was what?

What if going out West turns out to be a road to a nowhere job in a city where I don't know a soul? What if Karyn finds a new man—if not the computer book-salesman himself—and I feel like an intruder around Aaron?

Jamie also worried about how he could remain a growing presence in his son's life from 3,000 miles away. Then again, he did have visitation rights. Aaron could spend holidays and parts of the summer with him in New York. Molly would surely help with babysitting. Soon—knock on wood—there would be a little cousin to have as a younger companion, a surrogate sibling, and a home in Long Island with all the suburban trimmings.

True, I told Willis I was quitting tonight but wouldn't he, of all people, understand if I called for a do-over? He was the man who'd walked away from the woman of his dreams for journalism. Plus he likes me. Carla said so.

Ah, Carla. Unless Jamie had completely misread the moment, her wet kiss on the cheek in the bar was more amorous than platonic. She'd made it clear she didn't need a man, but there was also the matter of what she *wanted*. And while her life seemed as child-complicated as was Jamie's, maybe they could figure out a way to give it a go.

Of course, staying in New York for a relationship with Carla would also assume that he—and she, for that matter—would still be employed by daybreak. A man of Brady's wealth could not be so easily vanquished. He would use every resource available to discredit and punish those who had conspired to harm him. There were bound to be aftershocks from the earthquake Morris had triggered with the pressing of a computer key and the launching of the re-plated edition. They might continue for weeks or months. Even if he could stall a few days, Jamie would have to make up his mind without knowing what awaited the *Trib* and its workforce.

I need to get this over with as soon as I can. I have to decide by morning at the latest.

More than anything, Jamie wanted to do right by Aaron. That much he was certain of. But he could also appreciate that Morris had tried to do that with him when they lived under the same roof—and look what a mess he'd made of *that*.

At least Morris seemed to finally acknowledge that he could have tried harder, done better. Jamie, in turn, could finally see and appreciate the sacrifices his father had made for others.

"You were responsible for a lot of careers and families," Jamie had told Morris in the car.

"I just did what I could," he said.

"You did what you had to do," Jamie said. "There's a big difference."

Morris shrugged, uncomfortable with the compliment. "You know, if you told me yesterday that I would live to ever cross a picket line, I would have told you that you were out of your damn mind," he said. "What the hell? Maybe none of this stuff should ever be set in stone. Maybe you just have to live in the moment and make the best decision you can."

"Yeah, I suppose," Jamie said. "As long as you can make one and stick with it."

Jamie knew he was at that point now. There was no middle ground left for him to stand on, no way to straddle the line. He had to choose. He had to be less of a reporter and more of a columnist. Like Pat Blaine and—yes—Steven too.

He wished he could be sure, but there apparently was no sure thing.

Should he go to Seattle with Aaron and try to be the doting father he never had? Or stay in Brooklyn and try to build something with Carla and the *Trib* that his son might someday understand was worth fighting for?

He got into bed and drew the blanket up to his head.

Got to get some sleep and figure this out.

He predictably spent the next few hours tossing, turning and flip-flopping.

It was a little past six when he surrendered to insomnia. The boiler kicked on, sending bursts of steam through the old radiators. A garbage truck groaned as it passed by. From the other side of the wall, Jamie could hear his father's light snoring.

Jamie reached over to the night table and turned on a light. He swung his legs from the bed to the floor and looked around the room for something to read—a book, even a leftover Marvel comic would do. There was nothing. Only the *Trib* that he'd set down on the top of his old dresser.

He walked over and grabbed it, then returned to sit on the edge of the bed, his bare feet still on the carpet. He stared at the exclusive that within hours would be the talk of the town. *What a crazy story*, he thought. What a strange and totally unforeseen turn of events.

He would be getting calls for interviews—no doubt from the persistent Debbie Givens—to explain how he had gone from front-page humiliation to the *get* of a lifetime.

He studied the byline and mouthed the words: "By Jamie Kramer." He began reading the story, but lost concentration after the lead.

Damn, I slept so peacefully with Carla. But reading Aaron his bedtime stories—how cool had it been to watch his eyes gradually close, to hear him say he wanted me to stay?

So what would it be? Go to Seattle with his son or stay for a new-found celebrity?

The idea of relocating was thrilling yet scary. But so was the alternative of putting his life—professionally and personally—on the line with Carla and the *Trib*.

He would never know which path posed the greater risk or reward. He could only rely on his instincts, live in the moment, develop a plan.

Then again, what was it that Cal Willis had told him? The plan isn't the story. *It's only what gets you off your ass so you can go find it.*

It was daybreak in Brooklyn. Deadline was approaching, almost time for Jamie to begin his life rewrite.

The hardest part—the lead—would have to come first.

ACKNOWLEGEMENTS

The *Daily News* strike of 1990-91 happened a very long time ago but the memories of fear and loathing—along with friendship and loyalty— remain vivid and poignant. Thank you to my former colleagues who walked that line, put out the Real News and hung together through some mighty dark days.

A special thank you to John Gruber and Filip Bondy, longtime confidants. And to Jay Schreiber, who had to tear himself away from the line to go work for *Newsday*. On the subject of long ago, I owe a large debt to a great Staten Islander, Danny Colvin, for helping me to become a professional reporter and writer.

Neil Amdur, a terrific editor and journalist who knew an exhausted columnist when he saw one, helped get me started on this book by allowing me to take time off. Michelle Musler and Sophia Richman encouraged me to keep working at it. My father, the late Gilbert Araton, and my mother, Marilyn Araton, provided the voices in my head to finish it.

I have been blessed with two loving sisters, Sharon Kushner and Randi Waldman, and lucky to have such a caring extended family—my in-laws David and Ruth Albert, Dana and Hilary Albert, Ashley Stone and Allan Waldman.

My indefatigable agent, Andrew Blauner, found the ideal people for me to work with at Cinco Puntos Press. Being guided and edited by Lee Byrd was an education and a privilege. My deepest appreciation goes to John Byrd and Bobby Byrd for their vision and wisdom. Thank you to the rest of the team—Elena Marinaccio, Jessica Powers and Mary Fountaine.

Finally, to the greatest support group at home anyone could ask for: Beth Albert, Alex Araton and Charly Araton. Thank you for being there, always.

Harvey Araton
Montclair, New Jersey, Fall 2013

ABOUT THE AUTHOR

HARVEY ARATON is a longtime columnist and Pulitzer-Prize nominated reporter and columnist for the *New York Times*, who has written primarily about sports but also for the Sunday *Times* Magazine, Book Review, Styles, Real Estate, Home, Dining and Arts & Leisure sections. He is the author or co-author of six previous books, including *Driving Mr. Yogi* (Houghton Mifflin Harcourt, 2012), a New York Times best-seller, and *When The Garden Was Eden* (Harper Collins, 2011), which has been adapted for film by ESPN's 30 for 30 series. Another book, *When Soccer Moms Take the Field and Change Their Lives Forever* (Simon & Schuster, 2001) is being produced for feature film by Breaking Ball Films. Before the *Times*, Araton worked for the *New York Daily News*, *New York Post* and *Staten Island Advance*. He is also an adjunct professor of journalism and media studies at Montclair State University. Araton and his wife, Beth Albert, live in Montclair, New Jersey, and have two sons.

PRAISE FOR COLD TYPE

Harvey Araton writes, with keen insight, of a time when power was ebbing fast from both newspapers and their unions. It's an especially bittersweet tale he tells of the people who had grown up in newspapers and unions, as they struggle to adapt to this evolving new order. And, of course, what makes this even more evocative is that we're still trying to sort this all out.
—Frank Deford, author of *Everybody's All-American*, NPR commentator

Father and son face their demons, each other, and a depressingly realistic publisher in a newspaper yarn that made me yell, "Hold the Front Page" for Harvey Araton's rousing debut as a novelist.
—Robert Lipsyte, author of *The Accidental Sportswriter*

I've been waiting almost 25 years for something good to come of the *Daily News* strike. Now it has. But this wonderful novel captures more than a time and a place. Harvey Araton deftly turns the picket line into a metaphor for other divides, for those that separate journalism and commerce, heroes and goats, and most of all, fathers and sons. *Cold Type* is a love song to the real New York.
—Mark Kriegel, author of *Namath*

Fans of Harvey Araton's lively, engaging prose will love this vivid and heartfelt exploration of what it means to be a journalist, a son, a father, and a man.
—Pamela Redmond Satran, author of *Younger*

A gripping narrative and an insightful take on family, work, what loyalty means—and what it costs. Harvey Araton is a skilled writer who knows his way around the milieus he travels in this novel, whether it's a newsroom, a labor hall or a living room. But what really makes this worth reading is the heart you can feel beating underneath it all.
—Brad Parks, Shamus-, Nero- and Lefty-Award-winning author of *The Player*